Alex Barclay studied journalism at university, and worked for a period in fashion and beauty journalism as a copywriter for the RTÉ Guide. In 2003 she left the fashion industry to write *Darkhouse*, the first of two novels featuring NYPD detective Joe Lucchesi. She won the Ireland AM Crime Fiction Award at the Irish Book Awards for her third novel, *Blood Runs Cold*. Alex lives in County Cork, Ireland.

You can discover more about the author at www.alexbarclay.co.uk

I CONFESS

Edie and Johnny's dream had always been to buy and restore an old property and have their own luxury inn. On a remote west coast peninsula in Ireland, their dream becomes reality when they purchase an old convent — for if Johnny can see beyond the dark history of the place, then so can Edie. Soon they are playing host to five of their closest childhood friends, reuniting for an evening of laughter and nostalgia — or at least that's the plan, which is about to go horribly wrong . . . As the storm builds outside, the dark events that marred their childhoods threaten to resurface. And when a body is discovered, the group faces a shocking realisation: a killer is among them, and not everyone will escape with their lives . . .

Books by Alex Barclay
Published by Ulverscroft:

DARKHOUSE
THE CALLER
BLOOD RUNS COLD
BLOOD LOSS
HARM'S REACH
KILLING WAYS
THE DROWNING CHILD

ALEX BARCLAY

I CONFESS

Complete and Unabridged

CHARNWOOD
Leicester

First published in Great Britain in 2019 by
HarperCollins*Publishers*
London

First Charnwood Edition
published 2020
by arrangement with
HarperCollins*Publishers*
London

This novel is entirely a work of fiction. The names,
characters and incidents portrayed in it are the work
of the author's imagination. Any resemblance to
actual persons, living or dead, events or localities
is entirely coincidental.

A catalogue record for this book is available
from the British Library.

ISBN 978–1–4448–4476–4

Published by
Ulverscroft Limited
Anstey, Leicestershire

Set by Words & Graphics Ltd.
Anstey, Leicestershire
Printed and bound in Great Britain by
T. J. International Ltd., Padstow, Cornwall

This book is printed on acid-free paper

To *OMGP*
This is what it feels like to be seen.

Pilgrim Point

Beara Peninsula, Cork, Ireland

Darkness had travelled loyally with Pilgrim Point through all its incarnations, as if passed in the handshake between each fleeing owner and the hopeful successor whose eye he could barely meet. This anvil-shaped promontory on the south-west coast of Ireland had once been a battleground, and at various times in the centuries that followed, had been fought over, lost, regained, or relinquished.

The sufferings of each owner — and there were many — would at first be borne privately, but the anguish of their aggregate would eventually sound like an alarm, travelling east to Castletown, where it would turn to whispers at a retreating back. Pilgrim Point, now empty of life, would release into the silence a siren cry that would always be answered. Deep and discordant, it called to those of a darker persuasion. The greater surprise was the fine gold thread of its lighter melody and how its gleam, though rare, could attract to Pilgrim Point, in equal measures, those of more noble intent.

Perhaps its grounds had swallowed the consequences of so many sins that, under the feet of sinners, it felt like home and under the feet of the righteous, like a summoning. This despite stories of strange apparitions and untimely occurrences. There was also the curious fertility of its grass — stark against the dark stones of the ruins that marked it. This trick of nature kindled even the faintest hope of triumph, when it was doubtless nothing more than a pleasing cover for what lay beneath — the roots of sin itself. From under this vibrant green bed, it released a pale malevolence that rose like smoke to disappear into the late-evening mist.

Were you to pass through the black gates of Pilgrim Point now, you would find yourself on land cloven by a bitter feud between brothers. The path you must take marks the dead centre, its course as unbending as the will of the men who occasioned it. As you follow this path, you will feel as though the landscape is unfurling around you, ahead of you, and for you — in time with the fall of your foot or the galloping hooves of your mount. You will be rewarded, then, at the cliff edge with such astonishing natural beauty; this anvil pointing towards nothing but sky and wild Atlantic. Turn left or right and you will catch glimpses of lesser headlands, like runners that have fallen behind in a race. You have won. Or so you think. You won't know yet that, in fact, you have been won. Through the powerful sweep of the wind and the steady crash of the waves, you won't hear the voice of the true winner:

'I am Pilgrim Point, host of rulers and battles, victors and vanquished, the rich, the poor, the faithful, the lost. Who are you? And what will I make of you?'

For what does an anvil do but allow a thing to be hammered and moulded? And what confusion comes when it plays blacksmith too.

I should know.

I once lived there. And, I now believe, died.

In a Manor of Silence
Lord Henry Rathbrook, 1886

1

EDIE

'If you have a rich imagination you will never be poor.'

Edie's mother, Madeleine, had heard that from her starving-artist parents throughout her childhood, so although she grew up in a home blessed with the freedom of passionate creativity, it was caged, in her mind, by penury. Madeleine mentally rejected the advice, never realizing that she had, in fact, taken it — she married a rich man, having fallen in love with a version of him she had used her rich imagination to create. Before they married, she had brought Edward home to meet her parents, and Edward, weary of the constraints of his upper-class upbringing, had been charmed by her parents and their ramshackle home. He came alive in their company and expected their daughter would bring out the same spirit in him. It wasn't long after they married that he realized they were both running towards the life the other wanted to leave behind. Edie's mother was happy with

5

her beautiful home and her beautiful things, and a husband who travelled for business and left her to enjoy them. When he returned from his trips, she seemed as disappointed by the reality of him as he was by the sense that she might pick him up, look around, and try to find a suitable place to put him.

It was only when Edie was born that her father's dormant spirit and warmth found a home. He poured all his love into her, gave her all his attention. There was never any disappointment on Edie's face. She loved him just the way he was.

When Edie was eight years old, he brought the family to Beara on holiday. He had spent his most magical childhood summer there and had told Edie stories about fishing at sea or from the rocks on a pebble beach so secluded he used to pretend that it was his, that he had won it from a pirate in a game of cards. He told her about hiking mountains and hills, swimming in lakes and waterfalls, and diving off piers into the freezing Atlantic Ocean. He told her about friendly locals, and warm welcomes, and nights filled with laughter, music, singing, and dancing.

He made sure that Edie's first summer there was filled with all the same things, and for Edie, every day was like living in a fairy tale. Her father had spent the whole month of August with them, and by the end of it, had bought a beautiful house on a sheltered harbour. They called it Eventide. It had a boathouse and a summerhouse and a lawn that sloped down to a short rocky strand. By the following summer, she and her mother were living there full-time, and her father visited as often as he could.

He always stirred her sense of adventure, bringing her out to sea with him, or to storytelling nights in a candlelit cabin in Eyeries — a tiny village where all the houses were painted in different colours. He would leave books by her bedside, tapping their hardback covers, and saying, 'You'd like this one, Edie,' 'You'd get a kick out of this!'

They used to drive by the gates of Pilgrim Point, in those days a convent, and she would always look out for the mismatched stone finials on the pillars — one a lion, the other an eagle. Her father told her it was once a manor built by two English brothers, the Rathbrooks, who fell out, accusing each other of all kinds of transgressions that led them into a series of stand-offs that began with the alleged theft of a finial at the gate and ran right down to the edge of the cliff where one brother accused the other of regularly appearing, ghost-like, to frighten him. Both men denied the accusations levelled at them, abandoned the manor, and died estranged.

'Never be too proud, Edie!' her father had said. 'But don't let anyone get the better of you, either!'

Edie's mother, meanwhile, played only a bit part in Edie's childhood adventures. Her role would come when Edie had outgrown them, when she could prime her to do as she had done: look beautiful and marry well.

And in the middle, torn between who she was and who each of them wanted her to be, was Edie. But there was one thing her parents did agree on — her beauty. That, she realized, was her safest ground. When the waters got choppy, that's where she stood — fair-haired, smiling, long-limbed, and sunkissed — and that's where Johnny Weston found her. She had first seen him when she was fourteen years old. It was the Saturday of the August Bank Holiday weekend — the beginning of what was officially called the Beara Festival of the Sea, but was only ever referred to as 'Regatta'. It was the highlight of Beara's social calendar, when the town was filled with people, and the harbour filled with boats.

Edie was in the crowd, watching from the pier as Johnny, in red shorts, bare-chested and muscular, was playing Pig on the Pole. He and his opponent were sitting on a greased-up pole high over the harbour, each trying to topple the other into the sea with the slam of a pillow. Johnny won. He always won.

The first time they met was the following summer after Edie was crowned Queen of the Sea. Johnny came up to her in the square that evening to congratulate her. She was fifteen, and sober, and he was twenty and so drunk that all he did was sway in front of her, in awe, until he was dragged away. They kissed the following Christmas, when Edie had just turned sixteen. Johnny, her crooked-smile charmer — her first love, her only love, the only man she had ever slept with, and, like her father, a man who could do no wrong.

They were married twenty years now, with a twelve-year-old son, Dylan. They had left Beara for San Francisco the year they got married,

8

worked their way up in hospitality, moving around, making money in real estate and investments. Home for the past six years was the ski lodge they owned in Breckenridge, Colorado — a small, friendly resort town at the foot of the Rocky Mountains. They loved it there, but the plan had always been to buy and restore an old property and have their own luxury inn. They had no plans for an imminent move, nor had they considered Beara as a location — until Johnny arrived at breakfast one morning and told her the convent at Pilgrim Point was up for sale, rushing through talk of the view, and the architecture, the slashed guide price, and the years that had passed since they had been there.

★   ★   ★

She was watching him now from the balcony as he stood in the entrance hall below, picturing him welcoming their future guests. Johnny was a natural host, an entertainer, a storyteller rather than a conversationalist. He had a collection of anecdotes that Edie loved walking in and out of at parties, laughing at the punchlines and, over the years, chipping in her own lines.

He looked up at her, and his eyes brightened. 'How did the solo expedition go? Did you find Consolata's torture chamber?'

Edie shuddered. Sister Consolata had been the widely despised Vice Principal of the local secondary school when Edie was a student there. Sister Consolata had lived and worked at Pilgrim Point for forty years, and it was only after she

9

died that it was revealed she had owned it, that it was not owned by the order, as everyone had assumed. A wealthy uncle, who had bought it from the Rathbrooks, skipped over her elder brother to bequeath it to her.

'The only trace I found of her,' said Edie, 'was in every grim corner, and peeling wall, and threadbare carpet I looked at.'

Johnny jogged up the stairs to her. 'Come on — let's have on more look at the library.'

★ ★ ★

The library was on the first floor, at the rear of the convent, overlooking the sea.

'You have to admit,' said Johnny.

'It is spectacular,' said Edie.

Johnny walked over to the side window, and squinted through the stained-glass panel to a two-storey flat-roofed building nestled in the trees. 'I might see if I can drive the bulldozer that day,' he said.

Edie laughed.

'I'm not sure how gracious the Sisters of Good Grace were if they were shoving their guests into that shithole,' said Johnny. 'But you're right — it's the perfect spot to build.'

Edie narrowed her eyes.

'You did say that, didn't you?' said Johnny, frowning. 'Did you not say something about razing that to the ground, so we could build the perfect family home, featuring everything you've ever dreamed of under one roof, including your handsome husband, and beloved son?'

10

'You're beloved too,' said Edie. 'Especially when you're telling stories.'

'I don't know,' said Johnny. 'I'm sure that was exactly what you said earlier.' He looked across to the other side of the property. 'So, Consolata sold the acre with the Mass rock on it before she died. What was that about? Did she not trust the next owner not to make shit of it?'

'Probably,' said Edie.

'It would have been a nice feature to show the guests as we're guiding them down the jetty steps to their death. I mean, to our boat. I could tell them the story about our oppressors' — he winked at Edie — 'banning the poor Catholics from going to Mass, making them climb up the rocks and traipse across the fields to have a sneaky one.'

'There's no oppressing you, Johnny Weston.'

★ ★ ★

An hour later, Johnny and Edie stood, face to face, in the entrance hall.

'I know exactly what I'd do here,' said Edie, sweeping her slender hand around. 'Dark walls — somewhere between French navy and Prussian blue — custom blend, obviously.' She smiled. 'Some teal in there, antique gold somewhere, and — don't laugh — a deep raspberry, but subtle, like in an edging or maybe . . . ' She looked down. 'Maybe the centre detail of the tiles. Gothic, encaustic, original design, but I don't want it *matching* matching, so maybe a dusky black, a smoky grey as the

11

main colour, a fine line of antique gold.'

Johnny took her hands.

'Can you imagine,' said Edie, 'a grand opening, Regatta week, on the lawn . . . '

Johnny smiled his crooked smile and the scar on his chin went white.

'So that's a 'yes',' he said.

'Yes!' said Edie. 'Yes, it is!'

2

The Inn at Pilgrim Point
24 November 2018

As Edie approached the turn for the inn, she often thought of travelling the same road with her father when she was a little girl. She pictured the sun flickering through the bright leaves and across his face, the darker tan of his neck, his arms outstretched, the gleam of his wristwatch, his hands on the steering wheel, how he would turn to smile at her as she bounced beside him on the front seat, ready for adventure.

Today, a storm was raging across Beara. Edie's head was pounding from the clash of the rain as it hit the roof and the windshield, startling her with loud, sporadic surges. She drove through the black entrance gates to the inn, past the stone falcons mounted on each side.

'Daddy, I bought the manor! I changed the finials! They're matching, Daddy! They're like me and you!'

She drove towards the inn, picturing it through the eyes of her friends as they arrived for dinner later. It would be dark by then, and they would love the warm glow from the lights at the foot of the trees, and how the leaves made a canopy that softened the straight line of the drive. Everything had changed so much since they had all known it; she had made sure of that, because it had to change. She had walked the rooms and hallways on the day of the viewing, transforming them in her mind's eye in a way that felt magical. It was as if, with a flick of her wrist, she was plucking paintings from the walls, whipping tiles off the floors, rolling up carpets and then, with a sweep of her arm, replacing them with her vision of the future.

She wished she could be with her friends as they saw its newest incarnation. They would feel differently about it now — it was beautiful.

Edie's breath caught, and her hand went to her chest. She glanced in the rear-view mirror and saw, reflected back at her, the upward-tilted chin of her mother and the fastened joy in her eyes — the look that reminded Edie of things on shelves that, if you break them, you have to pay.

She felt a stab of anger at her blind faith in Johnny in the day of the viewing that, if he could see beyond the dark history of Pilgrim Point, then she could too. Johnny, who didn't believe in dwelling on the past, yet, she now realized, still saw them the way the outside world saw them when they first met — she the beautiful, privileged daughter of a wealthy English businessman and his devoted homemaker wife; Johnny, the handsome privileged son of the local doctor.

It didn't matter how absent Edie's father was nor that his adoration appeared like seasonal blooms in a vast lonely landscape. It didn't matter how remote Johnny's father was or how

14

desperately lonely his mother was, or that she had moulded her son into as close as he could be to the husband she really wanted, watching as her efforts were chipped away at by the husband she actually had. They saw what they wanted to see. And Johnny believed them.

★   ★   ★

As she came to the end of the drive, Edie caught sight of Johnny, standing in the conservatory with Terry Hyland, the contractor. Terry was a short, springy, gnarly-faced, man — the same age as Johnny, but looked a decade older. Johnny, at six foot two, towered over him, clearly questioning something, clearly unhappy about it, which was his default setting when it came to Terry. Terry had his arms folded as Johnny spoke, then would unfold them and stab a finger at the ground when he was responding to him. They glanced up, and pretended that they hadn't seen her. She guessed it was because they were both on a roll, and that if they could see her, that meant she could see them, which meant she might intervene.

She had no intention of intervening — there was too much to do before everyone arrived. The inn was closed for the season, and she hadn't brought any staff in for the night — she wanted to do everything herself, and to keep their evening with friends a private one. Her parents' dinner parties had been like that — hushed and behind closed doors . . . until they got rowdy and spilled out into rooms or hallways close enough that Edie could wake to the sound of their voices or the smell of their cigarettes.

She used to watch her mother prepare the house for guests, and she would always be given a job that, each time, she would carry out as if she didn't know that at least some part of it would be taken away from her or redone. The older she got, the less it happened, and, by the time her mother sent her out in to the world, she was proud to. When Edie was asked in therapy to think of something she might thank her mother for, that was it.

★   ★   ★

When she was fifteen, Edie had sat with her father at the table by the rocky shore at the end of their garden and told him that she hated her mother. He raised an eyebrow, but let her talk.

'You don't know what it's like when you're not here, Daddy. She's so strict. She has to control everything — what I eat, what I wear, who my friends are, what we do. She likes Helen. And she likes Jessie, but she never lets me go to her house. She hates Laura because she thinks she's 'unrefined'. And she thinks Murph's a . . . what's that word?'

'Boor!' said her father, laughing. 'I like Murph! He's a fun fellow, isn't he? A bit rough around the edges, like all the best people.'

'Yes!' said Edie. 'And his father is the sweetest, gentlest man.' She paused. 'What, Daddy?'

Her father frowned. 'Nothing. He is, he is. He's the stone chap, isn't he? Built those marvellous stone walls.'

'Daddy, you used to go fishing with him,' said Edie. 'Jerry Murphy.'

'Ah, Jerry Murphy,' said her father. 'Of course, of course. It's been a while.'

'All he does is sit in the house and read about history now,' said Edie. 'But he drinks a lot, so Mummy doesn't like that.'

Her father's gaze drifted out over the water. 'But he's a heartbroken man, isn't he?' he said. 'Lost his wife, lost his job.' He let out a breath. 'We'd give the man a pass for that, surely.'

It was the first time her father had crossed the united front he and her mother usually presented.

'Oh, Mummy does like Clare,' said Edie, 'but I think that's only because she's rich too.'

Her father leaned back from Edie a fraction and that one small move made Edie's stomach flip and the blood rush to her cheeks. She had never felt ashamed in his presence before.

'I'm sure your mother and I have both failed you along the way,' said her father, skipping past it, 'and I'm sorry that we did. But my advice to you is this — think of the past as a great big sea. It has delicious things we can feast on, a pearl here or there if we're lucky. There are other things that are best left there, though. And conditions are not always favourable — unseen currents, waves waiting to crash. It's best to take a quick dip, never wallow there, and certainly don't drown.' And he had smiled.

Her father was a prescient man. Edie still dived into that childhood sea, and fed on those creatures until she was sick. She had wallowed in the waters, crying into them, stirring up waves. There had been times when she hoped they would drown her.

★   ★   ★

Edie looked up at the walls of the inn. The rain on the granite had always looked to her like an oily film that could fall away from it in a single sheet. She had woken that morning, heaving and sweating, having dreamt that it had, and that she had watched, helpless, as it slid to the ground and rippled across the gravel towards her, and that she had stood, rooted, as it wrapped around her like a cocoon, and that she hadn't made a sound, even when it started to tighten around her neck. When she woke, she felt that she hadn't shaken it — not that she was bound by it, but that it hung over her like a threat. Daddy, what was I thinking?

Tonight, she and Johnny would be welcoming five of her closest childhood friends — Murph and Helen and Clare and Laura and Patrick. She waited for the joy to fill her heart. Instead, a thought came in to sink it: Five friends. No sixth — no Jessie.

All she could think of then was: I am the Ghost of the Manor.

3

EDIE

The Sisters of Good Grace Convent, Pilgrim Point
31 October 1988

Murph, Helen, Edie, Laura, and Clare were gathered at midnight by the chapel gate.

'Happy Hallowe'en!' said Murph.

'Where's your mask?' said Clare. 'You were the one obsessed with us wearing masks.'

'The elastic broke,' said Murph.

'The size of the head on him,' said Laura. 'As if they wouldn't know you if they looked out. Consolata up there closing her curtains: 'Surely, that's not that six-foot-four Liam Murphy goon running across my lawn. If only I could see behind that tiny plastic circle on his face — then I'd definitely know.'

'Have you seen the selection down in the shop?' said Murph.

'I think we have,' said Clare, looking around. They were all holding green Frankenstein masks.

'Monsters, the lot of us,' said Murph. 'Is there no sign of Jessie?'

'I wouldn't hold out much hope,' said Laura. 'She was down town earlier, pasted.'

19

'Oh, no,' said Helen. 'On her own?'

Laura nodded. 'Apparently, Consolata was at her again, the silly bitch.'

'All the more reason for her to come,' said Murph.

'I told Jessie I'd meet her,' said Helen. 'I don't know why she couldn't have walked up with the rest of us.'

'Leave her off,' said Laura.

'She needs to ease up a bit,' said Helen.

Murph nodded. 'She needs to get a grip . . . on these.' He held up a bag of cans.

They all laughed, but Edie knew they were all thinking the same thing — Jessie shouldn't be drinking, not as much as she did, not on her own, not at sixteen, not after everything she had been through.

Murph looked up the road. 'Here she is now. A dog to a bone.'

'Oh God,' said Clare, turning to Laura. 'You were right.'

Jessie waved with a can of cider as she swayed towards them, a white plastic Hallowe'en mask pushed up on top of her head.

'She shouldn't be climbing a wall in that state,' said Helen.

'Laura can heave her up one side,' said Murph, 'and I'll catch her on the other.'

They all put their masks on.

'Frankenfuckinglosers,' said Jessie, spreading her arms wide. She pulled her mask down. 'Boo!' She stopped like a soldier in front of them. 'But what's even scarier is I'm out of cider.'

They climbed over the stone wall, and ran alongside it, then slipped through the trees, and came
out by three flat-roofed buildings that were derelict now, but were once part of the industrial
school run by the nuns in the sixties and seven-
ties. Murph stopped at the long, narrow dormitory
block, crouched down by the door, and pulled
out a key from under a rock next to it. He stood
up and flashed a smile at the others, then unlocked
the door. They followed him into the pitch-black
hallway. Clare closed the door behind her.

'Ladies,' said Murph, turning on a torch, 'this
way.' He kept the beam low as he shone it on the
door to the left. He pushed it open, then stood
with one foot over the threshold. 'The living
quarters of whoever had to prowl the dorm at
night,' he said.

They others took a look inside. It was a makeshift
storage room now, with a timber countertop that
ran along three walls and was covered with broken
electrical equipment, cardboard boxes, crates of
empty bottles, containers, and paint cans. There
were more stored under the counter, along with
rolled-up carpets and paint-spattered sheets.

'Now,' said Murph, 'can I ask you all to adjourn
to the hallway for five minutes?' He looked at
them solemnly. 'I need to prepare the room.'

* * *

When they came back in, there was a picnic
blanket spread out on the concrete floor, with

21

church candles on two sides, and three more on the counter above. Everybody sat down.

'Right,' said Murph. 'Gather round.'

'Story time!' said Jessie, leaning sideways, steadying herself with her hand.

'Take the candle away from her,' said Laura.

'I'm fine,' said Jessie. 'Relax.'

Murph pulled it towards him when Jessie wasn't looking.

'Right,' he said, leaning in. He lowered his voice. 'It was a bright sunny day — '

'I thought this was a ghost story,' said Laura.

'I'm going for 'contrast',' said Murph.

'And bad things still happen on sunny days,' said Jessie. She knocked back a mouthful of cider.

Everyone exchanged glances.

'Relax,' said Jessie, lowering her can. 'I'm just wrecking you. You can hardly never mention sunny days again for the rest of your lives because of me!'

Murph let out a breath. 'OK . . . I'm going traditional: it was a wild night in Beara — raging storm, high seas, trees toppling, roads cut off. Five girls: HELEN, CLARE, EDIE, JESSIE, AND LAURA — '

'Noo!' said Edie. 'Not our real names! You'll jinx us.'

Laura rolled her eyes. 'Fuck's sake.'

'Leave her alone,' said Helen.

'And I want to star in this, if you don't mind,' said Clare.

'Me too!' said Jessie.

'Fine, then,' said Edie.

22

'Five girls,' said Murph. 'HELEN, CLARE, JESSIE, LAURA, and BABY EDIE . . . were driving out of town when, right in front of them, a towering oak fell from the skies and landed inches from their car. Laura tried to reverse, but behind them the hedge over the ditch split wide open and a river of mud and branches and stones poured through it, filling the road. The girls were trapped! What were they going to do? They were exhausted and so far from home. Then lightning struck, and pointed, like the needle of a compass, to . . . Rathbrook Manor — no more than a mile from where they sat.

'"Why don't we stay there for the night?' said Laura. 'There may be a boy inside that I haven't kissed yet!'

'"Nonsense!' said Clare. 'There's not a single boy in Beara that girl hasn't kissed!'

'"Yes — let's stay at the manor!' said Jessie, cracking open her fifth can of cider, looking up at the spires of the manor, which were a total blur, and, in fact, a tree.

'"No!' screamed Edie, screaming hysterically. 'I'll scream if you make me stay there!' she screamed. Hysterically.

'"Don't tell me you believe in the Ghost of the Manor!' said Laura.

'"Of course I don't believe in ghosts!' said Edie. 'It's just . . . I have nothing with me! How can I possibly wear the same outfit two days in a row?'

'The girls agreed that the manor was NOT haunted and so they decided to stay there, and they set off to walk the mile to the door. When they arrived, the manor was all locked up and in total darkness. Edie screamed. Laura punched her in the face and they walked on through the grounds until they stumbled across a dormitory. They peered in the window and saw row after row of iron beds, all of them empty. As they approached the door, it creaked open, and they all walked in. They each took a bed, side by side, and after hours talking about some ride they knew called Murph, they finally drifted off to sleep.

'In the middle of the night, Laura woke with a start to find herself staring silently at a ghost standing three feet from the end of her bed. Beside her, Helen woke with a start to find herself staring silently at a ghost that stood three feet from the end of her bed. The same happened to Clare, and then to Jessie. The last bed in the line was Edie's. When she woke to find a ghost standing three feet from the end of her bed, she was instantly hysterical, and she screamed at the ghost: 'Who are you?'

'And the ghost replied: 'I am the Ghost of the Manor. And I am yours.'

'Edie turned slowly to her left, and realized that each friend had a different ghost at the end of her bed.

'As each girl stared at the ghost before her, all five ghosts stepped forward into the silvery moonlight that slanted across the ends of the beds like the blade of a knife. Each ghost had died a different way: Laura's was bruised and broken, its eyeballs dangling from their sockets; Helen's was covered in tyre tracks, its limbs at odd angles; Clare's had half its head missing; Jessie's was pristine; and Edie's was covered in burns.

'The friends' mouths opened wider than a mouth naturally should, and their screams emerged as though ripped by the claws of a bear from the centre of their soul. But the source of their terror was not simply the apparitions that stood before them, nor the horror of their wounds. It was because each girl's ghost looked exactly like her, just . . . older — maybe ten years, maybe thirty, maybe fifty. But the likeness was unmistakable!

'Across this group of friends rippled the same realization: they had been RIGHT: the manor was NOT haunted. And this would be proven when, after they left, wherever they went, their ghost would reappear . . . some would say 'without warning'. But, of course, each ghost DID carry a warning, a GRAVE warning. For it was not the Ghost of the MANOR. It was the Ghost . . . of the . . . MANNER . . . of DEATH.

'And on that first night, as the friends were faced with the terrifying spectacle of the death that would befall them at some point thereafter, they were all struck by one thing: EDIE'S ghost, despite the burns that marked it, looked . . . the YOUNGEST.'

★   ★   ★

Everyone gasped, then gasped again as smoke started to rise around Murph.

Edie pointed. 'Oh my God — smoke!'

25

Murph was unperturbed. 'What?'

'I'm serious!' said Edie. 'There's actual smoke!'

'Where?' said Murph.

'All around you!' said Edie.

'There is!' said Laura.

Murph turned and looked. 'Oh Jesus, lads. I was warned! If you tell this story on Hallowe'en night, it'll come true.'

'What?' said Edie, getting to her feet. 'Why did you tell it? What do you mean, it'll come true?'

'Unless,' said Murph, 'we all say 'Sister Cuntsolata' three times backwards.'

Everyone looked at him.

Murph burst out laughing. 'It's a smoke bomb. Special effects, lads. Special effects.'

'You prick!' said Laura. 'Where did you get your hands on a smoke bomb?'

'I made it!' said Murph. 'A bit of this, a bit of that.'

Jessie reached into Laura's bag for another can. She turned to Murph. 'Can I still say Sister Cuntsolata three times?'

'You can, of course,' said Murph. A rush of white smoke appeared behind him.

'Right!' said Clare. 'Open the door, someone. I've seen my cousins with these — there's a reason you're only meant to use them outside.'

'Jesus — I know,' said Murph. 'Relax. It was only for a minute. Then I was going to fuck it out across the grass. I even have my protective glove lined up.'

'So you want to draw the nuns on us?' said Laura. 'Throwing it out across the grass? No fucking way.'

26

'To create a distraction,' said Murph.

Edie started to cough.

'The drama,' said Murph.

'Can you just put the fucking thing out?' said Laura.

'It's not on fire,' said Murph. 'It's fine. It's safe.'

'I'm happy here with my cans,' said Jessie, closing her eyes, smiling.

Helen and Laura exchanged glances. 'Locked,' Helen mouthed.

'Probably better off,' said Laura.

Murph was starting to disappear into a cloud of smoke. 'Okaaay,' he said, standing up. 'Maybe open the door.'

'Why are there flames, then?' said Jessie, looking up at everyone.

'What?' said Edie, panicked.

'If it's not on fire,' said Jessie. 'Murph said it wasn't on fire.'

'I can't see any flames,' said Clare.

'There really are flames,' said Jessie. She pointed into the corner. 'Are those not flames?'

Murph rolled his eyes, but then he turned around. 'Oh shit.'

Edie ran for the door.

Murph pointed to the corner. 'Laura! Throw me that sheet, and that brush.'

Laura grabbed them and flung them at him. He threw the sheet on to the flames and used the handle of the brush to poke at it. The smoke bomb was still smoking.

Edie cried out from the door. 'OK — this isn't funny! Murph!'

'What's wrong with you now?' he said.

Edie was holding up the doorknob.

'What's that?' said Murph. 'Did that come off? I didn't do that. I swear to God!'

Murph's eyes were so filled with fear that Edie started to cry. 'Oh, God! No! No! No!' She turned to the door and started slapping her hands against it. 'Help us! Help! Help! Help!'

'Shut the fuck up!' said Laura, lunging for her. 'For fuck's sake. We're going to get caught! We'll be fucked!'

'We're surely fucked if we can't get out,' said Murph, striding past Laura to the door. Clare and Helen followed.

'Seriously — how are we supposed to get out?' said Edie.

Behind them, Jessie stood up, swaying, holding her drink high, trying not to spill it.

Laura was pointing to the hole where the doorknob should have been. 'Can you not just turn the thing inside it?'

'You can't,' said Murph. 'You have to slide something in between the door and the frame to knock the latch back.'

Edie was sobbing.

'Shut up,' said Laura. 'It's not like we're not going to get out.'

'And I don't think that sheet worked,' said Jessie.

The others turned around, and saw the flames crawling along it.

'Jessie! Get up, for God's sake!' said Clare.

'Get over here!' said Laura.

'Will I throw some cider on it?' said Jessie.

'No!' said Laura. 'Get the fuck away from it!'

'Don't throw anything on it except water,' said Clare.

'Lads — what's in those bottles under the counter?' said Laura. 'Could any of them be water? Those ones look like camping bottles.'

Jessie bent, put down her can, and picked up a bottle.

'No, no, no!' said Clare. 'Don't let her near anything! Don't!'

Jessie started unscrewing the lid. 'I'm only smelling it.' She put it too close to her mouth, and tipped some on to her lips. 'Oh, God no,' she said, recoiling. 'That's kerosene.' She swung the bottle wide, and everyone watched, horrified, as it sent an arc of fuel across the room.

'Nooo!' said Edie, hammering on the door, screaming for help.

'Get her, Murph!' shouted Helen, pointing at Jessie.

Flames were starting to rise. Murph reached a hand towards Jessie. 'Get the fuck over here now.'

'I'm coming, I'm coming,' said Jessie. 'Relax.' But she took a step sideways, leaned too far, and then staggered back to the other counter.

'OK — don't move,' said Murph. 'You're OK, there's no fire there, but as soon as I get this fucking door open, head for Laura — her jacket's nice and white, grab the back of it, and go.'

Edie and Laura were slamming their hands against the door, screaming for help. Murph pushed in behind them and hammered at the door with the side of his fist.

They heard a shout from outside, 'Hello? Hello?' It was a boy's voice.

They all screamed. 'In here! In here! We're trapped!' They banged on the door again.

'Hold on!' he said. 'I have a key. Hold on! Stop banging!'

'It won't work!' shouted Murph. 'The lock's fucked. Who's that? Is that Patrick?'

'Yes!'

'Help!' Edie started screaming. 'It's Edie! Help!'

'Thanks be to fuck, Patrick!' said Murph. 'Thanks be to fuck!'

'OK — wait! Wait!' he said. 'I'll get something.'

'Hurry up!' said Edie.

'Hurry the fuck up!' said Laura.

They could hear him rattling around outside. 'OK, OK. Stand back a bit.'

'Jesus, I don't know if we want to do that,' said Murph.

'You've not much choice,' Patrick said. They could hear the sound of metal in between the door and the door frame. 'Get back!'

They all held hands, and took a small step back. They heard the bang of a hammer against the metal, and the ping as it slid off.

'Come on t'fuck!' said Murph. 'Jesus Christ! Hurry the fuck up!'

'Shhh!' said Helen, elbowing him. 'You're doing a great job, Patrick!' she shouted. 'Keep going. Keep going! Keep your eyes on it, your hand out of the way, and go.'

30

Patrick tried again and the door burst open. They all ran. When they were clear, Murph stood, bent over, his hands on his knees. 'Jesus, sorry, lads. I'm so sorry. Fair play to you, Patrick. Fuck's sake.' He looked at the others. 'Lads, — we need to get the fuck out of — '

'Where's Jessie?' said Clare.

Everyone looked around.

'What?' said Patrick. 'Was Jessie here?'

'Yes!' screamed Helen. 'Yes! Oh my God!'

Patrick turned and ran back.

'Edie — go!' said Helen. 'You're the fastest. Go!'

Edie ran, quickly catching up with Patrick.

Murph looked at Laura. 'Was she not hanging out of the back of you — Jessie?'

'What are you on about?' said Laura.

'I told her hang on to your jacket,' said Murph, 'because it was white and she'd see it!'

'I didn't hear you!' said Laura. 'I didn't hear anything about a jacket. I just thought she was coming out behind me!'

★   ★   ★

Edie and Patrick skidded to a stop at the side door to the dormitory as the wind tore a swathe from the black smoke billowing towards them. They froze. In the clearing, they saw Jessie standing, staring ahead, arms by her side. She was motionless, two steps from the exit, flames encroaching, high and loud and crackling. They screamed her name. She didn't blink. They screamed again. Jessie closed her eyes, and they

31

watched as she let the flames engulf her.

Edie grabbed for Patrick's arm, clawing at it with desperate hands, her fingers digging into his flesh. They turned to each other, wild-eyed, mouths open, chests heaving. In the fractional moment their eyes met, they made an unspoken pact: they would never mention what they had seen to another soul.

Or maybe it was a shared granting of permission — to lose the memory to a confusion of smoke or shock.

4

Edie parked at the bottom of the steps to the inn. She glanced down at the folder on the passenger seat — research she had gathered on the history of Pilgrim Point. She wanted to be able to talk to the guests about it, or include interesting details on the website or in printed cards she would leave in the bedrooms. When she bumped into Murph the previous summer, she told him her plans, and the following day, when he was meeting Johnny in town, he transferred four boxes of his late father's research into the boot of Johnny's car.

Edie opened the folder and saw two pages, titled *In a Manor of Silence*. In all she had read about Pilgrim Point, the words of Henry Rathbrook were the ones that resonated the most — even when she learned that they were not an extract from the handwritten manuscript of a published book, but were among the scattered remains of patient files discovered in an abandoned asylum.

Edie pulled up the hood of her rain coat, tucked her hair inside, and made the short dash up the steps. She pushed through the front door, and let it close gently behind her. Look where my rich imagination got me, she thought. The hall was exactly how she had pictured it on the day of the viewing. But how it looked and how it felt were on two different frequencies. Did it matter that each beautiful choice she had made could light up the eyes of their guests if the pilot light in their heart had blown as soon as they walked through the door? She would watch their gaze as it moved across the floors and walls, up the stone staircase, along the ornate carvings of the cast iron balustrade, and higher again to the decorative cornices of the ceiling, the elaborate ceiling rose, and the sparkling Murano glass chandelier that hung from it. Then she would graciously accept the praise that always followed, pretending not to notice the small spark of panic in their eyes or the tremor in their smile.

It was as if a signal was being fired off inside them: no, we don't smile at things like this, not in places like this, because something is not right. Something is wrong.

She would see some beautiful, eager young girl arriving with her young boyfriend who had spent a month's wages on one weekend, and he would beam as her eyes lit up, but Edie would see the rest. She knew it wasn't because this girl felt out of place — everyone was made to feel welcome at the inn because everyone was welcome. But sometimes Edie felt that the reason everyone was welcome was not because that was her job, not because the vast extravagance of the refurbishment had plunged them into an alarming amount of debt, not because a family has living expenses, and Dylan has to be put through college, but because she hoped that one day, someone would walk in and they would light up and it would be pure, there would be no strange

34

aftertaste, and the spell would be broken.

Edie shook off her jacket and hung it on the carved oak hallstand. She paused as she heard the sound of a door slamming, and heavy footsteps echoing towards her.

'Dad won't let me go to Mally's tonight!' said Dylan, stomping half way across the hall. He stood with his hands on his hips, his face red, his chest heaving.

'Dylan!' said Edie. 'Calm down, please.'

Johnny appeared behind Dylan.

'And why does it even matter,' said Dylan, glancing back at him, 'when you're all going to be here partying anyway?'

'Partying?' said Johnny. 'It's Helen's forty-seventh birthday — we're hardly going to be dancing the night away.'

Dylan looked at him, wide-eyed. 'Oh my God! That is so mean!'

Johnny stared at him, bewildered.

'Mom — did you hear that?' said Dylan. 'Just because Helen's in a wheelchair.'

Johnny did a double take. 'What?' He looked at Edie, then back at Dylan. 'Dylan — that had nothing to do with Helen being in a wheelchair. That was about us being so old that we don't have the energy to dance.'

'Well, that's depressing,' said Dylan.

Edie started to laugh.

'Well, I'd rather depress you than be accused of making fun of Helen,' said Johnny.

Helen was Dylan's godmother, and he was fiercely protective of her.

Helen was diagnosed with MS ten years ago,

35

and had been in a wheelchair for the past three years, and still, when Edie saw her, she could get hit with the unfairness of it. Even though Helen was such a part of their lives. Before the diagnosis, Helen had been fit, strong, the director of nursing in the local hospital, living with her partner, who left her as soon as her symptoms started to really show. She was still in the relapsing-remitting stage, but her condition was slowly deteriorating. She had an older sister in Cork, but they weren't close, and apart from her friends from the hospital, Johnny Dylan and Edie were the ones who helped her out the most.

'Jesus, Dylan,' said Johnny, 'you have to stop attacking people because of some assump-tion — '

'Says the guy roaring at Terry earlier,' said Dylan.

'I wasn't roaring at him,' said Johnny. 'We were having a . . . discussion.'

Dylan made air quotes.

Johnny turned to Edie. 'All that was going on with Terry is I asked him to board up the chapel windows properly, with decent timber, so they wouldn't look like an eyesore, and instead he throws up some bullshit with streaks of paint and black God-knows-what all over it. Do you want the lads arriving in and seeing that?'

'It'll be dark,' said Dylan.

'Not in the morning when they're getting the tour,' said Johnny. 'And what's with you defending Terry all of a sudden? Last week he was the worst in the world.'

'Because he thinks I'm the person who

36

smashed the windows!' said Dylan. 'Which, I'd like to repeat, I am not. Terry spots someone in jeans and a hoodie running away from the 'scene' and it's automatically me.'

Johnny gestured to Dylan's jeans and hoodie, and shrugged.

'Literally, everyone dresses like this,' said Dylan.

'But you can see where he's coming from,' said Johnny. 'He calls me to say he's caught you and Mally in the confession box in the chapel — '

Edie looked at Johnny. 'Can we stop this — '

'No,' said Johnny. 'He still hasn't given us an explanation.'

'Stop making it sound so creepy,' said Dylan.

'You were supposed to be in school!' said Johnny. 'The one day we're in Cork trying to get stuff done — '

'I don't know why he had to call you,' said Dylan.

'Here's why,' said Johnny. 'Health and safety. The chapel's a building site, basically, you had no hard hats on you — '

'Hard hats,' said Dylan. He rolled his eyes. 'Mally thought the whole thing was — '

'Why would I care what Mally thinks?' said Johnny.

Dylan looked at Edie. 'Seriously, Mom . . . what is his problem with her?'

'I don't have a problem with Mally,' said Johnny.

Dylan's phone beeped. He took it out of his pocket, and read the WhatsApp message. 'Well, I can't not go now,' he said. 'Because Mally's already on her way over here. In the rain. I can't suddenly go 'Oh sorry — go home. Oh — and I can't come back with you later.''

Edie turned to Johnny, her eyebrows raised. He gave her a resigned look.

'So she's going to be here for the day while your mother's trying to get the place ready for tonight?' said Johnny.

'They'll be over at the house,' said Edie.

'Obviously,' said Dylan. He looked at Johnny. 'Can I go now?'

'Yes,' said Edie.

'And can I go over to Mally's later?' said Dylan.

'Yes,' said Edie.

'Thanks, Mom.' He walked across the hall and they waited for him to disappear down the stairs.

'Why do you always have to do that?' said Johnny.

'Oh, good God,' said Edie. 'Grow up. What is your issue with him going over there, all of a sudden? I don't want to have to deal with any meltdowns tonight, and if he's over there — '

'She's a bad influence on him,' said Johnny. 'She always has to know everything. She's just in your face. She's . . . nosy. She's . . . '

Edie gave him a patient look.

'Look — I know she's no fan of mine,' said Johnny, 'but that's not the point. They're always . . . whispering and skulking about the place.'

'For God's sake,' said Edie. 'They're sixteen. Well . . . '

'And that's the other thing — why is a

38

nineteen-year-old college girl hanging out with a sixteen-year-old boy? It's weird.'

Edie raised an eyebrow. 'From the twenty-one-year-old with his eye on the sixteen-year-old?'

'That's different. And . . . different times.' He put his hands on his hips. 'And what makes you think he's going to have a meltdown?'

'Look at him,' said Edie. 'He's exhausted.'

'Because he was up all night watching Netflix!' said Johnny. 'He knows this is a big night, it's important to you, and — '

'Well, I hope it's important to you too — '

'Oh, for fuck's sake. I said 'you' because he doesn't give a shit what I think. 'He needs to get his head out of his arse!'

'He's sixteen,' said Edie. 'He's cripped with — '

'Oh God,' said Johnny. 'Anxiety — the Get Out of Jail card — '

Edie stared at him.

'Sorry,' said Johnny. 'But if he really had no control over his emotions, how am I the one who gets Angry Dylan and you get sad face? Or 'Hugs'?'

'We're not getting into — '

'No,' said Johnny. 'But — '

Edie shook her head. 'No — '

'You know what you should do,' said Johnny, 'show him some of your 'research' photos from the industrial school with those skinny little bastards running around out there — not a Netflick to their names.'

'He's already been rooting through my research,' said Edie.

39

'Jesus Christ. No wonder he has anxiety.'

'Why do you have such a problem with it?' said Edie.

'Because it freaks you out,' said Johnny.

'It doesn't freak me out,' said Edie. 'And I don't have time for this. I have too much to do.'

'I told you we should have got one of the chefs in,' said Johnny. 'We should have got staff in, full stop.'

'We're not going to get staff in when we're closed for the season,' said Edie. 'And we'd have to pay them. But the main thing, I told you, was that I wanted to make an effort for my friends — which I still do. I just need time.'

'Fine,' said Johnny. 'I'll leave you to it.' He turned to walk away.

'Johnny — wait,' said Edie.

He looked back. His eyes were bright with hope and Edie wondered what he thought she was going to say. 'Just . . . ' she said. 'Stop . . . waiting for him to change.'

Johnny frowned. 'What?'

'Dylan is all of what you see — the weight, the anxiety, the insecurity. But it's Dylan — aged sixteen. It might not be Dylan at eighteen or twenty or twenty-five. But . . . what if it is? I'm saying — if you're waiting for him to go back to being the happy little bunny . . . well . . . ' She paused. 'Maybe that won't happen.'

She raised her chin, blinked and hoped Johnny wouldn't notice she was fending off tears.

When she looked at him again, she could see the triumph in his eyes. He stabbed a finger at her. 'Don't you ever give me a hard time again

40

for grieving over that.'

'I'm giving you a hard time,' said Edie, 'for letting him see it.'

Johnny's eyes widened. 'Oh, and I'm the piece of shit? Because you can hide it better? These 'feelings' everyone is supposed to be all open about?'

'No one thinks you're a piece of shit,' said Edie.

'Oh, I think we both know Dylan does.'

'Don't be ridiculous,' said Edie. 'I've never got that from him.'

'Well,' said Johnny, 'maybe he raises his acting game when he's around a champ.'

Edie hated them both at this moment — individually, but mostly, as a couple.

★ ★ ★

The grandfather clock in the hall chimed four times. Edie closed the door to the bar behind her and stood with her back to it, pausing to release a breath into the dense silence. The storm had been building all afternoon, and she could feel the powerful push of the wind against the walls of the inn, like the shoulder of a fairytale giant who didn't want them there, who would keep pushing until they were gone. She knew that in her own house, the wind would be whistling through every broken part, reminding her of every unmet promise. 'Remember the monstrosity we said he'd raze to the ground? And replace with our dream home? Well, we live in it! And we've barely done a thing to it! But look at the beautiful fairy garden! You can see it from our bedroom! Look at the pretty lights! I go there when I'm losing my mind to try to make myself believe in magic again!'

She peeled herself away from the door and walked down the hallway. As she passed the dining room, a movement inside caught her eye, and she stopped. Mally was standing at the dinner table, taking a photograph with her phone.

Edie walked in. 'Hello, Mally.'

'Oh!' said Mally, startled.

'What are you up to?' said Edie, smiling.

'Just — I love what you've done!' said Mally, looking around.

The room had been transformed from elegantly formal into elegantly mismatched. The dining table still had its white starched linen table cloth, but there was a brown tweed runner on top, covered with fresh greenery and a mix of squat cream pillar church candles on slices of polished wood-cream taper candles in short brass candlesticks. The napkins were in muted blues and greens, with porcelain humming-bird napkin rings. The usual heavy silver cutlery was replaced with 1940s bone-handled knives, forks and spoons. The wine glasses were a collection of modern and antique — crystal, etched, gold filigree, all different, all beautiful.

Mally was staring at Edie, eyes bright. Edie sometimes wondered whether Mally was hopped up on ADD drugs. There was a wide-eyed, ner-vous intensity about her that could sometimes veer into something darker. And why would Mally be looking at place settings? She barely ran a hairbrush through her hair.

Edie's gaze moved down to Mally's hand. Edie had put a childhood photo at every setting, face down, peeping out from each napkin. Mally was holding Helen's. In it, Helen was sitting at her kitchen table in a white dress, her tenth birthday cake in front of her, candles lit. She was beaming at the camera, chin up, eyes scrunched tight, a pink paper crown on her head. Clare was standing to Helen's right, with her rosy red cheeks, looking like she was about to blow out the candles herself. Edie was in the back row, smiling serenely, her two arms neatly in front of her. Murph was standing sideways behind Clare, his arm up like a robot, but his head turned to the camera. His eyes were sparkling with mischief and he had three party blowers in his mouth. It looked like whoever had taken the photo had got distracted by him, because they hadn't waited for Jessie — the birthday girl's best friend — to make it into the frame. There was a glimpse of her at the edge — the end of her long black wavy pigtail, the sleeve of her bright pink dress.

Dylan appeared in the doorway. 'Hey, Mom . . .' He frowned when he saw Mally.

'I was admiring your mom's party styling,' said Mally. She held up the photo. 'Look at your godmother — she was so adorable!'

'She really was,' said Edie.

Edie smiled. She wondered would any of her friends realize how much effort had gone into the photo selection. She knew that Helen's tenth birthday was her favourite, and among the few photos she found, she had chosen the only one where Jessie wasn't right by her side. She hoped

Helen wouldn't notice the fraction of her, caught at the edge — she didn't want to see the sting of a painful memory on her face.

'Who's this?' said Mally, pointing to the picture. 'Is this the girl who died in the fire?'

Edie's eyes widened. 'Yes ... How did you know that?'

'Just a guess,' said Mally. She shrugged. 'I mean not a total guess — I read about the fire online and saw a photo.'

Dylan frowned at Mally. 'We have to go. It's insane out there.'

'I can give you a lift, if you want to wait,' said Edie.

'No,' said Dylan. 'What about your hair?'

'How many teenage boys would ever think of something like that?' said Edie.

'Only the ones who want something from you,' said Mally.

'Shut up,' said Dylan. 'I don't want anything, Mom.' He went up to Edie and gave her a hug. 'Have fun, tonight.'

'You too,' said Edie, kissing his cheek, before he pulled away. 'Be back at midnight and not a minute later.'

Edie went to Helen's place when they had left. She felt a stab of guilt that she was checking whether Mally had left a grubby fingerprint somewhere — Mally was never unclean, just dishevelled. She had left Helen's photo upturned. Edie picked it up. Helen had never said why her tenth birthday was her favourite, but maybe it was because it was the last summer before they all found out that bad things can still happen on sunny days.

5

JESSIE

Castletownbere
Saturday, 30 July 1983

The truck was parked in the square, twenty feet long, the side folded down to make a stage. A banner with JUNIOR TALENT CONTEST! hung from the front, flapping only once since the crowd had gathered; a single breeze on the hottest day of the year.

★ ★ ★

Jessie Crossan, eleven years old, was standing at the bottom of the wooden steps at the side of the stage. The quietest boy in her class, Patrick Lynch — his eyes bright with panic — was slowly shrinking through a tuneless 'Green Fields of France'. It was Jessie's father's party piece, and she knew all the words. She was singing them in her head to will Patrick along. She loved Patrick. He was so sweet, so shy. He brought jam sandwiches to school for his lunch, and something about that made her sad. When he had no lunch, she would make him take half

45

of hers. He would never have asked. She wanted to come to his rescue now, too; to run up on to the stage, and sweep him away like a superhero. Then dance. She had been practising for weeks.

Jessie didn't know any excitement like performing. She lived in a quiet house, with parents who didn't say much to each other, but when they sat side by side on the sofa, listening to her sing, watching her dance, she knew that was when they were happiest. She was sad they weren't there to watch her today — her mother was away, and her father wouldn't be back from work until dinner time.

Patrick went suddenly quiet, his pale hands intertwined, his knuckles white. His spindly legs had been shaking as soon as he stood in front of the microphone, but now the shaking turned violent, and he held a hand to his thigh to steady it. An older boy in the crowd — Johnny — shot out a laugh, and Patrick's head jerked towards the judges' table. There was the parish priest — Father Owens, jacket off, dabbing a handkerchief to his brow; Sister Consolata, Vice Principal of the secondary school — hands folded on the table in front of her, head tilted, legs crossed at the ankles, and the Sergeant, Colm Hurley, playing MC for the day.

'I forgot the words,' Patrick muttered, his gaze back on the floor.

'Do you want to go again, Patrick?' said Father Owens. 'Give it another blast?'

Patrick's eyes filled with a desperation that presaged tears.

Father Owens paused, then gave a hearty clap.

46

'Well, you did a great job, Patrick! That was a fine rendition!'

Patrick's eyes widened a fraction.

'Indeed, it was,' said Colm joining in the applause. 'Well done.'

'Yes!' said Jessie, louder than she meant to. She looked, full of hope, at Sister Consolata, who was staring up at Patrick with her tight smile and lifeless squint. Sister Consolata had a loud clap despite her tiny hands, and eventually threw two distinct ones into the fading applause. Jessie had worked out years earlier that this was Sister Consolata's way of giving marks out of ten.

Patrick, his head dipped, left the stage, and ran down the steps past Jessie.

'You were brilliant,' she said, but he didn't hear her.

★ ★ ★

Sergeant Colm had bounded up on to the stage from the front. He gave Jessie a warm smile. 'Up you come!' he said. 'Here she is, ladies and gentlemen — eleven-year-old Jessie Crossan, who — by the rig-out and the tape recorder — I'm going to guess will be dancing for us today. Is that right?'

Jessie beamed. 'Yes!'

She looked out at the crowd, and caught Sister Consolata running a chilling gaze up and down her body. She felt a spike of fear. Her parents loved her clothes, and loved her dancing, and so did all her friends. Instinctively, she searched the crowd for comfort, and found it in the smile of her best friend, Helen. Her next best friend, Laura, was beside her, with two thumbs up. Her other friends, Edie and Clare, were standing at the front, giving her matching ladylike waves. Murph was doing moves like a boxer. She tried not to laugh. She walked over to one of the speakers, and put the tape recorder on top.

'All business — look at her!' said Colm, and the crowd laughed.

Jessie gave him a nod.

'Right,' he said, 'she's got it all under control. In your own time.'

He jumped off the front of the stage, and jogged back to his seat.

★   ★   ★

Jessie hit Play on the tape recorder. She took to the centre of the stage. Then she knelt, one knee on the floor, one knee up, her head curled to her chest. The music started. And, at eleven years old, Jessie, with the innocence and enthusiasm of a girl whose parents were happy when they watched her dance, moved flawlessly through her own carefully choreographed routine to the song, Maneater.

She finished, arms in the air, joyful, expectant. She was met with silence. She was used to her parents' instant applause. Some sound. Any sound. But the crowd had fallen under the spell of Sister Consolata, whose moods could ripple out like a black-ink gauze, floating slowly down, and settling, wrapping around people, bridling them.

Jessie eventually lowered her arms, and a few scattered claps broke out. Her confused eyes finally found Sister Consolata, who was rising from her seat and heading towards her. With a stiff arm and pointed finger, she directed Jessie to exit the stage. She waited for her at the bottom of the steps, then stooped to meet her at eye level.

'That was a disgrace!' she said. 'An absolute disgrace.'

She stared Jessie down until she trembled.

★ ★ ★

That night, Jessie sat on her bed wearing just the loose pink cotton top of her summer pyjamas and a pair of underpants. Her diary was open, the tiny lock and key on the turned-down sheet beside her. She wrote the date at the top of the page, along with REGATTA!!!! She paused with the nib of the pen over the first line. After a while, she wrote:

Mammy is at a pilgrimidge in Knock. But she told Daddy I could open my parcel from Auntie Mona in Boston!!! I was so excited!!! It's not even my birthday until Thursday!!! The reason was because it had an outfit for the talent contest in it!!!! It was a shiny leotard and leggings from a proper dance shop. I love it so much! (she also got me a packet of 3 underpantses which is so embarrising). The Talent Contest was at three o'clock in the Square. It

*was rosting. Patrick Lynch sang Green
Fields of France. And I finally got to do
my dance! Maneater! Watch out boy she'll
cheer you up! Everyone loved it!*

*I'm so tired, but tell you the rest tomor-
row. Zzzzz.*

She never wrote in the diary again. She never saw
it again. The guards took it. They took her blan-
kets too. They took her sheets, and her pyjama
top, her pillow and her teddies, her hairband, and
her book. They took her father too for a while.

6

Edie stood in the shadows of the balcony overlooking the hall. She was wearing a dark green silk dress with three-quarter-length sleeves that had a small gold button at the cuff. She wore matching dark-green patent heels, and had a dark green bracelet with fine gold edging on her right wrist. Her hair was down, to her shoulders, and tousled, her make-up subtle, eyes with a hint of gold shadow and a smoky edge.

'Johnny's voice drifted up from below. 'I don't know where Edie is.'

'Agonizing over the details,' Clare said.

'Well, I hope so,' said Murph. 'I did my research, and I'm expecting a 'soothing five-star experience'.'

Johnny laughed. 'That was Condé Nast Traveller.'

'Murph reading Condé Nast Traveller,' said Clare.

'What do you think I read?' said Murph. 'The *Irish Field*? Which is an excellent publication, but not the point.'

'The place is amazing, lads,' said Laura. 'It's like . . . I don't know how ye did it.'

'It's magnificent,' said Clare. 'Helen — you must be used to it at this stage.'

'No,' said Helen. 'Still impresses me every time. But we're usually over at the house.'

'Probably a shithole too, is it?' said Murph.

They all laughed.

'Speaking of shit,' said Laura, 'what was with the reviews on Trip Advisor?'

Edie closed her eyes.

'Laura!' said Clare.

'What? I was disgusted,' said Laura. 'About the afternoon tea and the cream being off, and the whole thing being a rip-off? I'm saying it because I know there's no way that's true.'

'It wasn't,' said Johnny. 'But that's a conversation for another time.'

Edie took a deep breath, straightened her shoulders, and walked to the top of the stairs. 'Hello!' she said, beaming. They all cheered.

'Here she is now,' said Murph. 'Lady of the Manor.'

Edie laughed. 'You're all so welcome! I'm sorry I wasn't here. What an appalling hostess! I had a few things to take care of.' She looked at Helen. 'Happy Birthday! You look stunning.'

'It's the blow-dry,' said Helen, waving a hand at it. She had thick, shiny short brown hair that fell across one side of her face. It was an old-fashioned cut but it was perfect on her. She never wore much eye make-up and always wore a pair of glasses to complement whatever outfit she had on. Tonight, they were black. She was wearing a red wrap top and a long black taffeta skirt, and red shoes with a square gold buckle with pearls on the toes.

'It's not the blow-dry,' said Edie. 'It's everything.'

'And she's got the tits out,' said Murph. 'Looking amazing.'

Clare hugged Edie. 'I'm blown away.'

'I can't believe this is your first time here!' said Edie.

'Ours too,' said Laura, pointing at herself and Murph.

'Yeah, you ignorant bastards,' said Murph.

'We didn't want to lower the tone,' said Johnny.

'Says your man,' said Murph, tilting his head toward him. Then he looked at himself in the long mirror, and ran his hand down the sleeve of his navy jacket. 'I think I scrub up very well.'

'You do,' said Edie, opening her arms wide. Murph gave her a huge hug, and lifted her off the ground. 'I miss my Murph hugs,' she said.

'So, I heard Father Lynch is coming,' said Murph when he put her down.

'Please have some new jokes for tonight,' said Laura.

'He'll always be Father Lynch to me,' said Murph.

'Yes — he's coming,' said Edie. 'Helen bumped into him in Cork and said 'Come on down'.'

Murph looked at Helen. 'He still looks like a priest. I know he does.'

'No,' said Helen. 'No, he does not.'

'Is he still in the States?' said Laura.

'I thought he was in Dublin,' said Clare.

'He is,' said Edie. 'I think he was in New York before that.' She looked at Helen. 'Isn't that what you said?'

Helen nodded.

'Jesus,' said Johnny. 'I never thought I'd see

such excitement over Patrick Lynch coming to something.'

'It's not excitement,' said Edie. 'It's — '

'Curiosity,' said Clare. She looked at Johnny. 'You were too old when Patrick was on the scene — you were off doing your Munster thing. You only remember him from when he was a child.'

'I hope he's had a shower,' said Johnny.

'Ah, Johnny,' said Clare.

'It's not like I'm going to say it to his face,' said Johnny.

'Sure, no wonder he smelled,' said Laura. 'The child was a mobile sweatshop. And he couldn't have been more than six. Polishing the church when he should have been out kicking a ball.'

'I'm sure I saw him with his arm in a sling at one stage,' said Clare.

'Still at it?' said Murph.

Clare nodded.

'Imagine my two polishing a church,' said Laura. 'They'd be up taking a shit in the font.'

'Laura!' said Clare.

'Don't pretend you're shocked,' said Laura.

The doorbell rang. Murph's eyes widened, then he mouthed, 'Is that him? I hope he didn't hear.' He mimed a shower over his head.

Everyone laughed. Johnny walked over and opened the door. A blast of wind and rain swept in with Patrick. He had his head bowed against it, the hood of his black jacket up. He pushed it back and smiled at everyone.

'Welcome!' said Johnny, shaking his hand. 'Let me take your jacket.'

'Thank you,' said Patrick.

Clare flashed a glance at Edie, her eyebrows raised. Laura was less subtle. Edie tried not to laugh. Patrick was six foot two, broad-shouldered and muscular. He was wearing a tight black long-sleeved sweater with three black buttons at the neck, and black trousers. He was fresh-faced, his teeth were perfect, his brown hair cut with a neat side-parting.

Even Murph and Johnny were staring at him.

'Father Lynch,' said Murph, extending his hand.

Laura rolled her eyes.

'Mr Murphy — you haven't changed a bit,' said Patrick.

'I wish I could say the same to you,' said Murph. 'You're showing myself and Johnny up. The ladies can't know this is possible at our age.'

Edie glanced at Johnny.

Patrick hugged everyone. 'You smell divine!' said Clare.

Laura stifled a laugh. Edie's eyes widened.

'Right,' said Johnny. 'To the bar.'

Murph and Patrick strode after him.

★ ★ ★

Clare turned to Edie.

'I did not say that on purpose,' she said.

'I know you didn't,' said Edie. 'Your face!'

Laura looked at Helen. 'You dirty bitch. That's why you invited him.'

'Obviously,' said Helen.

'What's his scoop?' said Clare. 'Is he married?'

'We need a bit more time to start getting that

info out of him,' said Laura.

'He looks single,' said Clare.

''Looks single',' said Laura.

'He doesn't look like he has the weight of the world on his shoulders . . . that marriage brings,' said Clare.

The others laughed.

'What's he up to, these days?' said Laura.

'He's in hedge funds,' said Clare.

'What does that mean?' said Laura.

'That he's rich enough to wear a jumper and hiking boots to a five-star establishment,' said Helen.

Edie laughed. 'As if I'd care.'

Clare raised her eyebrows. 'I saw you giving a frowny look at his jumper.'

'What?' said Edie. 'No, I did not.'

'So, you're telling me Patrick Lynch is rolling in it,' said Laura.

'Oh, yes,' said Clare.

'From nothing,' said Laura. 'Fair play to him.'

'Murph made a huge effort,' said Clare.

'The navy jacket and shirt,' said Edie. She nodded her approval.

'Never thought I'd see the day — Murph in velvet,' said Laura.

'It suits him,' said Helen.

'God, when I think of him, the poor divel,' said Clare, 'going from one house to the next for his dinner, making everyone laugh, and how sad he'd look, heading off. And the worst part of it was it wasn't like he was going home to some savage who was going to beat him.'

'Heartbreaking,' said Edie. 'And Mum would

never let him stay for dinner. It was so awkward. And she would have known what was going on.'

'That time he was in our house and the packet of ham fell out from under his jumper,' said Laura. 'And Mam would have been happy to give it to him.'

'Oh, no,' said Helen. 'I can just picture his little face.'

'And remember,' said Laura, 'the time he — '

'Let's remember,' said Helen, 'that we all had that little face once.'

'And,' said Clare, 'is there not some unspoken agreement that we forget each other's childhood shame?'

7

MURPH

Castletownbere, 1981

Murph stood outside his mother's bedroom. He hadn't seen her for two days. He put his ear to the door. He could hear a man's voice, but it wasn't his father, because his father was at work. He could hear the voice coming closer to the door, so he bounced away, and took a few steps back down the hallway. When he heard the door open, he pretended he was walking towards it. Dr Weston appeared with his big leather bag, closing the door gently behind him.

'Hello, Liam,' he said. He gave a nod.

'Can I go in to see Mammy?' said Murph.

'Not today,' he said. 'She needs to rest.'

Murph frowned. 'She's resting the whole time.'

Dr Weston started to walk down the stairs.

Murph came after him. 'Can I not just go in for a little minute?'

Dr Weston gripped the banister. Murph froze. 'What's so important that it can't wait 'til tomorrow?'

'You said tomorrow the last time,' said Murph.

'Well, I'm saying it again, now.' He gave a nod, and then he looked up at Mm. 'Sure, you're a big lad, now. Aren't you able to look after yourself, and not be bothering your mammy?'

Murph's face flushed. Dr Weston's three sons were all big lads, rough and tough. Murph knew they were older than he was, but when they were his age they were the same. Johnny, the one who played rugby, was fourteen but he was a bit of a bully, and Murph wasn't sure being tough was all it was cracked up to be.

Murph stayed where he was on the stairs until Dr Weston left. Then he turned and ran up to his mother's room. He put his ear to the door again. There was no sound. He let out a sigh, then ran downstairs, and out into the front garden.

★　★　★

Jerry Murphy drove up to the house, and parked the van in the drive. He jumped out, and reached Murph in four strides, sweeping him off the ground, and throwing him up on his shoulders.

'I'm too big, Daddy!' said Murph.

Jerry held on to his son's little calves, and walked him around the side of the house. 'Do I look like a man who can't carry a smallie like you on his back? Sure, amn't I doing it right now?' He slid his hands down to Murph's ankles, and lifted them, tilting him back, making him grab for the back of his shirt collar to pull himself up. 'Daddy!' he said, tapping him on the head.

Jerry laughed. When they got around the back,

he swung Murph down on to the ground beside a small pile of red timber slats. 'Right,' he said, 'you and me are going to make a little house.'

'What kind of a house?' said Murph.

'Ah, for one of your little cousins for her dolls. Now — grab me that hammer over there.'

He knelt down, and Murph stood smiling at the top of his head; his father was always helping people, and Murph loved helping him do it. And he loved hearing the things people always said about his father: 'That's a man you can rely on,' 'That's a man who'd never let you down,' 'You could call Jerry Murphy any time, day or night,' 'Jerry Murphy'd give you the shirt off his back.'

★   ★   ★

When the little house was built, Murph stood back and put his hands on his hips.

'I don't know, Daddy, if she's going to be mad about it.'

'What?' said Jerry. 'What do you mean? After all our hard work.'

'No — I know,' said Murph. 'But . . . are you going to be cutting holes in it later? For the windows?'

'Jesus — I hadn't thought of windows.'

'And is it not supposed to have a floor in the middle to put furniture on?' He glanced at his dad. 'It looks funny.'

'It looks funny, you think. What does it look like to you, so?'

Murph frowned. 'I don't want to be mean. I know you wanted to do a nice job on it. But it

60

looks a bit . . . like a kennel.'

Jerry stood up, and laughed. He put his hands on his hips. 'Jesus — you're right.' He started rubbing his face. 'Amn't I some eejit? Let me see if I have anything at all in the van, so we can sort something out.' He disappeared around to the front of the house.

Murph heard a knock from the upstairs window. He took a few steps backwards so he could see properly. His mam was standing at her bedroom window with a big smile on her slender face, her eyes huge, her dressing gown up high around her neck. She waved at him, and he waved back. She pointed down at the little house, like she wanted to get a better look. Murph went over, and dragged it on to the grass where she could see it. She smiled.

'I think I have something for that house!' Jerry shouted.

When Murph looked up, Jerry was standing a distance away. Between his two boots was a little ball of fur that he let go as soon as Murph turned.

Murph jumped as a tiny black-and-white border collie pup shot towards him. By the time Murph crouched down, the dog was flinging himself into his chest, wriggling against him, trying to lick his neck. Murph stood up with him, hugging him tight, and they rubbed the sides of their faces together. Then Murph settled him into his arms, with his front paws up on his shoulders.

'Daddy!' said Murph. 'I love him!'

He held the dog up to show his mam. She beamed down at him from the window.

Jerry laughed, and patted the back of Murph's head. 'Sure, you're best pals already.'

'Thank you, thank you, thank you,' said Murph, and he looked up again, but his mam was gone. 'And thank Mammy for me.' He paused. 'Or could I thank her myself later?' His eyes were shining.

Jerry squeezed Murph's shoulder. 'You can, of course.'

Murph beamed.

'So,' said Jerry, 'what are you going to call your new pal?'

Murph thought about it. 'Rosco.'

Jerry laughed. 'From the television? The lads that climb in the car through the window?'

Murph nodded. 'Rosco P. Coltrane.'

Jerry patted the dog's head. 'Rosco P. Murphy, it is so.'

★   ★   ★

That night, Murph woke up to a terrible choking sound, his heart pounding. He got up, and went to the door, pressing the handle down slowly, and edging the door open. He heard the sound again, and it was coming from downstairs. His chest tightened. He wanted to go into his mammy and daddy's room, but he wasn't allowed. This time, he knew they wouldn't, though, because he was scared. And his mammy always told him to come to her when he was scared. He crossed the hallway, and opened their door gently. He walked in on tiptoes, and up to the bed. His mother was asleep, and even though she was asleep, she looked tired, and he didn't want to wake her. His daddy wasn't there, so he thought maybe that was him downstairs.

★   ★   ★

He sneaked down and stuck his head in to the dining room. He saw his father inside, sitting in the dark, his back against the wall, his legs out in front of him, his chin to his chest. His arms were loose at his side, and he was sobbing and sobbing. A rush of fear swept over Murph. He'd never seen his father cry. He went up to him, then turned his head away for a moment from the smell of whiskey. He looked down and saw an empty bottle by the leg of the table. He had only ever seen his father have one glass, and not even finish it.

'Daddy!' he said. 'Daddy!' He patted his shoulder. 'It's OK . . . it's OK. I'll . . . ' He tried to think of what his mam would say to him when he was small and he was having a nightmare or he was worried about something and he couldn't get to sleep.

'It's OK, Daddy,' he said. 'No one's coming to get you.'

He knelt down beside him, looking at his shirt, soaked with tears. He was thinking of his mam again, and what she would say.

'What is it, Daddy? Did someone say something to you?'

His father raised his head, confused. After a moment, he focused. 'Liam.' He tried to sit up. 'Liam . . . '

'Yes! Daddy — are you all right?'

Jerry shook his head slowly. 'No, no . . . no, no.' He started to sob again. Murph started crying too, because he didn't know what was wrong, and that was even scarier. He thought again of what his mam would say. He knelt in close, and put his hand on his father's shoulder.

'If I find out,' said Murph, 'that anyone was being mean to my . . . ' And his mam would say 'to my little man', so Murph said, 'If I find out that anyone was being mean to my . . . little dad . . . '

And his dad, all six foot four of him, with his big head, and his huge hands, and his broad shoulders, started to shake, and then Murph realized it was because he was laughing at the same time as he was crying, and Murph didn't care what he was laughing at, because he was laughing, and his dad reached out and grabbed his face like it was a football, and he looked at Murph with such love in his eyes that Murph thought his heart would burst.

★   ★   ★

The next morning, nothing was mentioned at breakfast about what had happened. When Murph came home after school, he went out to play with Rosco in the garden. When his dad came home from work, he ran to him, and gave him the tightest hug.

'Come on a way over with me,' said Jerry, 'and we'll sit on the wall.'

His father turned to him when they sat down.

'Liam,' he said, 'you know, now, the way Mammy's not well . . . '

Murph nodded.

'Not well at all.'

Murph nodded again.

Jerry put a hand to his chin. 'Do you know something?' he said. 'I think that woman would hug you every minute of the day if she could.'

Murph smiled, and his shoulders went up to his ears.

'But you know that's a small bit harder for her, now she's not well.' He paused. 'And that's all that is. She's a bit weak.' He patted Murph on the head. 'But you'll always be her little man . . . no matter what.'

8

Johnny waited outside the bar until everyone had caught up. He pushed open the door and guided everyone through with a sweep of his arm. The room had a mix of mahogany panelling and slate-grey walls, thick carpet in charcoal grey, and small round tables with green leather chairs. A log fire burned and crackled drawing everyone's attention until Murph boomed, 'No way,' and crossed to the opposite wall. Johnny, Edie, and Helen laughed.

Murph looked back at Johnny and Edie, his eyes gleaming. 'Is that . . . is your drinks cabinet an actual confession box?'

'Yes, it is,' said Johnny.

Murph shook his head, smiling.

'It's a little kitsch,' said Edie, 'but we couldn't resist.'

'I love honesty bars,' said Murph. 'But I prefer lying, filthy, cheating bars.'

'It's superb,' said Clare. 'Is it from the chapel?'

Johnny nodded. 'There were four of them, which was a bit much when you think of the size of it. We kept one where it was, ripped the other three out, and had this one restored.'

'Look,' said Murph. 'It actually accepts sins.' He pointed to a slot, and pulled out the drawer underneath. There were folded-up notes inside. He picked out three. ''Stole a bathrobe', 'Filled my purse with croissants at breakfast', and 'Had impure thoughts. Followed through.' Fair play to them. I hope the purse one was an American or she wouldn't have got far.'

'Is anyone weird about it?' said Clare. 'The sacrilege of it all.'

'No one's complained yet,' said Edie. She put her hand on the small of Johnny's back. 'Well done, by the way.' She gestured around the room. 'He set this all up.'

'He's got the fire on, the candles, everything,' said Laura. 'Never thought I'd see the day.'

'I do this all the time,' said Johnny, frowning. 'Why is everyone so surprised?'

'Jesus — I don't know,' said Murph. 'Maybe because of this.' He pointed to the wall beside the confession box. 'Johnny's glory wall under a picture light, in case we might miss it.' There were framed newspaper cuttings, Munster team photos, shots of Johnny on the pitch, at award ceremonies, with celebrities. Murph pointed to one: 'New Zealand, 1989. You played some game.'

'How you didn't end up playing for Ireland is beyond me,' said Clare,

'I agree,' said Edie.

'Thank you, ladies,' said Johnny. He walked over to the drinks. 'Right — what are you having?'

'The time of our lives,' said Murph.

Everyone put in their orders, and Johnny started to make the drinks.

'Speaking of time,' said Clare, 'this is very early for pre-dinner drinks. This could go horribly wrong.'

Johnny handed her a gin and tonic. 'Starting now.'

'That's my fault,' said Helen. 'I can't last very long in the evenings these days. So apologies to all of you for tomorrow's hangovers.'

'Who says I'm going to have a hangover?' said Clare.

'As Johnny hands everyone a massive drink,' said Helen. 'You'll all be dying in the morning.'

'Not me,' said Patrick, pointing to his 7UP.

'Do you not drink?' said Laura.

'No,' said Patrick. 'I gave up years ago.'

'Why's that?' said Laura. 'Health reasons?'

Patrick nodded. 'I guess so. Stopped one January and never looked back.'

'Hey — that's Clare's line,' said Johnny. ' "Never look back".'

' "Eyes ahead" is my line!' said Clare.

'It's "eyes ahead",' said Murph at the same time.

'Relax, the pair of you,' said Johnny.

Clare looked around the room. 'You're all an appalling influence and I know I'm going to end end up in some 'District Court Judge in Drinking Shame' situation.'

'We're well tucked away here,' said Johnny. 'What happens in Pilgrim Point stays in Pilgrim Point.'

'I'd say any fart I crack off tonight after a rake of pints will go well beyond the boundaries,' said Murph.

'Any development on the spa?' said Clare.

'Well, the plans are drawn up,' said Edie, 'but before we can put in for planning, we have to get an archaeological survey done. And there's no point getting it done at this time of year, so we're looking at March for that. And on and on.'

'Ooh,' said Murph, sucking in a breath, 'Johnny fucked up there.'

'What?' said Edie. She flashed warning eyes at Murph. 'No, he didn't.'

'Sorry,' said Murph. 'He just looked a little — '

'Bored,' said Edie.

Johnny frowned. 'I'm not bored, I'm — '

'I'm teasing,' said Edie. 'The chapel is Johnny's thing.'

'The chapel's not 'my thing',' said Johnny. 'It's — '

'Jesus, lads,' said Murph. 'You've got visitors. Did your mammies not teach you anything?'

'So, what are the plans for the chapel?' said Patrick.

'Well . . . ' said Johnny.

'Well . . . ' said Edie.

'What I think we should be doing,' said Johnny, 'is corporate events or yoga retreats or conferences or gigs or whatever. We're in the perfect spot — away from it all, no mobile coverage unless you want to use WhatsApp, no distractions — '

'And the views,' said Clare. 'And the Wild Atlantic Way.'

Murph turned to Edie. 'And what do you think you should be doing with it?'

'Not talking about it tonight,' said Edie, giving him a bright smile.

'And on and on it goes,' said Edie. 'That's why it's sort of . . . in limbo.'

69

'Or 'under renovation', as I like to call it,' said Johnny.

They fell into silence.

'So,' said Johnny, turning to Laura, 'how are you? How are the kid . . . s?'

'Good one,' said Laura. 'Yes, I've more than one. And they're alive. After that . . . well, Mammy's on the lash, isn't she?' She took a long sip of her drink.

Murph laughed. 'Johnny's like 'thank fuck we got that out of the way'.'

'I hate people banging on about their kids on a night out,' said Laura.

'It was a genuine question,' said Johnny.

'And have you any more question . . . s?' said Murph.

'Ah, give him a break,' said Laura. 'He's had a fair few knocks to the head over the years. Children: Séamus, seven, Paddy, five: healthy, happy, and tapped.'

'And the father?' said Johnny. 'Both Frank's?' He smiled.

'Johnny!' said Edie.

'I see a lot of Brad Pitt in Séamus,' said Laura.

Johnny turned to Clare. 'What about your lot?'

Clare smiled. 'Children: Ava, nineteen, Lucas, fourteen, Marco, twelve. Husband: Alan, forty-eight. Cuddly toy. Toaster. Microwave oven.'

'Not a child to my name,' said Murph. 'Until the knocks on the door start.'

'Not a child to my name, either,' said Patrick.

'Any woman on the scene?' said Laura.

Patrick shook his head. 'No.'

'Man?' said Clare.

Patrick smiled. 'Also, no.'

'And would you like to meet someone?' said Clare.

'I would, I suppose,' said Patrick, 'but it's hard enough, these days. And I wouldn't be one for internet dating.'

'Multiple women on the go, here,' said Murph. 'No apologies.'

'I hate to stop you mid-candid admission,' said Clare, 'but do you mind if we sit down?'

'Of course,' said Edie. 'Sorry.'

'No,' said Clare, 'it's my shoes.'

'Remember 'don't puke on my shoes', 'take off my shoes',' said Murph.

'Oh, God,' said Laura.

'And the gas part was you were talking to yourself,' said Murph. 'Laura, pasted, forehead down on a white plastic table — '

'That I had to climb under,' said Helen, 'so I could take off the shoes.'

'Well, of course you did,' said Murph.

There was a chorus from the others, ' 'I couldn't say no!' '

'Do I say that a lot?' said Helen.

They all laughed. 'Yes,' said Edie.

'Yes!' said Murph. 'It's why we all love you.' He turned to Laura. 'There's not many who'd risk climbing under a table when you're gearing up.'

'And she managed' to have the wherewithal to tell me make sure the shoes were 'out of splashing distance',' said Helen.

'Ah, lads,' said Laura. 'Clare — you were right. We need to be allowed to forget this shit.'

71

'Sure, that's no craic,' said Murph.

'Right, everyone,' said Johnny. 'Go — sit. I have a few things to check on and I'll be back.'

Helen let Johnny pass, and pulled Edie to one side as everyone else sat down.

'Am I sensing tension?' said Helen.

'Where?' said Edie.

'Johnny and Patrick?' said Helen.

Edie's eyes widened. 'What? Why do you say that?'

'Do you really think Johnny believes I randomly bumped into Patrick last week, and just said, 'Come on down for my birthday dinner', given that the last time I laid eyes on him was when he came to say his goodbyes to Sister Consolata in the hospital — and she's dead — what? Ten years?'

'Why would Johnny not believe you?' said Edie.

'Apart from him or his wife usually being the people who drive me to Cork?' said Helen. 'For which I am eternally grateful, obviously.'

Edie smiled. 'Pleasure. But — you could have been up there with anyone.'

'I know — I told him I was with one of my nurse pals, but I'm just . . . questioning the wisdom of your plan. And I was wondering if you were too. Johnny looks on edge.'

'Johnny always looks on edge,' said Edie. She caught Helen's expression. 'Sorry — that's awful. Just . . . you're making it sound like I'm doing something terrible, when all I wanted was for Patrick to see the inn. That way, if the investment thing becomes a real issue, and

72

Patrick is interested, it won't be a bolt from the blue — he'll have been here, seen what we're doing.'

'You don't feel bad, lying to Johnny?' said Helen.

'No,' said Edie. 'No. The inn is . . . we need investment, Patrick has the means, he's our friend.'

'But the last time you saw him was three years ago. And that was because you needed a favour.'

'Yes — about the inn,' said Edie. 'Because I knew he was in hedge funds, I knew how success-ful he was, and unlike anyone else I could have asked, he knows Beara. This was a big investment — you know that. Johnny and I were in the States at the time. Patrick was in New York. All I asked him to do was meet me for a chat. And he could have said 'No' if he didn't want to help. I'd have done the same for him. And he was the one who offered to view the place, so . . . ' She shrugged. 'Look — he's a nice guy.'

Helen nodded.

'I couldn't have approached just anyone, saying that I wasn't sure whether or not my husband had a clue what he was doing,' said Edie. 'And I wouldn't have known what a third party would need to be able to give me informed advice. Nor would I have known how to actually gather it all together without Johnny being on to me. I knew what Patrick did, he knows us both, and he knows the property, and after looking at everything, he said, 'Go for it!' So he believed in it as a business, which — in my mind — makes him the most logical person to approach as an investor.'

'No — I know,' said Helen. 'It makes sense — sorry. This is my issue. I think I'm feeling guilty because Johnny's so good.'

'He is good,' said Edie, 'which is the whole point of Patrick being a possible investor — to actually relieve Johnny of pressure.'

★   ★   ★

Helen glanced up at Edie. 'Clare — incoming.'

'What's going on here, ladies?' said Clare. 'It all looks very serious.' She narrowed her eyes. 'Are we setting Helen up with Patrick?'

Edie and Helen laughed. 'No,' said Edie.

Laura came up behind Clare. She glanced back at Patrick and Murph. 'Murph's on about horses.'

'I was about to say that I'm not sure I believe Patrick Lynch that he's single,' said Clare.

'Why would he lie about that?' said Edie.

'I don't know,' said Clare.

'I totally believe he's single,' said Laura. 'I'd say the mother frightened him off women for life. You look back and you think, was she well in the head at all?' She paused. 'In fairness, my two will probably think the same about me.'

'Well, he's made a success of himself,' said Helen, 'so she must have done something right.'

'Whatever went on in that house,' said Laura. 'Good enough for her, the mother died before she could cash in.'

'Laura!' said Clare.

'What?' said Laura. 'She was an oddball. Was she ever outside the door? Remember, you'd go

74

by the house, and if the door was open, you'd see the Sacred Heart . . . '

'Sure, every house had a Sacred Heart back then,' said Helen.

'They did not,' said Laura. 'And none were in your face like that.'

Edie glanced over at him. 'Poor Patrick.'

'Not any more,' said Laura.

The others laughed.

'Right,' said Edie. 'I'll be back. I have a few last-minute bits to do.'

'I'm mortified,' said Helen, 'Honestly. I don't mind if we have spaghetti on toast.'

Laura rolled her eyes. 'How about nuggets and chips? Would you eat them if she landed them up in front of you?'

'Yes!' said Helen.

'You would, of course,' said Laura. 'Sure, you can't say 'no'!'

The others laughed.

'What?' said Helen.

'Your catchphrase,' said Clare. ' 'I couldn't say 'no'!' '

'It is not,' said Helen. 'Is it? Did I say that a lot?'

Edie smiled. 'You still do.' She put her hand on Helen's shoulder, and gave it a squeeze. 'There are worse catchphrases to be known for.'

⋆ ⋆ ⋆

Edie did one last check of the dining table. She stopped at each place setting, turned the childhood photos right side up, and stood them

75

against a wine glass. When she reached Patrick's, there was the sound of paper crinkling under-foot. She stepped back and crouched down. There were two pages on the floor — lined, yellowed, ripped from a notebook, both rigid from where a red or black biro had moved back and forth across them with such force, it had broken through the page in places. Edie took them in her hand, and stood up. Her legs went weak, and she reached out for the back of the chair to steady herself. There were crude drawings of faces on each page — circles for heads, black Xs for eyes. The first had a crooked line for a mouth, and a jagged head wound, spurting blood. There was a hammer drawn beside it. The second had a large circle for a mouth, a noose around its neck and a rope that disappeared off the top of the page. HA HA HA HA HA was written to the right of it, and under-neath: BYE BYE PATRICK LYNCH.

9

PATRICK

Castletownbere, 1981

Patrick was nine years old, standing in the kitchen doorway. His mother was at the sink, an empty chair beside her. She looked at him and nodded down at it.

Patrick shook into stillness. He knew he was to get up on the chair, but he didn't know what he'd done. Nothing bad had happened in school that day. He always behaved himself. He was never late, he was always polite.

Mrs Lynch's eyes widened. She moved towards him, reached into the pocket of her apron, and whipped out a piece of paper. She unfolded it and held it up. Before he had a chance to focus on it, she pushed it closer to his face. 'What's this nonsense?' she said.

Patrick pulled his head back so he could see. It was a page she had ripped from his religion copy. On the top half was a picture he'd drawn of a boat, with a boy beside him. The sun was shining, the sky was a skinny blue strip at the top of the page, the birds were waiting for fish. What was causing the problem that his mother was pointing at now were the huge smiles on the boy and the man.

'It's not nonsense,' said Patrick.

His mother turned the page around to face her. She read out loud what he had written on the lines underneath the picture — in the voice she used when she wanted him to hear himself: ''I am fishing with Daddy. We are on the boat. We are catching so much fish. We went to Dursey Island on the cable car. There was a sheep in it. It was so funny. We had a picnic. Then we went home.' She looked up at the title. 'So that's 'My Best Day' by Patrick Lynch. Have you ever seen such nonsense in all your life?'

Patrick's face burned, and the heat seemed to flush through his whole body. His mother was glaring at him, waiting for him to reply.

Patrick shrugged.

'Don't you shrug your shoulders at me!' She shook the picture again. 'And a big red tick beside it and a 'VG, Patrick!' I'll VG her when I see her.'

'Don't, Mammy! She's so nice.'

'Nice!' said his mother. 'Nice?'

'What's wrong with it?' said Patrick, brave, tentative.

His mother looked at him, her face pinched, lines like arrows piercing the tight circle of her mouth.

'What's wrong with it?' she mimicked.

'Why don't you like it?' said Patrick.

'Like it?' she said. 'This?' She rattled the page again.

Patrick shook his head. 'No.' His eyes darted

everywhere before they tried to settle on hers, but he couldn't even manage that. 'Why don't you like it when things are nice?'

His mother stared at him. 'Get up on that chair now this minute.'

Patrick walked towards the sink behind her, his heart hammering, his eyes never leaving the picture. She was holding it between her thumb and index finger like it was dirty. He just wanted it back. It was his favourite picture and it was his favourite imaginary day. He knelt up on the chair. She lowered her left hand into the sink, and he watched the page disappear after it.

Patrick let out a moan. 'No, Mammy; Mammy, no!'

Mrs Lynch lifted her hand slowly from the water, and tossed the picture to one side, where it clung, briefly, to a bucket of potato skins.

The same hand went into the sink again, and she rattled the dishes around to make space. Patrick jumped at the speed her right hand came down on the back of his neck. She plunged his head under the water, and his forehead struck the edge of a thick glass tankard. His scream, reflexive, and submerged, sent a rush of bubbles from his nose and mouth.

'Jesus Christ Almighty!' said Mrs Lynch, yanking him up. 'You could have split your head open on that!'

When she was angry, her sentences came in a low snarl with highs like sparks from embers. She plunged him under again.

He had time to taste the water, and it tasted of cabbage and fish and bleach. She pulled him out again, and he hung from her grip, gasping, and red-eyed. Then she gave him three hard shakes — his prompt.

'Sorry, Mammy,' he said. 'I'm sorry! I'm sorry!'

She held him there, spluttering, his head bowed, a string of saliva hanging from his lip, until, eventually, her body relaxed.

★ ★ ★

Sorry was his mother's drug. She needed to hear it for every transgression, real or concocted. She had never heard it from the husband she had kicked out. Not even on the last day she had seen him, when he left her to her insanity, and her fury, and their seven-year-old son, whose blond hair glowed red under the flickering bulb of a Sacred Heart light.

10

Edie left the dining room, the pages of the notebook wrapped inside a napkin, gripped tight in her trembling hand. She stopped, briefly, in the hallway and let out a long breath. Johnny jogged up behind her. She jumped.

'Hey, hey, hey,' he said. 'What's up?'

'Oh!' said Edie. 'Nothing! It's . . . ridiculous. I'm . . . nervous about dinner.'

'You need to get some more Prosecco into you.' He looked at her. 'Or maybe not. You're white as a sheet.'

'I bent down and got up too quickly,' she said. 'You were right, though — I don't know what I was thinking, cooking.'

Johnny put his hands on her shoulders and made her loosen them out. 'Breathe. It's our friends. No one cares. Everyone's drinking away, happy out.

'You're playing a blinder.'

'Thanks,' said Edie.

'What do you want me to do?' said Johnny.

'Keep everyone entertained for five minutes. I need to nip to the office. Then I'll get the starters.'

'I can do that,' said Johnny.

'It's fine — go do your thing.'

She walked down the stairs in to the office, her legs shaking. She went over to the safe, crouched down and punched in the code. She pulled open the door and slipped the pages into one of her folders and closed it again.

★ ★ ★

Edie stood outside the honesty bar, the heels of her hands pressed against her eyes. She straightened up, took in a deep breath, smiled, and opened the door.

'Ladies and gentlemen,' she said, 'Dinner is now served.'

Everyone cheered. Johnny held the door open as they filed out and followed Edie down to the dining room. Edie checked she had everyone's attention before she opened the tall double doors with a flourish. The chatter petered out as they walked in. Laura banged into the back of Helen's chair when she stopped just inside the threshold, her hand to her mouth.

'Oh Edie,' was all Helen could manage. 'Oh Edie,' she said again, lifting her hand and waving it in front of her, as if to introduce the room. She turned to the others. 'You can imagine what this is normally like — formal, elegant . . . Edie. And this . . . This — '

'Designer forest clearing,' said Clare.

Everyone laughed.

Helen's eyes, when they met Edie's were shining. 'Now, this,' she said, 'This is what it feels like to be seen'. Edie bent down to hug her. 'Thank you,' Helen whispered in her ear. They embraced for a long time, before pulling apart, both laughing and wiping away tears. 'And thank you, Johnny.'

'Pleasure,' said Johnny. 'Absolute pleasure.'

'Come in. Come in, everyone,' said Edie.

'I'll go get the starters,' said Johnny.

'Thanks,' said Edie. She turned to the others. 'I didn't do place names, but I did do place photos.' She smiled.

Clare found hers first. 'Oh, thank God — no perm.' She squinted at it. 'And it looks like I've got the hang of Immac.' She ran a finger across her upper lip, and made a face.

'That state of me!' said Laura, holding her photo up. 'I haven't changed a bit.' She leaned into Murph's. 'What's yours?'

He gave her a sad smile as he handed it to her. 'Me and the love of my life.'

'Aw, Rosco,' said Laura. 'Everyone loved Rosco.'

'He was my best pal,' said Murph. 'No offence to any of ye. But his coat was so soft. And you were all wearing those scratchy duffel ones at the time. And you were cold auld bitches. 'Get off me', 'get off me'.' He sat down.

'Well, Jesus — Rosco ran away from you altogether,' said Laura, sitting beside him.

Murph looked at her. 'Too soon. Too soon . . . '

Laura squeezed his hand.

'Sorry, Murph,' said Edie. 'It was the only photo I could find of you that wasn't a big group one.'

'I know,' said Murph. 'Dad — the king of Beara history — and I go through his things after he dies, and I'd say from eleven on, he has one photo. Of his only child. And hundreds of photos of miserable-looking skinny bastards from here. I'm not talking about you, Edie. And I'm

83

definitely not talking about Johnny. The industrial school, obviously.'

Johnny walked in with a tray of starters, and set them on the sideboard inside the door. Edie went over to help him.

Edie's eyes were on Helen. She was lost in her photo, teary. She looked up at Edie, 'Thank you,' she said, smiling. 'Thank you.'

'Are those sad tears or happy tears?' said Murph.

Helen laughed, picking up her napkin to dab her eyes. 'Happy, of course!'

Murph reached across the table for Helen's photo.

'Aw, look at Jess,' said Laura, pointing to her.

Murph leaned back in his chair and called over to her, 'There's been a devastating turn of events.'

Edie spun around to him, her eyes wide, her hand to her chest.

'Jesus,' said Murph, holding up his hands. 'I was just going to say I had no napkin.'

Edie laughed a shaky laugh. 'That is devastating for me.'

'Right,' said Johnny, watching her rearrange the plates. 'I don't think there's much more we can do here.' He put his arm around her waist and squeezed. Edie squirmed out of his grip.

'Sorry,' she said, 'just . . . give me a minute.'

As she walked to the table, she straightened her shoulders and smiled as she handed out the starters. Johnny watched her as he did the same at the other side of the table.

'Did I hear Kevin Crossan died?' he said.

'That was last year,' said Laura.

'The poor divil.' said Murph. 'That must have been hard, all the same. People thinking he had something to do with what happened to Jessie.'

'Ah, not everyone thought that,' said Laura.

'There was a fair few did,' said Murph. 'I mean, I always liked Kevin, but we were so young at the time. Later, I was thinking: OK — Jessie's mam was away, Kevin was minding Jessie, and he says he hears nothing at all — no one coming into the house, no screams from Jessie, no one leaving. Does that make sense to anyone?'

'He said he had the TV blaring,' said Laura.

'It wasn't a big house, though,' said Murph. He turned to Helen. 'OK — you were right next door. Did you not hear anything?'

'Have we not had this conversation?' said Helen.

'I don't know,' said Murph.

'Mam and Dad were out,' said Helen. 'They got a 'babysitter' in.' She looked at Laura. 'Laura's Miriam.'

'Miriam?' said Laura. 'God — they must have been desperate.'

'Everyone was desperate for babysitters Regatta weekend,' said Helen. 'And no — I didn't hear a thing. But Miriam had lent me her Walkman — '

'Jesus — you had more luck than me,' said Laura. 'She'd literally ask you to clean her room top to bottom before she'd give you a go of it.'

'How do you remember shit like that?' said Murph.

'Sisters,' said Laura. 'They scar you.'

'OK — forget about that for a second,' said

85

Murph. 'So your dad said there were no signs of forced entry.'

'Ah, Murph — of course there weren't,' said Laura. 'Everyone left their doors open.'

'Do you really think Kevin did it?' said Clare.

'No,' said Murph. 'I'm just saying I could never wrap my head around the whole thing.'

'A lot of people were saying that the only reason Jessie said the rapist was wearing a mask was to cover for her dad,' said Patrick.

'Oh, God — that's a depressing detail,' said Clare. 'I hadn't heard that.'

'Well the man's life was ruined, either way,' said Murph. 'As if he hadn't been through enough. All it takes is a few people thinking you're guilty, and you're fucked.'

'Well, I never for a second thought Kevin was guilty,' said Clare. 'My heart went out to the man. Can you imagine? Finding your child in that state.'

'Three stab wounds,' said Murph. 'There was no way she was meant to survive that.'

They all went quiet.

'But she did,' said Helen.

'The little fighter,' said Clare.

'But, then, do you wonder?' said Laura. 'She was told the whole time how brave she was — apart from Cuntsolata — and how strong she was, and that she was a miracle, and all the rest of it. And she could have been going around for years trying to believe that, because why wouldn't you? And inside, she could have been in bits.'

Edie and Patrick exchanged accidental glances.

'Jesus,' said Johnny, 'I'll never forget Dad

86

coming home that night. He was one of the first on the scene.' He shook his head. 'He did what he could for her, waiting for the ambulance, but . . . he wasn't right for a long time after that.'

'I don't think anybody's dad was right after it,' said Clare.

'None of ours were — I think they all thought, 'it could have been my daughter'.'

'I remember Daddy having to go away on business the next day,' said Edie, 'and he was terribly upset. I'm sure I was clinging to him for dear life. And he said to me, 'I would never leave you if I thought you weren't safe.'' She paused. 'And that was all it took. God — there was nothing he could say that I wouldn't just believe one hundred per cent.'

'Lads . . . I saw the state of her in the hospital,' said Laura. 'And — '

'What?' said Clare. 'How?'

Laura nodded. 'The Thursday after. Her birthday.'

'Good Lord,' said Clare. 'Was that not a bit much — your parents sending you up there at that age?'

'Sure, look — nobody knew anything back then,' said Laura. 'Poor Mam was only thinking of Jessie lying there on her birthday with no friends, as if she'd done something wrong herself.'

'Your poor mam,' said Edie. 'That was very sweet.'

'And woefully misguided,' said Clare.

Laura turned to Helen. 'How did you . . . ?'

Everyone looked at her, waited.

'How did I what?' said Helen.

'Nothing,' said Laura.

'It's obviously something,' said Murph. 'You have to tell us now.'

'Just,' said Laura. 'How did you look after Consolata in the hospital? Like, I know it was your job, but . . .'

Helen shrugged. 'She was a patient, like any other — '

Laura raised her eyebrows. 'Like any other psycho bitch with a shrivelled — '

'No more cider for Laura!' said Murph. He checked the time. 'Or it'll be a very premature Rage O'Clock, followed swiftly by Tears O'Clock . . .'

Everyone laughed.

Laura turned to Helen. 'Sorry — I wasn't giving you a hard time — '

'I know you weren't,' said Helen. 'But no-one likes to think they'll end up in hospital and be laughed and joked about — '

Laura nodded. 'Fair enough. You're right.' She paused. 'You always just . . . say shit.'

Helen laughed. 'Sure, you're the same yourself!'

'No, no, no,' said Laura. 'You're honest. I'm horrible. You give a shit. I'm just mean, I think.'

'You're not mean,' said Helen. 'You're funny — '

'I'm a bitch, lads, amn't I?' said Laura.

'No!' said Edie.

'Will you stop it?' said Helen. 'You're honest, and funny, and you're tough. And we all love you for it.'

'Shh!' said Johnny, holding his hand up. 'Did anyone hear — '

The lights flickered. Everyone looked around at each other. There were two loud clicks, then buzzing, then the beeping sound of dying electronics. Then the lights went out.

11

LAURA

Castletownbere
12 June 1988

Laura walked down Main Street, her arms out from her sides to keep from sweating into Miriam's T-shirt. Everyone had been asleep when she got dressed. Miriam would see her at Mass, but there was nothing she could do about it then. Laura smiled. She touched the sides of her short blond hair, feeling the ridges where the mousse had hardened, then started to backcomb the front with her fingers. She finished it, looking at her reflection in Wiseman's window. The same T-shirt was hanging on the mannequin for £20. Laura laughed.

When she got to the square, she could see someone lying on one of the benches, their arm hanging down over a grey canvas bag with an empty naggin of vodka sticking out of it. It was Jessie's. Laura went over. Jessie was curled up, barefoot, wearing a short, tight black dress, her thick dark hair covering her face. It reminded Laura of the waves in a storm you knew could drown you. She took a step closer, then froze:

90

Sister Consolata was marching towards the bench. Laura ducked down between two parked cars, pressing her back against the dirty tyre, pulling her knees to her chest.

★ ★ ★

Sister Consolata leaned down to Jessie and shook her hard by the shoulder. 'Fifteen years of age, lying on a bench like a down and out,' she said. 'And you with a perfectly good bed up at home — '

Jessie raised her head a little, and swept her hair off her face. She shielded her eyes from the sun, gave a half-smile, and flopped back down. 'Is that the bed your Saviour saved me in, Sister?' she said, flinging her arm out, letting it hang there.

Laura's eyes widened.

'And to what end?' said Sister Consolata.

Laura leaned out and saw the rage on her face, then shrunk back into her hiding place.

'To what end?' Sister Consolata repeated.

Laura's body was still, her heart pounding.

Jessie sat up a little, her head loose on her neck. 'I did not die, Sister!' She swung her arm. out again. 'Do not stand at my grave and weep!' She laughed.

'I surely won't,' said Sister Consolata.

'Don't!' said Jessie. 'I am not there! I did not die!'

'Remember what I said to you the last time,' said Sister Consolata. 'You broke your parents' hearts, and you broke their home.'

Laura's hands were pressed against her mouth. She stuck her head out again. Sister Consolata's gaze travelled the length of Jessie's body. She gave a sharp nod. 'All dolled up to see who's looking at you. Surely be to God, you, of all people . . . '

Jessie was staring at her, confused.

'Well, you know now,' said Sister Consolata, 'that men will do more than just look at you.'

Jessie didn't move, didn't say a word. Neither did Laura.

Sister Consolata shot a short blast of air from her nostrils. 'Indeed and you didn't die.'

Jessie started to sob, and Sister Consolata, her head tilted, stood watching her. When Jessie's cries quietened, a cough broke the silence. Laura's head turned slowly towards the sound. Her eyes widened. Patrick Lynch was standing behind the bench, staring at Sister Consolata. Jessie was looking up at him, open-mouthed.

'Leave her alone, Sister,' said Patrick.

Sister Consolata glared at him, her eyes lit with anger, her face twisted in disgust.

'It wasn't her fault,' said Patrick.

Sister Consolata's face was sucked into a tight frown. 'How dare you — '

Patrick locked eyes with her. 'Same as it wasn't your fault . . . about that dog.'

Sister Consolata's frown flickered. Then she narrowed her eyes, huffed one last time, and walked away.

Jessie leaned up on her elbows, and smiled at Patrick. 'Thanks.' She slid her legs down off the bench, so he had room to sit beside her.

'What dog?' said Jessie.

'It doesn't matter,' said Patrick. 'What matters is . . . you.'

They fell into silence.

'You just want to be normal,' said Patrick.

Laura frowned. He was such a weirdo. She leaned out to look. Jessie was nodding at Patrick, tears spilling down her face.

'And, you know something,' said Patrick, 'you are normal.'

Jessie bowed her head, let out a long breath.

'But, then, you're not, at the same time,' said Patrick.

Jessie looked up at him.

'Because,' he said, 'you have a magical smile, and a magical laugh. And you're a magical dancer.'

Laura frowned. He is mortifying. She started to get up.

'You're the only person who gets it,' said Jessie. 'You always know what to say.'

Laura froze, eyes wide. Since when did Jessie and Smells ever say a thing to each other? She sat back down.

'You do know it wasn't your fault,' said Patrick. 'It's not any child's.'

'Sometimes, I don't,' said Jessie. 'Sometimes, I think, if she says it enough times . . . '

Patrick took a book out of his bag. He opened it where it was bookmarked. 'I found this and I thought you'd like it.' He handed it to her.

She read out loud. 'To the child you once were. You are crying now, you are lost, and you are afraid. But hurt is not your fate. I promise you that one day, you will be loved to safety. There will be arms wrapped around you to hold you tight, and never let you go. One day, someone will look you in the eye with a love so fierce, it will remind you of pain. But in that beautiful torment, you must be brave. Know that you can be loved that much, and can love that much in return. That will be your home. And it will be unbreakable.'

★ ★ ★

When Jessie told Laura, and Clare, and Edie the story the next day, she started it when Sister Consolata arrived at the bench and finished at the punchline. Laura laughed just as loud, and was just as shocked as anyone else that when Sister Consolata said 'Indeed and you didn't die', Jessie replied, 'And tough tits to you I didn't, Sister!' '

12

Edie rose from the table, her eyes flickering with fear in the candlelight.

Johnny's frown softened as he looked at her. 'Hey,' he said. 'Are you OK? Did you get a fright?'

Edie shook her head. 'No . . . yes. I . . . no, but the lights! What's going on?'

'You look shitless,' said Laura.

'Do I?' said Edie.

Johnny looked across at Murph. 'I blame you.'

'For the lights?' said Murph.

'For all this research you've been feeding her,' said Johnny. 'That Rathbrook guy, seeing people disappear one minute, then reappear the next. That freaked her out completely.'

'Hello?' said Edie. 'I'm right here.'

'And do you believe in ghosts, pet?' said Murph.

'No,' said Edie. 'I do not. My 'fright' was how can I bake my desserts?'

'That is a five-star fright, in fairness,' said Murph. 'Luckily, I can solve the dessert and the lights problem in one simple move: bring out the birthday cake.'

Edie smiled.

'And that,' said Murph, turning to Johnny, 'is how to satisfy your wife.'

Johnny got up and squeezed Murph's shoulder as he walked past him to the door. When he stepped into the hall, he heard banging at the front door. He went over and opened it. Terry Hyland was standing three steps down, dressed in black rain gear with a high-vis vest over it, his head bowed, rain pounding down on his hood. He was holding a torch in his right hand, and tilted the beam up as he raised his head.

'Are you trying to blind me?' said Johnny.

'What's the story with the power?' said Terry. 'I was driving by and — bam. Lights out. Is it the storm, do you think?'

'How the fuck would I know?' said Johnny. 'Do you have the key to the boiler room? I was looking for it after you left earlier.'

'I do,' said Terry.

Johnny let out a breath. 'Well, would you mind taking a look at it?'

'Sure, isn't that why I'm here?' said Terry. 'These things have a mind of their own half the time.'

' "These things" don't have a fucking mind,' said Johnny. 'One wire goes here, the other goes there . . . how hard can it be?'

'Hard as it is to get a bob out of you?' said Terry, with a smile. He swayed back on his heels.

'The bang off you,' said Johnny.

'Yerra, relax,' said Terry. 'It's Saturday night. I've a few pints on me and I was about to have a few more, but I said if a man is stuck . . . I suppose I'm an awful prick for doing that, am I?'

Johnny hovered in the doorway. 'Is the power gone to the whole area?'

'No, no,' said Terry. 'Your fairy garden's still lit up. And I've got power at my place, the Jameses next door have theirs. It could be the chapel's the problem.'

'For fuck's sake,' said Johnny. 'Why?'

'Well, I won't know 'til I take a look at it,' said Terry. 'There could have been a cable cut if a spade hit it or if a drill hit something in the chapel.'

'And who would have done that?' said Johnny, 'seeing that you were in there this morning, and no one else was in after you.'

'Did you have your eyes on it for the day?' said Terry.

'Well, I'm presuming you locked the thing after you,' said Johnny, 'but I don't know why I'd do that.'

Terry walked up to the top step, and waited for Johnny to move.

'Would you mind going around the back?' said Johnny, 'and I'll let you in.'

'I'm getting soaked.'

Johnny was already closing the door. He went downstairs and ducked into the wine cellar. He used the torch on his phone, pulled an envelope out from the back of a shelf, went over to the table, laid out four fat lines of coke, and snorted them. By the time he got to the back door, Terry was standing with his sour, wind-burned face up against the glass. Johnny let him in.

'What kept you?' said Terry. 'It's blowing a gale.' He pushed past Johnny.

'And while you're at it,' said Johnny, 'could you have a look at one of the suites for me — '

'The stables?' said Terry. 'Where the fine fillies go.'

Johnny gave him a patient look. 'Yes.'

'What's wrong there?' said Terry.

'There are a few roof tiles loose by the look of it, and if anything flies off and ends up going through my conservatory window, it won't be me paying for the glass.'

'Well, we know that,' said Terry. 'But I'd need someone with me for that.'

'You're always fucking missing something, aren't you?' said Johnny.

'Eleven grand, last time I checked,' said Terry.

'I told you,' said Johnny. 'I'm happy to pay any man for the work he's done. But if it's half done? Not my fucking problem. And can you keep the head down? I've got people here, and I don't want them — '

'Knowing a thing,' said Terry, winking. 'Of course, of course.' He turned away and rolled his eyes. Then he yanked open the back door and stepped out into the wild night.

Johnny closed the door behind him. 'Fucking prick,' he said.

'Fucking prick,' said Terry, his words lost in the wind.

★　★　★

Edie made her way slowly towards the dining-room table, her face glowing in the candlelight from Helen's birthday cake — three-tiered, chocolate, with a thick red ribbon and bow. On top, a red-icing *Helen* was written in perfect cursive script.

Murph stood up, and started to sing 'Happy

98

Birthday'. He stopped when Johnny appeared in the doorway.

'Did you start without me?' said Johnny.

'Oh!' said Edie, glancing back.

'I assumed he was coming in behind you,' said Helen. 'Sorry, Johnny.'

Edie set the cake down in front of Helen. Murph started singing 'Happy Birthday' again, and everyone joined in. Johnny stood by the table, poised with a bottle of champagne.

'Champagne too!' said Helen, her eyes bright.

When they finished singing, she closed her eyes, and blew out her candles. Everyone cheered. Johnny popped the champagne, and filled everyone's glasses.

Murph looked at Helen. 'Did you even make a wish?'

'Don't turn into Laura,' said Murph. 'That's my wish for you.'

Helen looked around the table. 'Thank you so much, everyone. You are so good to have all come. Especially on a night like tonight. And thank you to Edie and Johnny — '

'For plunging us into darkness,' said Murph.

'Terry's here to sort it — relax,' said Johnny.

'Terry who?' said Murph.

'Terry Hyland,' said Johnny.

'What?' said Murph. 'What are you doing getting that prick in?'

'I didn't 'get him in',' said Johnny. 'He just showed up — he was driving by and he spotted the lights go. Plus — 'that prick' is the likely source of whatever's just gone wrong. He was out dicking around in the chapel earlier and he's

99

now saying the problem might be there.'

'Well, don't let me lay eyes on him,' said Clare.

'Why?' said Johnny.

'He did a job for Dad and overcharged him by about two grand, knowing the poor man has dementia. Dad was on his own in the house when he came and Mam didn't find out for ages, and because it was cash, there was this big rigmarole.'

Patrick stood up, 'Excuse me,' he said.

'Are you going to the jacks?' said Murph.

Patrick paused.

'Murph, for God's sake — have some manners,' said Clare.

'What? I've loads of manners,' said Murph.

Patrick laughed. 'Yes, Murph — I am going to the . . . men's room.'

'He can't even say it,' said Murph. 'Well — enjoy.'

Patrick walked out the door laughing.

'Are you hammered or what?' said Laura.

'No,' said Murph. 'I don't know where I was going with that. I think part of me was going to get him to grab me something from the bar . . . or maybe just hear my confession . . . and I chickened out then because he's looking so snazzy. Like too snazzy to be serving me drinks.'

'But me and Johnny can?' said Edie. 'Thanks.' She was smiling at him.

'He's had the biggest makeover, maybe,' said Murph. 'Maybe he even has the tightest ass.'

'You're not well in the head,' said Laura.

'Can I tell my Terry Hyland story?' said Helen.

'You can,' said Murph, 'as long as you go along with the peer pressure thing. We've made

100

our minds up he's a bollocks. So . . . as long as your story fits in with that, fire away.'

'Absolutely,' said Helen, smiling. 'Well, it's as simple as this — when I was getting some modifications done to the house — he didn't charge me a penny for labour.'

'I knew it!' said Murph. 'He charged you millions, the bollocks.'

Helen laughed. 'I couldn't believe it. And he'd given me a quote and everything. And at the end of it all, he says, 'I won't take a penny from you, now, Helen, after all you did for the mother when she wasn't well.' She was in the hospital for a few weeks, not even anything serious, and I treated her no different to anyone else. It brought a tear to my eye. And then he says, 'Sorry for your troubles', which I love.' She laughed. 'Death, MS — '

Murph sat back in his chair and stretched his hands behind his head. 'Didn't yer man Terry have a thing with Patrick's mam, come to think of it? Maybe that's why he fucked off.'

'Terry and Mrs Lynch?' said Laura. 'Jesus.'

'Mrs Lynch didn't have things with anyone,' said Clare.

'Well, she obviously had a thing with at least one man,' said Murph, 'unless that fella I've been admiring all night is a hallucination.'

'Where did you get that idea from — Mrs Lynch and Terry?' said Helen.

'I heard he'd be in and out of the house,' said Murph, 'and, sure, there was only so much she would have been getting done to it.'

'And where was Patrick's dad when this was

101

going on?' said Helen.

'Long gone,' said Murph. 'Actually — dead at that stage. This was when we were in fifth or sixth year.'

'Did Patrick ever say anything to you about it?' said Laura.

'Like what?' said Murph. 'You won't believe who Mam's — '

'I meant about his dad,' said Laura.

'His dad died the same year as Mam,' said Murph. 'I remember Patrick coming up to me one day and asking me something or other about it. I don't think his mother gave a fiddler's the man had died.'

13

PATRICK

Castletownbere
12 January 1984

Patrick was sitting at the kitchen table doing his maths homework. The sink was full, and the tap was dripping. He didn't know why his mother always did that — fill the sink, leave the dirty dishes in it. It made his stomach tighten. He wondered if she was leaving it there, like a threat hanging over him, like he wasn't too old to be put through it again.

He heard a knock at the door. He paused, his pen hovering, then heard the flap of his mother's slippers as she went down the stairs. She opened the door. 'Sister Consolata. Come in.'

Patrick could hear her shoe catch on the threshold as she crossed it, then the click of the latch. After a short silence, he heard his mother: 'What is it, Sister?'

Patrick's heart started to pound. He wondered if he was in trouble. The voices outside dropped to a murmur and he stood up, glancing at the doorway, tempted to listen from there. Before he had a chance to move, they appeared in the kitchen.

'Patrick,' said Sister Consolata with her tight nod. She was holding a package that was wrapped in a plastic shopping bag.

'Sit down, Sister,' said Mrs Lynch. 'Are you sure you won't have a cup of tea?'

A flash of irritation sparked in Sister Consolata's eyes as she lowered herself on to the chair opposite Patrick. 'No, thank you.' She paused. 'I'm afraid I'm here with some bad news.' She patted the package on her lap.

Patrick tried to figure out how bad news could have anything to do with what was in the shopping bag. His mother sat to his left, the three of them making a tight triangle. He could feel his mother's head turned towards him as if she was expecting whatever this was to be his fault.

Sister Consolata looked at Mrs Lynch. 'It's about . . . Patrick's father.'

A rush of panic swept over Patrick.

'We don't know the full circumstances of what happened,' said Sister Consolata, 'but your father's body was found in Courtown harbour.'

Patrick stared at her, his mouth open, then turned to his mother. Her shoulders had straightened and her chest was high. Her eyes met his and his stomach turned at what he saw in them.

'He didn't leave a note,' said Sister Consolata, looking at his mother.

Patrick frowned. 'What do you mean? 'Didn't leave a note'?'

'Your father killed himself,' said Mrs Lynch, her voice flat.

'What?' said Patrick, 'But — '

'Your father lived a sinner, died a sinner,' said his mother.

Patrick frowned.

'You know it's a mortal sin to kill yourself,' she said.

'Daddy wasn't a sinner,' said Patrick. 'He was — '

'Is it not a sin to drink the food off a child's plate?' said his mother. 'Or to hand over his school uniform to a stranger at the races and pray for a horse and the man up on his back? They were the prayers your father prayed! Not a single one for his own son, not a single one for his own soul. He prayed for the money for the stout he could drink while he cheered on whatever four-legged animal he hoped would pay for the next round.'

Patrick looked at Sister Consolata. She had her head bowed. 'Will there be a funeral. Sister?' he said.

She looked up at him. 'I'm afraid that by the time the news came to me, he had already been laid to rest.'

Patrick's eyes widened.

His mother hopped up and banged her fist on the kitchen table. 'In a pauper's grave! A sinner's grave! That's what you get when you kill yourself — a grave with not a mark on it! Do you not get it all? Lived a pauper, died a pauper. Lived a sinner, died a sinner! Did you want to go to the grave with him? Is that it? Are you sorry you're here? And not cold in the grave beside him? Are you?'

Patrick shook his head. 'I'm not sorry, no.' He

looked over at Sister Consolata. 'But . . . can I go to his grave? I want to. I want — '

'You'll go nowhere near it!' said his mother.

'But — '

'Your mother's right,' said Sister Consolata.

Tears welled in Patrick's eyes.

'He has a new woman, now,' said Sister Consolata. 'Down in Courtown. And he has a new son. And it wouldn't be right.'

Patrick felt like she had reached into his chest and ripped his heart from it. He turned to his mother.

'That's the first I heard of it,' she said. 'And good luck to them!'

'How old is he?' said Patrick, wiping tears from his face, turning to Sister Consolata.

'Who?' said Sister Consolata.

'The son,' said Patrick.

Sister Consolata frowned. 'Eight on his last birthday. I'm trying to picture the birthday cake. Your father sent me a photo.'

'Eight?' said Patrick. 'But . . . Daddy only left . . . five years ago.' He shook his head. 'That can't be right.'

'Well, let's just say, it wasn't his first trip to Courtown,' said his mother, a triumphant look on her face.

Sister Consolata rose from the chair, and took the package with her. 'I'm sorry for your troubles,' she said to Patrick. Mrs Lynch followed her into the hallway.

Patrick sat at the table, white-faced, staring down at his copybook and all the equations he could solve faster than anyone else in his class

106

but he could not figure out how one minute you could be doing your maths homework and the next, someone could walk in, throw a grenade into your life and walk out and leave you behind and you have no father and half a brother and there's nothing you can do about any of it. But it wasn't even a grenade. It was too cold. It was like a handful of icicles.

He could hear Sister Consolata muttering in the hallway. He got up and slipped his feet out of his school shoes, and walked in his thick white socks to the door to look out. Sister Consolata was handing his mother the package.

'I washed them as best I could,' she was saying. 'They were in no fit state.' She paused. 'But you might want nothing to do with them.'

'Well, I'll take them off your hands, anyway. Sister,' said his mother. 'Did the new woman not want them?'

'I don't know,' said Sister Consolata. 'I can help you with anything you might need to do . . . get whatever certs . . . for the widow's pension — '

'Oh, I've done all my waiting around for money from that man,' said his mother. 'I gave that up long ago.'

★ ★ ★

Patrick lay curled on top of his bed that night, still in his school uniform, sobbing into his pillow. Eventually, he drifted off to sleep, but woke in the middle of the night, his cheek hot and red against the damp pillow. He listened.

107

There was no sound in the house. He got up and quietly made his way down the stairs. He pulled open the door to the cupboard underneath. Behind a stack of phone books was the package that Sister Consolata had left. He took it out and brought it to his bedroom. When he opened it, he smelled air tinged with laundry detergent and bleach. He slid out what was inside: his father's black rain jacket, a pair of battered black lace-up boots, his father's faded ID card, and a key with a metal keyring on it, shaped like a boat. He felt a stab of recognition. It was almost identical to the boat he had drawn for his perfect imaginary day with his perfect imaginary father.

14

Clare turned to Murph. 'Were you serious about multiple women on the go? Are you ever going to marry a Whateverhernameis?'

'Not a hope!' said Laura. 'It's same old, same old. Remember — we'd be out in Cork, you'd arrive in with whatever Whateverhernameis — '

'And the fact that's what you called them,' said Edie.

'With love,' said Murph. 'Always with love. And behind their backs.'

'You'd show up,' said Laura, 'drop her off with us, and we'd be the ones who ended up mad about her and devastated when it was all off. And you'd make sure every other woman in the place was taken care of — even if they were complete randomers.'

'What is it with you?' said Edie.

'I don't know what you're talking about,' said Murph, doing side-eyes.

Helen's back straightened, her chin tilted upwards. 'As soon as someone falls for Murph,' she said, 'he loses all respect for them.'

'It's the Groucho Marx thing,' said Clare.

'It's a sign of weakness,' said Murph. 'I can smell it off them!'

'You're such a gobshite,' said Laura.

'Murph,' said Edie, 'that's terrible.'

Murph spread his arms wide. 'Ah, look at me,

though. I'm hardly — '

' 'Poor me. Sure, who'd want me?' ' said Laura. 'Get a grip. You'd make a lovely embarrassing husband and mortifying dad.'

'And you'd make a shit therapist,' said Murph.

'Which is why I'm not a therapist,' said Laura.

'Which is why I'm not married,' said Murph. He paused. 'They're not connected, but you get the gist.'

Edie, Laura, Helen, and Clare were all looking at him. 'Oh, God,' he said, 'are you going to make me go for counselling now?'

'Jesus, we don't give that much of a fuck,' said Laura.

Helen looked at him. 'Some day, you might wake up and think, 'what a waste of my heart'.'

'Big heart,' said Edie.

'Yeah,' said Murph, 'that's exactly the kind of shite I wake up thinking.' He turned to Laura. 'And are you happy? Signing up to one man for the rest of your life?'

'Get lost,' said Laura.

'Imagine if there was Google Maps in the nineties,' said Murph. 'Every time they updated, there'd be a different guy on the path outside Laura's place, hi a blur, running in or out, depending on whether she was on the cider or not.'

Laura rolled her eyes.

Murph turned to Clare. 'Yourself and Alan . . . you're together how long?'

'Twenty-two years,' said Clare.

'Look at her — all starry-eyed,' said Murph. 'I do mention yourself and Alan the odd time to people.' He looked at the others. 'You know the

110

way there's always one couple that you go
— now, they're rock solid.'

Laura and Edie exchanged glances.

'Thanks, Murph,' said Edie. 'And what are
myself and Laura?'

'Papering over the cracks,' said Murph.

Edie laughed. 'You are right about Alan and
Clare, though.'

'I'm a lucky woman,' said Clare. 'God, I
wouldn't fancy being on the singles scene at this
hour of my life.'

'Jesus,' said Murph, looking at Patrick — 'now
it's us getting attacked. It's like a Lazy Susan of
insults. Four of us taken out in ten seconds.
Have we left anyone out? Do we need to spin it
again?'

'I'm still reeling from the fact you know what a
Lazy Susan is,' said Clare.

'But here's some advice for you, Clare — if
you ever do end up on the 'singles scene' — God
forbid — calling it that would keep you on it for
the rest of your life.'

'I'm not saying there's anything wrong with
being single,' said Clare, 'but when you're married as long as I am, the idea of dating is terrifying.
It sounds to me like everyone just shows up with
a giant carpet bag of life experiences, empties it
out all over the table, and points out the crappi-
est bits.'

'Are you mad?' said Laura. 'I left that big bag
in my wardrobe when I met Frank. In with all
the skeletons. Then I sold the wardrobe on Done
Deal and bought a white dress with the pro-
ceeds.'

'But do you ever wonder why some fuckers get married?' said Murph. 'Like, do they just pick the same road they've seen everyone else go down, and they're halfway along it, and they realize they've lost sight of everyone else up ahead, and that, actually, they could never really see the bits further along the road, and suddenly they go, 'Fuck'. And, at this stage, they're holding someone's hand on one side, and they look down at the other hand, and there are a couple of smallies hanging off that. And now . . . now they're responsible for a whole pile of other lives. And they're not trapped . . . but they're not free. They can't go back, though — they can never go back. All they can do is walk on with whoever's holding their hands or they can go on away ahead on their own. Or do they listen out for the echo of someone else's 'Fuuuuck', and leg it up to them, and see what their story is.'

Everyone looked at him. He looked into his glass. 'What IS this shit?'

Laura laughed. 'Did you ever think . . . some fuckers get married because they fall in love? And they stay in love? And that love . . . is a beautiful thing?'

'Are you messing with me?' said Murph. 'Was that all just bits of an Ed Sheeran song?' He turned to Helen. 'What about you?'

'Oh, they're lining up at the door,' said Helen.

'And rightly so,' said Murph.

Laura put her empty glass down. 'No one warns you about the kids thing, though.' She eyeballed Murph and Patrick. 'Don't do it, lads. Don't have kids.'

Murph looked at her. 'What — did you think I was about to run into town for one?'

'I'm serious,' said Laura. 'You need to know this. While I have you. I love my babies, they're mental, and I love them to bits, and don't get me wrong — I wouldn't be without them, but . . . no one tells you. No one who's had kids is going to tell you it was a massive mistake because it's so awful. I love them, I do. But I sat down one day, and I realized: I'm never going to South America again — '

'That's rather specific,' said Clare.

'It's never going to happen,' said Laura. 'I know it won't. I loved it. I loved everywhere I went. And I'll never see any of those places again — '

'That's ridiculous,' said Clare.

'It's not,' said Laura. 'Every penny goes on the kids.' She paused. 'Unless . . . has anyone spotted a slippy tile or a lump somewhere in the carpet? I could trip, crack my head open and sue the shit out of Johnny and Edie. Next stop — South America.'

'You could be a mule,' said Murph. 'All expenses paid.'

'Seriously — this is my life,' said Laura. 'I make dinner, I feed the kids, I make their lunches for the next day, I feed Frank, I resent the whole lot of them, I fight with the kids at bedtime, and the minute they're asleep, I feel so guilty that I want the kids back up again to hug them and say I'm sorry, so I fight with Frank instead. Then I prick around on Facebook 'til two in the morning, then I give out to myself, go

113

to sleep, get up, and do the same shite all over again. And at the weekend — more of the shite, less of the pricking around on Facebook. Like, I'm not a prison officer at all if you think about it. I'm actually a prisoner — at work, at home. And in between, I'm a prisoner in a Nissan Micra.' She paused. 'I'm looking at those photos of us, and our little faces, and it's just . . . sad. It's making me sad.'

'Oh, God,' said Murph. 'Is it Tears O'clock already?'

Edie and Clare exchanged glances. Clare glanced down at Laura's glass.

'What?' said Laura, looking at her. 'What was that face in aid of?'

'What face?' said Clare.

'That was judge face,' said Laura.

'Don't be ridiculous,' said Clare.

'At least you get paid to judge now,' said Laura. 'The rest of us have to do it for free.' She turned to Helen. 'You must get judged a lot these days.'

Johnny and Murph gave shocked laughs. Patrick held his breath. Clare shook her head at the Prosecco bottle Edie was holding.

Helen laughed. 'Thank you, Laura! Thank you! I do!'

'It must be a pain in the hole,' said Laura.

'It is!' said Helen. 'People see the wheelchair and it's like they make up their mind about something — it could be anything — I can see it happening and I'm thinking: What's going on this time?'

'Like . . . what?' said Murph. 'They don't start

114

talk . . . ing . . . slow . . . ly . . . to . . . you . . . do they?'

She laughed. 'They do! Or they're afraid to talk to me in case I'm mentally impaired and I'll suddenly start flapping about the place and they're mortified. Or the pity eyes.' She held up her hands. 'And I do get it — it's not like I'm going around waiting to be offended. I just want to have the chats, half the time. Unless I'm exhausted or I've a headache or . . . ' She shrugged. 'It's the same as anyone.'

'Well, I'm definitely going to have a headache in the morning,' said Laura. 'And I'm definitely going to have trouble walking later. So I'll know exactly how you feel.'

Everyone laughed.

'OK,' said Edie, standing up. 'Can we raise our glasses to the kindest, most caring woman I know — '

'All of us know,' said Murph.

Everyone stood up.

' — who has been looking after us for as long as we can remember,' said Edie, 'who's come to our rescue on so many occasions we've lost count, who's done the same for every single patient who's walked through the door of the hospital — '

'Even Consofuckinlata,' said Laura.

'Who also,' said Edie, 'went above and beyond to help Johnny and Dylan and me settle back home . . . ' She paused, her hand to her chest. 'Sorry — I'm getting emotional, now. But, Helen — seriously, I've no doubt I speak for all of us when I say you are the most selfless person we

115

know. And it's not just about what you do for us. It's your warmth, and your smile, and that calming look in your eye that has this . . . effect. Like — '

'Two Xanax,' said Clare.

'I couldn't have said it better myself,' said Edie. 'So . . . to Helen!'

'To Helen!'

Helen took a long sip of champagne. 'I shouldn't be drinking this — '

'Get it in to you!' said Murph.

'Thank you, everyone,' said Helen. 'And thank you, Edie. You're far too good.'

'And while we're here,' said Edie. 'Another announcement. Thanks to Helen's design input, the inn has been awarded a five-star rating from a UK website that rates hotels on wheelchair-friendliness.'

Helen's eyes were wide.

'Look at her — stunned,' said Murph. 'Fair fucking play.'

'So, on a selfish level,' said Edie, 'thank you for giving me one of my proudest moments.'

'I loved doing it,' said Helen. 'I should be thanking you.'

'Ah, lads, you're making me puke, now,' said Laura. 'What have I ever done for anyone?'

'Do you want me to answer that?' said Murph.

'Murph!' said Edie.

'What?' said Murph. 'I'm saying credit where credit's due.'

'Seriously, though,' said Laura, turning to Helen. 'Fair play. There's nothing you wouldn't do for anyone.'

'Would you stop it, the lot of you?' said Helen. 'You'd think I was a saint.'

'You are!' they all said.

15

HELEN

St Gabriel's Hospital
Castletownbere, 2006

Sister Consolata was sleeping, her hands folded on top of the tight covers. Helen stood by the window, staring out over the harbour, lost in the sparkling strip of the moon's light on the water.

She turned around and walked over to Sister Consolata's bedside. She noticed that everything on the locker had been moved to the left; the statue of the Virgin Mary, the Bible, the prayer book, the rosary beads. In their place was a black, leather-bound book that she recognized, but knew didn't belong there. There were two red rubber bands wrapped around it, barely containing what had been slid between the pages.

She picked it up. She realized then it was Father Owen's diary. She glanced at the door, then rolled the rubber bands off. It sprung open on a page with two In Memoriam cards wedged in the gutter. She opened them and saw two familiar faces from town, and read the prayers. Then she flipped through the rest of the diary,

118

letting it fall open wherever it was at its fullest, catching brief glimpses of raffle tickets, addresses written on scraps of paper, lists of Ministers of the Eucharist, a menu for a takeaway that was no longer open and, towards the back, in Father Owens' flowing, slanted script, the beginnings of a eulogy. Then:

Sister Consolata's kindness . . . insert examples . . .

Helen raised her eyebrows. 'Good luck with that, Father,' she whispered.

She closed the diary, wrapped the rubber bands around it, and put it back. She turned to Sister Consolata and watched her chest rise and fall as she slept, her face remarkably serene.

Helen shook her gently awake. Sister Consolata opened her eyes, and slowly focused on her. She frowned and turned to look at the clock.

Helen smiled and nodded. 'I know, Sister. It's late. Were you asleep? Did I disturb you?'

Sister Consolata tried to bat her away with her hand.

'Do you know where I was today, Sister?' said Helen, her eyes wide, arms spread. 'I was in hospital myself! Getting great news! A diagnosis! Multiple Sclerosis! Thirty-five years of age! Can you believe that? M Fucking S! That I've seen so many patients with over the years! So I know it all!'

A frown flickered across Sister Consolata's face. Helen leaned in and smoothed down the top sheet. She smiled. 'Are you at peace, Sister?'

Sister Consolata closed her eyes, as if to answer yes.

'Good for fucking you,' said Helen.

Sister Consolata's eyes snapped open.

Helen bent close to her ear: 'Because how the fuck does the whole thing work? That a bitch like you gets to be in the whole of their health until this hour of their life, and still get to be at fucking peace? After all the shit you did. With everything you put Jessie through. Do you remember that, you auld bitch?'

Sister Consolata's eyes were wider then, fearful.

'Good enough for you!' said Helen. She glanced towards the diary on the bedside table. 'Did Father Owens hear your confession?'

Sister Consolata blinked.

'Oh, you want me to know that, all right,' said Helen. 'Sure, no wonder you're at peace. All your shite's been taken care of — is that it? You've said your bit and off you go.'

Sister Consolata tried to swallow.

'Did you lay it all out for him?' said Helen. 'For Father Owens? Did you say? 'I confess to . . . tormenting a poor child right up until the last? Do you think Jessie'd have been as drunk that night if she wasn't trying to block out the poisonous shite you kept coming out with? Did you tell Father Owens you blackened the name of a lovely man like Jerry Murphy? Did you tell him — Jesus! — I could go on and on! INSERT EXAMPLES! There's enough of them! So, did you? Did you name your sins?'

Sister Consolata gave a few weak coughs and

120

pointed towards her mouth. Helen paused, then reached for a foam swab from the bedside locker, dipped it in water, and ran it across her lips. Sister Consolata closed her eyes, and rested her head back down on the pillow.

Helen's heart pounded. She put her hands down on either side of Sister Consolata's shoulders, and used all her weight to tighten the covers across her chest. 'Answer me, you bitch. Answer me! Did you name your sins?' She pushed her hands down hard one more time, then took them away. Sister Consolata's head lifted, then landed without a change crossing her face.

'Nothing?' said Helen. 'Nothing? Not a word?'

She reached down and whipped the pillow out from under Sister Consolata's head, holding it over her face in a white-knuckle grip, her biceps bulging against the short sleeves of her uniform. 'I could do it,' she said. 'I swear to God. And no one would be any the wiser.' She came closer with the pillow. 'Answer me, you bitch. Answer me! Did you name your sins?'

Sister Consolata's lips parted and with two gnarled fingers, she beckoned Helen down to her. Helen paused as she leaned in, momentarily trapped by the venomous black of her eyes. A shiver ran up her spine as she lowered her head.

Sister Consolata whispered: 'Did you name yours?'

16

Helen raised her hand. 'OK, I hate to be the bearer of boring news, but I'm going to have to go to bed. I'm shattered. It's suddenly hit me.'

'Nooo,' said everybody. 'Don't go.'

'I don't think the party's going to end if I'm not here,' said Helen.

'But there'll be less boobs in it!' said Murph. 'Fewer. Jesus — what kind of example am I to my students?'

'Helen — no! Please don't go,' said Laura.

'Laura's Party Break-up Panic,' said Murph. He looked at Helen. 'If you're wrecked, can't you fall asleep where you are?' He paused. 'Ah, come on, lads — I'd say that to anyone who was in any kind of a chair.'

'Lads!' said Helen. 'No one is offending me! I have enough strangers walking on eggshells around me. I definitely don't need you lot at it.'

'Fine,' said Clare. 'But don't go to bed.'

'See — this is why people need to get hammered,' said Murph. 'No fading.' He looked at Helen. 'Can anyone do anything for you? Can we do anything to stop you leaving?' He pointed to the wheelchair. 'Is there a brake on that thing you can't reach?'

They all laughed. 'No, but thank you,' said Helen. 'And I will see you all for breakfast.'

Murph and Laura exchanged glances.

' 'Helen Maguire was always known for her optimism',' said Murph.

'Are you writing my eulogy already?' said Helen.

'See?' said Murph. 'You can't say a thing without her taking offence.'

Helen laughed. 'You know I'd love to stay, but I just can't.'

Edie stood up. 'Come on — let me show you to the stables.'

'Is there no room at the inn?' said Murph. 'Anyone want to lay me in the manger? I could do this all night.'

'Can I come for a gawk?' said Clare. 'I love converted stables.'

'Who says they're converted?' said Murph. 'I'm telling you — they don't give a shit.'

'I wouldn't mind a nose in the library too,' said Clare.

'Ah, lads,' said Murph, 'are ye all going to be off now talking about curtains and shite? And I'll be stuck drinking the honesty bar dry? On 'Guys Go Free' night?'

'Well, I've no interest in sitting around talking about curtains,' said Laura. 'So, I'm with you.'

'No one's going to be talking about curtains,' said Clare. 'But nosing was always going to be part of the deal.'

'And we won't be long,' said Edie. 'We're not going to keep Helen up if she's wrecked. And it's not like we did much to the library. I mean — we spruced it up, but we didn't want to be the owners who — '

'Turned it into a casino,' said Murph.

'Not that I had any great attachment to it,'

123

said Edie. 'I think the viewing was the first time I'd been in it.'

Murph nodded at Patrick. 'You were a big reader. You used to go up there too, didn't you?'

'Did you?' said Clare.

Patrick looked at her. 'Yes.'

' "Why are you so surprised?' said Murph, mimicking her.

'I'm not surprised,' said Clare. 'All I'm saying is I didn't know that.'

'Well, you were hardly in the place morning, noon, and night,' said Murph.

'No,' said Clare. 'Wednesday afternoons. And maybe during a few free classes. And the odd Saturday. And mid-term breaks. And — ' She paused. 'It's amazing I had any friends.'

'We needed you for the table quiz,' said Murph. 'To win a prize sponsored by your dad. Covered in boats.'

' "Covered in boats',' said Clare. 'One boat. Tastefully ironed on to an anorak.'

'That everyone's mams would iron over by mistake,' said Laura.

'Ooh — Clare's fierce proud of Daddy,' said Murph.

'I'm 'fierce proud' of his logo . . . designed by his daughter,' said Clare, pointing to herself. 'I drew the boat part. I was ten, so don't judge. Daddy got them to add the gold around it.'

'And then he cut loose in a merchandising shop up in Cork and slapped it on everything,' said Murph.

'My dad definitely had a polo shirt,' said Edie, nodding.

'And I'm sure I saw Laura with a g-er,' said Murph.

Patrick looked at him. 'What's a g-er?'

'Ah, Patrick,' said Murph. 'A g-string — the things women stop wearing when they catch sight of their arses properly in those changing rooms with the three mirrors.'

Clare, Laura, and Helen nodded.

'Except Clare,' said Murph. 'She still wears them. 'Eyes ahead'.'

Edie looked across the table at Patrick. He was staring off into space.

'Patrick,' said Edie.

He looked over at her and she smiled. 'Could I ask you to do me a favour, please?'

'Yes, of course,' he said.

'While we're gone — would you mind going down to the cellar and grabbing a couple of bottles of Prosecco? I asked Johnny, but he probably got distracted.'

'I'll go,' said Murph. 'I don't mind.'

'Not at all,' said Patrick, standing up. 'Stay where you are.'

★　★　★

Patrick walked across the hall, his black hiking boots silent on the tiles. He went down the stairs and was guided by emergency lights to the wine cellar. A soft light glowed from inside. He walked in. Ahead of him, was a tall wooden table with a metal worktop. Johnny was leaning over at one end, his nose buried in the tail end of a fat line of coke. He looked up, saw Patrick, and jumped.

125

Patrick raised his hands, palms out.

A flash of anger crossed Johnny's face. He glanced down at Patrick's boots. 'Did you wear them especially?'

'Especially what?'

'To be a sneaky prick.' He smiled. 'So . . . what has you down here?'

'Edie asked me to bring up two bottles of Prosecco.'

Johnny turned around, and scanned the shelves. He pulled out two bottles, and put them on the table. 'You didn't see this, by the way.' He gestured to the coke.

Patrick nodded. 'I didn't see anything. But . . . she doesn't know?'

'Why do you give a shit?' said Johnny.

'I don't,' said Patrick. He reached out and took the bottles. He was about to turn away, but he stopped. 'Why the hostility, as a matter of interest?'

'Hospitality, surely,' said Johnny. He flashed a smile.

Patrick sucked in a breath. He eyed the coke. 'I'm not sure that agrees with you.'

'And I'm sure' said Johnny, 'That I don't really give a fuck.'

⋆ ⋆ ⋆

Dylan and Mally ran across the front gardens of the inn, staying close to the hedges that bordered the car park. Rain was pouring down, and they both slipped in the same water-logged hollow, crying out, grabbing for each other, then righting

126

themselves. They laughed, then shushed each other.

'This is insane,' said Dylan.

'I know — I love it!' said Mally.

'If we get caught, we're dead.'

'You're always saying that,' said Mally. 'We did get caught! And we're aliiiive.' She spread out her arms.

'Yeah, but I'm already in trouble,' said Dylan.

'Don't be a wuss!' said Mally. 'And stop making me talk — I'm getting rain in my mouth. I literally have puddles in my mouth. Ducks will literally fly in. That's how I'm going to die.'

'I am not a wuss,' said Dylan. 'You're the one who's all 'No — I can't drink, my mom will kill me'.'

'Mam can literally smell blood,' said Mally.

'Stop saying 'literally'.'

'But she LITERALLY can,' said Mally.

'I know!' said Dylan. 'It's your favourite excuse to risk . . . nothing. All the danger in our lives happens entirely on my property.'

'Danger,' said Mally.

'Trespass is danger!' said Dylan.

'*Your* property,' said Mally, mimicking his voice. 'Cut to: your parents lying dead in the kitchen and you, clutching their will in your fist and shaking it in the air in triumph.'

''Literally I'm going to choke to death on ducks,'' said Dylan, mimicking Mally's voice.

They both laughed.

They kept running until they came to the trees that curved around the chapel.

'Do you have the key?' said Mally.

'Yes!' said Dylan. 'See? Theft is also dangerous.'

'Forgive us our trespasses,' said Mally, joining her hands and looking up.

Dylan turned the key in the door.

'I love that you have a chapel,' said Mally.

Dylan glanced back at her. 'You love that we have a confession box.'

'Terry totally thought we were having sex in there,' said Mally.

'He was probably all 'is nothing sacred anymore?'.' Said Dylan.

Mally held her hand to her heart. 'The truth,' she said. 'The truth is always sacred.'

'Well, I confess,' said Dylan, 'that recently, I've been lying quite a lot to my parents.'

They high-fived each other. 'Anxiety,' said Mally, 'the Get Out of Jail Card that keeps on giving.'

'Oh my God — you're so mean!' said Dylan. 'I do have anxiety!'

'I know, I know,' said Mally, 'but some of it is fake news. You're lucky your mom is so nice.' She paused. 'But I do think your dad is onto you. I try to frighten him away with my glare when he gets too close to the truth.'

17

DYLAN

Pilgrim Point
17 November 2018

Dylan was kneeling in the confession box, shifting his weight from side to side before finally settling.

'You wouldn't want to have had a lot of sins,' he said.

'No, my child,' said Mally, looking up from the opposite side. She slid back the grille, and made a sign of the cross.

Dylan passed an XLR cable through to her. She took it, and plugged it into a large diaphragm microphone, set on a small stand in front of her.

'Ready?' said Dylan.

'Yes,' said Mally, pulling her long, dirty-blond hair back, twisting a red elastic band around it. 'Yes, I am. The fashion-backward pony tail is in place. Which means business.'

Dylan pulled on a pair of Bose headphones, and checked his laptop screen. 'Say something,' he said.

'Sinnah!' boomed Mally. 'I cast out — '

'Shhh!' said Dylan, staring up at her, wide-eyed. 'We'll get caught.'

129

'Sorr-ee,' she said, shrugging. 'I just . . . the power!' She gestured around her. 'It's going to my head. You common penitent.' She paused. 'Or are you . . . penitent?'

'That's better,' said Dylan. 'I've got your levels.' He hit the track pad, and a red dot appeared on screen. He nodded.

Mally started to speak:

'You are listening to episode one of the true crime podcast: Girl Eleven, Girl Sixteen: The Jessie Crossan Story.

'On July thirtieth, 1983, in the small fishing town of Castletownbere on the Beara Peninsula in Cork, an eleven-year-old girl put on her pyjamas, got into bed, and wrote in her diary about the wonderful day she had just had. It was the first Saturday of Regatta week — the high point of Beara's social calendar — when the town is filled with people, the harbour is filled with boats, and the pier glows with the multicoloured lights of the funfair.

'Jessie's 'Best Day of the Year' had begun at breakfast when she got to open an early birthday gift from her aunt in America. That afternoon, Jessie danced in a talent contest on the square. She didn't win, but, in her heart, she did. She closed her diary, turned out the light, and went to sleep a happy girl. It was eight thirty p.m.

'Three hours later, Jessie's father was to walk into her room to discover his daughter's almost lifeless body, lying on her now blood-soaked bed. Jessie had been beaten, raped, and stabbed multiple times. There were no signs of forced entry. And her rapist was never caught.

'Though Jessie survived her horrific attack, she was not to live for much longer. Five years later — on Hallowe'en Night, 1988, Jessie lost her life in a fire that tore through a derelict building in the grounds of the Sisters of Good Grace Convent on nearby Pilgrim Point.

'Jessie's parents, devastated by their daughter's rape, were already under strain, and their marriage did not survive the trauma of her death. Her mother moved away, never to return, and passed away in 2004. Jessie's father, Kevin, remained in Beara. Where fathers in similar circumstances might hound detectives investigating the case, Kevin seemed to come to terms with the possibility that Jessie's rapist would never be found. Some would say the fight drained out of him through the cracks in his broken heart. Others would say that it was not in Kevin's interest for the guards to find the culprit. Sadly, it was under that cloud of suspicion Kevin Crossan lived until his passing in 2017.

'It seemed there was no one left to fight for justice for Jessie. Until a new sergeant came to town. Known for her keen eye and her methodical approach to investigations, Valerie James was a newly promoted sergeant when she moved from Cork city with her family to start a new life in the close-knit community.

'James inherited the Jessie Crossan rape case — a case long-since gone cold. With daughters of her own, James felt a particular resonance with the case and vowed that Jessie's rapist would be brought to justice.

'But conscious of being a stranger in a small

town and with no local connections, this was a vow James shared with only her family and a small circle of trusted friends. If she were to solve this case, she would have to separate the facts — the physical evidence, forensic evidence, sworn statements — from the conjecture and rumour that, in a small town, can often be mistaken for the truth.

'How do I know all this? I am Mally James. And the woman who made that vow is . . . my mother.'

Mally spread her arms, and bowed. She took a drink from her Diet Coke, and stretched her legs.

'The acoustics are awesome,' said Dylan. 'It's the insulation panels.'

'Mally looked at him. 'Stolen insulation panels, my child.'

'Borrowed,' said Dylan. 'It's not like we attached them to the walls.'

'So,' said Mally, 'What do you think?'

'The 'How do I know all this?' is lame. So is the sentence about the cracks in the heart. And some of it is a tiny bit too dramatic.'

'But it IS dramatic,' said Mally. 'And so sad. I feel like I know her now.'

'That's because you keep asking Mom about her. 'Hey, Edie, love your make-up, so what about that dead friend . . . ?''

'Dark,' said Mally.

'Plus, by the way, your mom obviously doesn't trust my parents because they haven't a clue — pun intended — about this vow she made.'

'But I'm sure they want the guy to get caught

132

too,' said Mally, 'so they'd be delighted Mam was being so secretive.'

'Unlike her daughter,' said Dylan. 'She would go mental if she knew what you were up to.'

'It's a college assignment,' said Mally. 'It's not like it's a court case and I'm like emailing a link to the jurors. It's only for my lecturer.'

'Your *journalist* lecturer?' said Dylan.

'Ooh,' said Mally, 'I forgot that part. But I won't do it if it's not confidential obviously. But if I *can* do it, that means when Mam does solve the case, he's going to be like pointing at me from the top of the class going, 'This one breaks stories! First for her!''

'Or,' said Dylan, 'he'll be 'Mally James: Future Journalist Most Likely to Be Fired/Jailed/Shot because of Poor/Illegal/Both Journalistic Practices.''

'I'm literally on the pilot episode and you're shooting me down. It's not like I'm doing a whole series closely following the progress on the case.'

'Oh my God — you totally are! Nosing through your mom's files the whole time.'

'I meant not following it 'out loud' — like, in my assignment.'

'Everything you said there was true,' said Dylan. 'Your mom would go nuts.'

'Well, that's the risk you take when you leave your curious daughter — I heard that too — when you leave your *inquisitive* daughter at your desk in the station while going to find your purse to give her money for her lunch.'

'Yeah — what a bitch.'

'And I haven't nosed in a while. Which is killing me.' She paused. 'OK — can I read you the new developments bit? It's not quite finished.'

'Yes, but I'm not recording. We have to go.'

'OK, OK,' said Mally, checking her notes. 'Right: the first new development is the kind that one usually sees in reverse: a missing box of evidence — which included items of Jessie's clothing — reappeared. As DNA testing was not available to investigators in 1983, this has opened up the possibility that a DNA profile of Jessie's attacker could be obtained.

'The second development came from the same box of evidence — in the form of Jessie's diary. A seemingly insignificant detail was discovered by Sergeant James in the last entry Jessie made — only hours before the rape. In it, Jessie mentioned three pairs of underpants sent to her as part of her birthday gift by her aunt in America. When Sergeant James went to check the items of clothing taken into evidence, she discovered that not only was the underwear not there, neither was there any record of them in the inventory of items taken away from Jessie's bedroom that night: a pyjama top, matching shorts and a hair band. In Jessie's mother's statement at the time, she said it was Jessie's habit to wear either a nightdress or a pyjama top and bottoms to bed, but that she did not wear underwear. To Sergeant James, this meant that this rapist may, perhaps, have taken away trophies from the scene.'

'That is beyond creepy,' said Dylan.

They heard a rattle at the chapel door.

'Who's that?' said Mally.

'How would I know?' said Dylan. 'Not my parents, anyway — there's no way they'd be back from Cork yet.'

'Hello? Hello?' It was a man's voice.

'It's Terry,' said Dylan. 'We're dead.'

18

Murph stood up from the dining-room table and reached out to Laura. 'Come with me.'

She frowned. 'Where?'

'Just do as you're told,' said Murph, taking her hand.

'Where are we going?' said Laura.

'Shhht.'

As they walked down the hallway, Terry was coming towards them. He slowed.

'Did you see Johnny, lads?'

'He's around somewhere,' said Murph.

'How are ye enjoying the night?' said Terry.

'Grand out,' said Laura, without breaking her stride.

Terry nodded as they passed.

Murph laughed when they were out of earshot. ''Grand out' meaning 'Fuck you'!'

'Good enough for him, the skeevy bollocks,' said Laura.

★ ★ ★

Terry met Johnny coming up the stairs to the basement. A flash of irritation crossed Johnny's face.

'I had to come in,' said Terry, shrugging. 'I couldn't find you. Have you five minutes? There's something you need to see in the chapel.'

★ ★ ★

Murph held open the door to the honesty bar for Laura and she walked through. He turned on the flashlight on his phone and started checking each bottle, tilting the labels into the light to read them. He glanced back at Laura.

'Right,' he said, 'I'm taking you on holiday. We are going on the Pisco.' He held up a bottle of 1615 Pisco Torontel. 'I'm assuming you went to Peru on these South American travels of yours.'

Laura's eyes lit up. 'Ah, Murph — you're a dote.'

He put his arm around her and squeezed her shoulder. 'Well — it might take you back. But I'm hoping it'll take you forward too.'

She looked up at him.

'Don't shut your life down, girl,' he said. 'You've another fifty years in you, yet. Nothing to stop you.' He paused. 'Apart from those shite-looking kids.'

Laura laughed. Murph poured the drinks, and raised his glass. 'The life!'

'The soul.'

'The ass.'

'The hole.' They clinked glasses.

He gestured to the window. 'Madame, a seat? Overlooking the pitch-black?'

They sat opposite each other, and drifted into a brief silence.

'Do you not think it's fucked up, though?' said Laura. 'That they bought this place? After everything . . .'

'But you know Edie,' said Murph. 'Look at the

137

renovation job she did on Johnny'

Laura laughed.

'Mind you,' said Murph, 'I think he's already started the demolition job.'

'Ah, leave him alone,' said Laura. 'In fairness, the place always gave me the creeps, even when I was a child. I'd hear Dad talk to Mam about it when it was an industrial school and he'd be called up to 'put manners' on the boys — that's what Consolata would say to him. There were a couple of 'Houdinis' he'd call them. He was told they were under 'strict supervision' by one of the Brothers but they'd still manage to get out and they'd be found wandering the roads or drinking down in The Anchor. He said it was the boys making a big show of saying their prayers were the biggest brats. They'd be in and out of the chapel the whole time, Consolata thinking she was doing the Lord's work. He couldn't for the life of him figure out how they got out, except for one of the Brothers being in on it.'

'Sure, of course they were,' said Murph.

Laura eyed him. 'Are you getting any weird kind of vibe tonight?'

'No,' said Murph. 'What kind of vibe?'

'Between Johnny and Patrick,' said Laura.

'I thought you were going to say, 'Johnny and Edie.''

'What?' said Laura. 'Are you serious?'

'No — I just wanted to shit-stir. But no — I'm not getting a weird vibe anywhere.'

'I'd say Johnny's not too happy not being the fittest man in the room.'

Murph sucked in a breath. 'Harsh.' He sat

138

back and looked around, stopping at Johnny and Edie's wedding photo on the sideboard, gesturing to it with his glass. 'Do you think they'll make it to twenty-five?'

'Sure, why wouldn't they?' said Laura.

'It's a bit like doping, though, isn't it?' said Murph.

Laura's eyes widened. 'He's not cheating, is he?'

Murph raised his eyebrows. 'You tell me.'

'Me?' said Laura. 'Would you fuck off?'

'No. I'm going to fuck right on.' He smiled. 'Come on — was he giving you the glad eye at any stage?'

Laura sputtered into her drink. '"The glad eye"! I couldn't tell you the last time I heard that.'

'Well, just so you know — my eyes are always glad to see you . . . every time I fondly reminisce about your . . . skills.'

'Jesus. Don't remind me.'

'Excuse me' said Murph. 'You should be very proud of yourself.'

Laura rolled her eyes. She turned her head to the window.

'Are you actually mortified?' said Murph.

Laura looked at him. 'Not about you. But I do look back sometimes and think, 'What was I like?''

'You were amazing!' said Murph. 'Johnny and I used to always say Laura gives the best — '

'Jesus Christ!' said Laura, sitting up, glancing towards the door. 'Would you shut up?'

Murph laughed. 'She'd hardly give a shit at this stage, would she?'

'Of course she'd give a shit.'

'She always knew Johnny was a boyo.'

'Not with me she didn't.'

'Ah, she must have had her suspicions,' said Murph.

'Are you mad?' said Laura. 'She'd never have thought Johnny'd lower himself to me.'

'Mind you — if she knew you fucked up his Final Trial for Ireland — '

'Murph — shut up! And I did not fuck up his Final Trial. That was all Johnny.'

Murph tipped his glass towards Johnny's glory wall. 'Do you not think, though, that if you hadn't happened to bump into him in Dublin that night — wasn't he on his way back to The Shelbourne? — then he might have been tucked up in his bed and not out punching the head off someone in Leeson Street?'

'Why are you going on about that now?' said Laura. 'Are you trying to make me feel like shite? That was Johnny's call. It's not my fault he fucks things up for himself. And, anyway, I was the one got him out of trouble. Now, can you just shut up about it? I'm trying to enjoy the thing he actually hasn't made a balls of.'

After a while, Murph turned to her. 'Do you reckon she ever got into the swing of blow jobs in the end — Edie?'

'The shit that goes through your head,' said Laura.

'I'd say yourself and Frank are at it the whole time — are you?' said Murph.

'You need help,' said Laura. 'Has it been a while?'

'Bless me. Father — it's been three weeks since my last indiscretion. Laura's here beside me, Father. You remember her — one of your biggest sinners. Would you like to say a few words to her? Do you miss her? I know I do.'

★   ★   ★

Johnny and Terry stood inside the chapel, their eyes on the wall to the left, where Terry was shining the beam of his torch through the outline left behind when one of the confession boxes had been ripped out. Spray-painted in red, was the word KERR-O-SENE, and beside it, the stick figure of a girl, and around her head, a crown of flames.

Johnny turned to Terry. 'Jesus Christ. Don't tell Edie. Fuck's sake. Don't tell anyone.'

'Can you smell it?' said Terry. 'It smells fresh.'

141

19

JOHNNY

Castletownbere
23 December 1989

Johnny was stretched out on the sofa, one leg on the floor, the opposite arm up over his head. His green rugby shirt rode up, showing a taut stomach. The doorbell rang. He lifted his head, and through the net curtains could see a squad car.

'Fuck.' He got up, slowly. 'Fuck.'

He paused at the mirror, ran his hand through his hair a few times, and steadied his gaze. His eyes were pinched from tiredness. His jaw twitched. He scraped a fingernail down the corners of his mouth, and wiped it on his jeans. The doorbell rang again. He tucked in his shirt and walked into the hall, as his mother was sticking her head out of the kitchen.

'It's only Laura's dad,' he said. 'It's grand.'

'OK, so.'

He waited until she went back into the kitchen to open the door.

'Johnny,' said Colm. 'Would you mind if I had a word with you?'

'No, no,' said Johnny. 'Not at all. But . . . could you maybe come back around eight? I'm in the middle of something.'

'I'm kind of in the middle of something myself,' said Colm.

'Oh,' said Johnny. 'Well, can we talk outside? The mother's got a migraine.'

'I don't mind where we talk, boy.'

The hairs on the back of Johnny's neck stood up. 'Good, good. Right.'

Colm stepped off the porch, and gave Johnny room to come out. Johnny floundered.

'Will we sit on the bench, so?' said Colm.

Johnny glanced at the white iron bench in front of the living-room window that his mother had got the previous summer, and that, for some reason embarrassed him. 'OK, so.'

'How did last weekend go?' said Colm.

Johnny glanced briefly towards him.

'The Final Trial,' said Colm. 'I heard you were up in Dublin. You made the probables, I'm told. Within a hair's breadth of making the Ireland team. And then . . . ' He paused.

Johnny's eyes were on a gnome he had never noticed in the front garden, whose expression looked like how he felt: uh-oh.

'Do you know why I might be here talking to you about a game I no more give a damn about than . . . '

Johnny rubbed his jaw. 'No, Sergeant. I don't.'

Colm nodded. 'Of course, you don't. So, here's how it went. The Friday, I'm guessing, you headed up to Dublin, you had your team meeting, went off for the couple of pints afterwards to settle the nerves ... The plan was to go back to The Shelbourne at around ten o'clock, maybe, to get a good night's sleep before taking advantage of an opportunity that most boys could only dream of.'

Johnny's heart was pounding. He started to smile at the gnome.

'Did something funny happen next?' said Colm. 'Was it funny what happened next? When you bumped into my daughter up above to do her Christmas shopping? Seventeen years of age.'

Johnny went very still.

'And before I go any further,' said Colm, 'if you let on to Laura that we had this little chat, I will give you the land of your life. And you won't see it coming, you prick.'

Johnny swallowed.

'And you're thinking: But why would Laura tell her dad she was with me in Dublin? No one was supposed to know! That was a secret! Do you want to know how I know? Well, while you're out gallivanting around Dublin, I'm fast asleep in my bed, hundreds of miles away, and I get a phone call. From Kevin Street Garda Station. And I'm thinking to myself: Why, now, would I be getting a phone call from a garda station in Dublin in the middle of the night?'

Johnny glanced at him and Colm was expecting it, so they locked eyes. Johnny broke away fast.

'Oh, it turns out they'd brought in some local lad I might know from Castletownbere,' said Colm. 'From a very respectable family, a fine rugby player, plays for Munster, apparently

144

. . . because he was caught, buckled drunk, throwing punches around Leeson Street at three in the morning.'

Johnny frowned.

'Can you remember a bit of it?' said Colm.

Johnny let out a breath.

'Well, you obviously don't remember the part where my daughter, at seventeen years of age, asks a guard to call her daddy: 'We have your daughter here with us, Sergeant.'' Colm turned to Johnny, grabbed a handful of his shirt, yanked him to his feet. Johnny was broader, three inches taller. Christmas lights from the tree in the living room flashed green and red on their faces.

'How fucking dare you?' said Colm. 'I don't know which made me sicker — having to hear that or having to hear myself say what a fine young man Johnny Weston is.'

'I didn't ask her to — '

'Of course you didn't!' said Colm. 'Do you think I don't know that? You didn't know your own name is what I heard. Laura was frightened out of her wits. Do you know what it must have took for her to have a guard make a phone call like that to me in the middle of the night? And to save your skin?'

Johnny shook his head. 'Honestly, I wouldn't have — '

'Honesty doesn't come into it with you,' said Colm. 'Could you look me in the eye right now and honestly tell me that that wasn't you I saw climbing out my daughter's bedroom window the Bank Holiday weekend?'

'Last Bank Holiday?' said Johnny. 'Laura was

145

away with Edie that weekend.'

Colm erupted. 'Do you think I came down in the last shower? Jesus Christ, you have some neck, boy. Some neck. You haven't an ounce of respect in you. Not an ounce.'

'I don't know what you want me to — '

'Do you think I came down in the last shower? I'm asking you,' said Colm.

'No. No. I don't.' said Johnny.

'If there's one thing I can't stand — it's a lad like you — wanting for nothing, his father working hand over fist to send him off to boarding school to put manners on him, and he swans back home like he owns the place. How in the name of God you got a lovely girl like Edie Kerr to go out with you is beyond me.'

He grabbed Johnny's shirt, and shook him hard. 'Have you anything at all to say for yourself?'

Johnny thought about it. 'Thanks for . . . thanks for sorting that out.'

'There's nothing I wouldn't do for my girls,' said Colm.

Johnny nodded. 'I know, I know.'

'So if I was you,' said Colm, stabbing a finger at him. 'I'd stay the fuck away from both of them. Stay the fuck away from Laura, and stay the fuck away from Miriam.'

20

Edie and Clare stood in the stable yard arch watching the rain pouring down.

'I'm not looking forward to this,' said Clare, pulling up her hood.

'Can I keep the guest jacket, though?'

'Yes!' said Edie, pulling up her own hood. 'And the Hunter short wellies.'

'The suites are beautiful,' said Clare.

'Do you think she enjoyed the night?' said Edie.

'Helen? She had a ball,' said Clare. 'You do know she's gone to bed by choice and not because she was having a bad time.'

Edie laughed. 'True, but there's something about someone going to bed early.' She turned to Clare. 'Are you enjoying the night?'

'Yes,' said Clare.

'Right,' said Edie, gesturing ahead. 'Let's brave this.' They walked down the path to the inn.

'I still can't get over Patrick,' said Clare.

Edie laughed.

'Seriously,' said Clare. 'Money and power. They're like Spanx for men.' she paused. 'Tiny dick, probably.'

Edie leaned away from her. 'Clare Brogan!'

'Edie Kerr!'

'You brat!'

They exchanged glances. 'You're actually blushing,' said Clare. 'And we both just used our

147

maiden names. Is that the night that's in it or are we about to be doomed? To . . . the singles scene.'

They laughed.

'Though I'm sure Patrick's having the time of his life,' said Clare.

'Probably,' said Edie.

'I think we can all take some credit for how well he turned out,' said Clare. 'He had no life until he started hanging out with us.'

'I know,' said Edie. 'I remember being so conscious that he knew we wanted to be friends with him, not just because he saved us, but because . . . ' She paused. 'Well, we never gave him a chance, did we?'

'But we weren't mean to him, either,' said Clare.

'I suppose so,' said Edie.

'And all he had to do to gain one life was to save four,' said Clare.

'Poor Jess,' said Edie.

'Poor Murph, more to the point.'

They arrived at the back door of the inn. Edie turned the latch and they walked into the boot room.

Clare inhaled. 'Love that smell. So . . . laundry room to the left and . . . ?'

'Miscellaneous to the right,' said Edie. She walked down the hallway and glanced back. 'What do you mean 'poor Murph'?' She stopped. 'But — he knows no one thinks it's his fault.'

'Well, of course everyone says that,' said Clare. 'And most people believe it. But Murph never will.'

'But all the rest of us made it out alive,' said Edie.

Clare shot her a glance. 'Like two out of three ain't bad?'

'No,' said Edie, irritated. 'Just — '

'I'm kidding,' said Clare. 'Look, you can understand that's going to stay with him. It's Murph, for God's sake!'

'I know,' said Edie, 'but — '

'Enough!' said Clare. 'Take me to the library.'

★   ★   ★

Laura stood outside in the smoking area, her shoulders up to her ears, squinting as she took a drag on her cigarette. She saw Johnny walking by, his head down, holding the hood of his rain jacket closed under his chin, the wind inflating it.

She shouted over. 'You look like you're walking to school.'

Johnny stopped. 'Hey,' he said. 'What are you doing out here?'

'Jesus, I don't know . . . '

He laughed, and came over. He pointed to her cigarettes. 'Can I rob one?'

'Yes, you bollocks.'

'What's that for?'

'Your crack earlier. About the kids being Frank's.'

'Relax,' he said. 'It was a joke.'

'It doesn't mean it wasn't ignorant.'

'You're such a cranky bitch.'

Laura rolled her eyes.

'How are you, anyway?' he said. 'You're looking great.'

'I look like shite. I'm wrecked.'

149

'No, you don't.' He held eye contact with her.
'Stop that,' she said.
'Stop what?' He smiled.
'That's how it always started.' She turned away and blew out a straight line of smoke.
Johnny laughed.
'How are you doing?' said Laura. 'You look a bit . . . under pressure.'
'No, no. Just a lot going on.'
'The place is fabulous. I've driven by enough times. And I had a good gawk at it online. Lovely royal engagement photo of you and Edie. 'About us'.'
'Livin' the dream.'
'Is it massive work?'
Johnny shook his head. 'Unfuckingreal. We had no idea.'
'Myself and Frank got a kitchen extension and it was nearly the end of us.'
'Multiply that by a million. We were arguing over a door knob at one stage.'
'And is it doing well for ye?'
'Ah, you have to take a hit the first few years. But I may have made a couple of miscalculations. Things like being closed from November to February. You know yourself — the business is just not there. But other than that, we're getting the bookings, the reviews are great . . . apart from the shite ones. People are coming back. When the spa's done and the lap pool's in, and the chapel turns into whatever we actually agree on, that'll make a big difference.'
'So, go on — tell us,' said Laura. 'Who wrote the bad reviews?'

Johnny's head jerked towards her.

'I knew it!' she said. 'I knew you knew something.'

Johnny shook his head. 'No . . . it wasn't anyone. I don't know who it was.'

Laura nodded. 'You're a shit liar.' She took a drag off her cigarette. 'I'll get it out of you before the night's out.'

Johnny gave her a resigned look.

'It's someone local,' said Laura. 'Does someone have it in for you?'

Johnny raised an eyebrow.

'Are you serious?' said Laura. 'I was only joking.'

'Don't say anything to Edie.'

'Sure, I don't know anything! Tell me! Who am I going to tell?'

Johnny glanced at her. 'No . . . '

'It's someone I know,' said Laura. 'Is it?'

'You're such a pain in the hole.' He paused. 'Kind of.'

'You have to tell me now.'

'It's a weird one,' said Johnny. 'So not a word to anyone. Because that would be a serious shitshow.' He tilted his head to the right. 'The Jameses.'

'Next door?' said Laura. 'Fuck off.'

'Seriously.'

'There's no way — '

'Well — I got it traced and it was their IP address.'

'That can't be right.'

'I know.' He shrugged.

'But who would it be?' said Laura. 'It's hardly

Val, and she a guard. No way'

'Mam's well in with her — she'd have a lot of respect for her.' She paused. 'And it wouldn't be Seán. He's a dote. Who's left? The kids? How old are they?'

'The youngest girls are whatever age — still having bouncy castles for their birthdays,' said Johnny. 'There's a son, Cian, he's sixteen, but he's harmless. And the eldest is Mally — she's nineteen. But she's Dylan's best bud. I'm trying to figure out if she hates us more than she loves Dylan.' He paused. 'Well, not 'us' — me.'

'Why does she hate you?' said Laura. 'I mean, does she know who you are?'

Johnny rolled his eyes. 'Sadly, she does — a fat dad who fights with her best friend and 'doesn't understand him'.'

'Still, though — a review like that would be a bit extreme. Like, she's nineteen. She'd want to have a bit of cop on at that age.'

'What — like us?' said Johnny.

Laura smiled. 'Seriously, I don't know what to make of that.'

'Me neither,' said Johnny.

'What are you going to do? Does Edie know?'

'She does not,' said Johnny. 'Are you mad? She'd have a meltdown. So don't say a word.'

'Of course I won't. Jesus.'

Johnny took another drag off his cigarette. 'I wasn't smoking, either.'

Laura took a packet of Silvermints out of her pocket, broke them in half, and handed them to him. He laughed.

'What's so funny?' said Laura.

'Nothing. Just you.' He put them in his pocket, put his arm around her, and gave her shoulder a squeeze. She patted his hand.

'Where were you off to, anyway?' said Laura. 'You looked like you were on a mission.'

She looked up at him. They locked eyes. Laura's flickered briefly wider.

'Right,' said Johnny. 'You've got your drink, you've got your cigarettes — is there anything else?'

Laura opened her arms wide.

'Aw,' said Johnny. He smiled and gave her a brief hug. She watched him walk away, then flicked the end of her cigarette through the dark like a little red meteor.

★ ★ ★

Clare and Edie sat in the library — Edie on the sofa, Clare in the window seat.

'You look very elegant,' said Edie, getting up to grab a box of matches horn a shelf by the fire. Clare turned back to the window and looked through her reflection into the black night.

Edie lit two red taper candles on the mantelpiece. 'That's better.'

'It is,' said Clare, without turning around.

'Will you be all right here for a little while?' said Edie, turning towards her. 'I need to go down and behave like a hostess.'

'You're being the perfect hostess.'

'Abandoning everyone.'

'Stop,' said Clare. 'You were bringing one of your best friends to the beautiful suite you clearly spent a lot of time preparing especially. You've taken me to my favourite spot, and, don't forget, everyone is dying to have a gawk about the place. And what's the alternative? A group tour? I have no doubt we'll all find our way back to the bar in no time.'

'Do you want me to bring you up a drink?' said Edie.

'Stop!' said Clare. 'Stop worrying about us. Do what you have to do and I'll be back down.'

'OK,' said Edie. 'See you in a while.'

Clare stood up and walked over to the window that overlooked the rear garden. She leaned in, and tilted her head.

'*Bonjour*, Clare!' she said. She smiled, and it quickly faded.

21

PATRICK

The Sisters of Good Grace Convent
26 October 1988

Patrick was pushing the lawn mower across the grass at the front of the convent, his arms fully extended, his head half-bowed between them. It was the last cut of the year. It was a mild afternoon and his black-and-white football jersey and black tracksuit bottoms were stuck to him. As the severed blades of grass flew up around him, he was thinking about all the As in Maths he had got and how he would make millions that he would grow into hundreds of millions. He stopped for a moment, and glanced up at the convent. He could see a shadow in the window of the library and he knew it was Clare and for the first time, his heart skipped. She came every Wednesday afternoon and the nuns always let her because she was one of the smartest girls in school and she had run out of books to read. Patrick knew that half the time she was in the same corner, looking out the window. Always in the same place — sitting on top of the table, the book on her lap, her feet on a chair, looking up from it to look down over the garden. He didn't think she was going to come today. He thought she might be too embarrassed. Last week, Sister Consolata had made a show of her in class. She had caught her in the middle of writing I HEART PATRICK in her homework journal and she'd picked it up and said to the whole class, 'Oh. You love Patrick, do you, now?' and Clare's face had gone as red as he'd ever seen a face go, and he knew his had done the same from his corner of the classroom. And Sister Consolata had said to her, 'Do you want to finish it, Clare? It must be far more important than anything I've got to say. You've only one letter to go. Go on — pick up your pen. What comes next? Pick up your pen! If it's so important! Pick it up!'

Clare picked up her pen and her hand was shaking.

'What's next?' said Consolata. 'P-A-T-R-I-C?'

Clare was just crying, staring down at the page.

'What comes next?' Sister Consolata was saying to her.

And Clare said. 'K, Sister,' and everyone was trying not to laugh and Patrick's face was hot but at the same time, he wanted to take his hands from on top of the desk and slide them under it.

He was surprised that Clare had come back to the convent today. Her love of books must have been greater than her embarrassment or greater than her shame or greater than her hatred for Sister Consolata. Or maybe it wasn't her love of

156

books, it was her love of him. He looked up at the window again, and she was still there. He waved up at her, but the sun was so bright, he didn't think she could see him. Then he remembered she was getting French grinds from Mademoiselle Autin, the visiting French teacher and everyone loved Mademoiselle Autin because she looked like a movie star. It didn't make a whole pile of sense to him when Clare was already top of the class at French.

He bowed his head and kept mowing. He thought about the future, where he had his own home, a mansion, and he would stand at the window, and wave down at a student like him, then come down, and give him a bottle of Coke in the heat, and a one-hundred-pound tip, and explain to him how he could turn that into a fortune, so he could become a millionaire too. He would tell the boy he could use the pool if he wanted to, and he could bring his friends if he wanted to. Then he would head back into the house where he would stand at the bay windows at the back, and watch his beautiful wife — looking like Wonder Woman and Jessie Crossan — walk towards him in a bikini that was still wet. Then he thought of Clare with her even bigger breasts. Then he thought of her short frizzy hair and the darkness of the hair all over her — on her arms and above her lips and by her ears and he thought of how she was shorter and fatter. Then he thought of how she was closer.

★ ★ ★

Shafts of bright sunlight slanted through the gaps in the blinds of the library windows. He was hidden behind one of the tall bookshelves, his crooked left arm above him, his forehead resting against it. In front of him, just below his eyeline, spread open on a gap he made on one of the shelves was a brochure for Playtex bras.

In his other hand, he was holding his dick as he stared down at a pretty brunette in a white bra that was more modern than the ones he brought in off the washing line for his mother. His breathing was fast and shallow, and his hand was working harder and harder, and he could feel the tightness of the waistband of his tracksuit bottoms, pushed down at the back, and the breeze from the window drifting across his skin and he closed his eyes at the feeling, and breathed the air deep. His forehead shone with grease, and sweat. He smelled of cut grass and petrol. His legs shook. He lifted his eyes from the page, and pictures of Jessie flashed into his mind until he went back to the model, whom he didn't know, and who didn't bring him any guilt, and then he fought again for Jessie to get out of his head, because she did something to his heart too, and she had been hurt, and he was as bad as any man who would do a thing like that, and he groaned, and he clenched his teeth, and his eyes were back on the model, on her breasts this time, and no face was in his head. His eyes went lower but the photo ended at the model's waist and he found himself thinking about Clare and all the hair she might have and how he would cup his hand tight around it and search with his fingers

158

for where it was wet and he could push a finger inside her.

He gripped himself tighter, lost in how that dark hot hole would suck his finger deep and how his finger would suck back and how he would have to push harder to go further and how that hole wouldn't want to let his finger go until it knew that he was putting something longer and harder in there and he looked down and it was so much longer and harder than any finger and his breath quickened and deepened and there was a rushing sound in his ears that happened when his body was reduced to one body part, and breath, and nothing could break through.

She was standing beside him. To his right. A chill shot up his spine like a yanked piano wire. He stopped breathing, then turned his head. It was Clare. His breathing started up again at the relief it wasn't Sister Consolata. Clare's mouth was open, her eyes wide, widening again when they moved down his body to where his dick was still hard, still in his hand. She looked up and their eyes met. Patrick looked down and back up at her. 'Do you want to . . . '

Clare's eyes were like dolls' eyes broken, open, but she was frowning too and Patrick felt like his heart had leapt to the base of his throat, and it was lodged there and that it was wrong, but, still, that it needed to be there, like the pin in a grenade.

'Sorry,' he said, his voice trembling. 'Sorry . . . I thought . . . 'He was pulling up his tracksuit bottoms when the elastic snapped back against him and he came and there was so much of it and it shot past and some of it landed on the edge of the shelf. They both gasped.

'Sorry,' he said again. 'Sorry . . . I thought you . . . I thought you . . . liked me.'

Clare's eyes fluttered with rapid blinks. She took two steps backwards.

'Don't tell anyone,' said Patrick. He was about to reach out for her with his sticky hand and they both froze. 'Sorry,' he said. 'Sorry. Please. Don't. I'll be dead.'

Clare shook her head, firmly, quickly. 'I won't,' she said. 'I promise.'

'Thanks,' he said.

Clare turned her head sharply and walked towards the door with such calm purpose that he thought he had dreamt the whole thing.

22

Murph left the bar and walked down the hall to Reception. Johnny was walking towards him.

'What the hell's going on with the lights?' said Murph, gesturing around. 'I mean, obviously it suits me, but . . . '

'He's some useless piece of shit, Terry,' said Johnny.

'Well, we know that,' said Murph. 'But is he making any progress?'

'I'd need to find him first.'

'You literally couldn't have got a worse guy — '

'Would you shut up about it?' said Johnny. 'I fucking know.'

'Look,' said Murph. 'I'm just a forty-six-year-old man standing in front of a way-older, less-attractive man, asking him why the fuck he hired a particular tradesman.'

Johnny looked confused.

'Wasted on you,' said Murph. 'Don't worry about it.'

'Quick one,' said Johnny. 'Have you talked to Patrick much?'

Murph nodded. 'I was chatting to him there — he was having a look at your plans for the spa — said he needed to talk to you about it.'

'What?' said Johnny. 'Why?'

'I don't know,' said Murph. 'I hate all that shite.'

'And it's definitely hedge funds he's in,' said Johnny.

'Yeah — what's that got to do with anything?' said Murph.

'Not vulture funds.'

Murph laughed. 'You know they only buy places that are fucked, right?'

Johnny laughed.

'In fairness, though — he did view it when it was up for sale.'

'What?'

'Your face — would you relax? *Viewed* it. Didn't put in an offer. Nothing weird is going on. Patrick is not here to run off with your inn.'

'It's not that,' said Johnny. 'It's . . . ' He shrugged.

Murph let out a dramatic gasp. He leaned into Johnny, eyes wide. 'Maybe he's back for vengeance! Against the boarding school prick who bullied him!' Murph did a voice-over voice: 'Inn Escapable: the story of Patrick — the boy who waited thirty years to grow muscles, so he could finally face down the rugby hero he hadn't realized had let himself go.'

Johnny laughed. 'You prick.'

'Right,' said Murph. 'Are you OK now?'

Johnny nodded. 'Where are you off to?'

Murph turned around and started walking away backwards. 'None of your business.' He shrugged and held his hands out. 'You've lost control of the crowd, Johnny. And you know what happens then?' He shook his fists in the air. 'The crowd goes wiiild.'

Helen looked around her suite — elegant, understated, and now award-winning.

Edie had included every item on the wish list she asked her to write — all the things that would make a wheelchair-user's stay the most comfortable possible: a door to the en suite wide enough for the wheelchair to get through but not too heavy that she couldn't open it herself, mirrors — mounted at the right height — in the bedroom and the bathroom, room for the wheelchair at both sides of the bed, room to open the wardrobe door and be in front of it, clothes rails at the right height, grab rails by the sink, grab rails by the toilet, shower with a drop-down seat, emergency pull cords in convenient places.

She started to cry.

Edie walked down the hallway and slipped in the door to the Billiard Room.

'Oh . . . my God! Murph!' she said, startled. 'What are you doing in here?'

Murph was sitting alone in the dark, staring out the window, holding an empty glass on the arm of the chair. He glanced briefly at her but turned back to the window.

'Are you all on your ownsome?' said Edie.

Murph nodded, but didn't look at her. Edie walked to the window and looked out. 'The silence.' Some of the force had gone from the

163

wind and the rain had stopped. 'I'd say it's only a lull, though.'

Murph didn't reply. She turned around to him. He looked up at her, his eyes damp.

'Sorry,' he said. I'm a bit worse for wear.' He pressed his thumbs into the corners of his eyes.

'Oh, no,' said Edie. 'What is it?'

Murph showed her the photo he was holding in his left hand.

'Aw — you and Rosco,' said Edie. 'What is it? Talk to me.'

Murph let out a long breath. 'I suppose . . . I'm listening to you in there and all Helen's done for everyone . . . and . . . ' He shrugged. 'What have I done, except — '

'Make everyone laugh?' said Edie. She touched his shoulder. 'Move.' He did, and she sat down on the arm of the chair.

'Thanks, but . . . ' He let out another breath. 'Who have I saved?'

'Saved?' said Edie. 'Gosh, who have I saved? What do you mean?'

'Do you know when the weirdest thing hits you?' He held up the photo again. 'I couldn't even save Rosco. A dog.'

'Because he's a dog and he ran away, didn't he?' said Edie. 'And it's sad but that's what dogs do.'

'He was last seen headed for here, as a matter of fact.'

'What?' said Edie.

'Rosco used to come here with dad when he was working. Until Consolata fired him.'

'Why?' said Edie.

'I don't know,' said Murph, 'but one night

164

— he was in a bad way with the drink — and he was saying something about her blackening his name with her lies. He was in an awful state.'

'When was that?'

'It wasn't long before Mam died. It was right before first year. The same year poor Jessie . . . '

'Imagine firing a man whose wife was dying of cancer,' said Edie.

'Yup,' said Murph. 'Maybe Rosco was coming up to eat the face off her.'

'I know you loved him,' said Edie, 'but — '

'It's not that,' said Murph. 'It's . . . Mam . . . Dad . . . Rosco. And then Jessie.'

'Ah,' said Edie.

Murph shook his head. 'I killed Jessie and that's that. I know no one wants to say it out loud, but it's a fact. I could have killed you all. My pals. Because I wanted to make you laugh. I mean, I wanted to scare the shite out of you — that was the main thing . . . '

Tears welled in Edie's eyes. 'Oh, Murph.' She patted his shoulder.

He looked up at her and gave her a sad smile. She blinked back tears. Then she reached out, took his hand, brought it to her lap and squeezed it tight. 'You didn't kill Jessie. And you couldn't have saved her. Neither could I and neither could Patrick.'

'You must have had therapy.'

'It's not that,' said Edie. She squeezed his hand again. 'She didn't want to be saved.'

'What?'

'Patrick and I were there. At the end. We saw what happened.'

'What do you mean 'saw what happened'?'

'She wanted to go,' said Edie. 'She wanted to go.'

Murph looked up at her, wide-eyed.

'She was so damaged,' said Edie. 'So, so damaged.'

'But why didn't you say anything?' said Murph.

'It would have been too much for her parents to bear,' said Edie. 'It was horrifying. That's all I'm going to say. I can still see it. And I thought . . . I don't know. I thought that it was one thing for everyone to think 'she was drunk, it might have slowed her down, she wouldn't have felt a thing' but quite another for them to imagine what we saw, to know it was a choice she made.'

'Are you sure, though?' said Murph. 'It must have been so hard to see.'

'Sadly, we could. We talked about it. Once. A few months later. And we both saw the same thing.'

Murph shook his head. 'That's shocking.'

'I'm so sorry I couldn't say anything — it was too much.'

'I'm sorry for the pair of you having to see that,' said Murph, 'but it's all the same to me — it's still all my fault.'

'It isn't,' said Edie. 'I hate to think you think that.'

'It's OK,' said Murph. 'It is what it is.'

Edie stood up. 'Can I get you anything before I go?'

'No, no — I'm fine out,' said Murph. He sat up. 'Do you know where Laura is? She was only supposed to be going to the ladies.'

'God knows,' said Edie. 'Will you be all right here?'

Murph nodded. 'Yes. I'll get a grip.'

Edie smiled. 'Good. You should be enjoying yourself.'

'I am!' said Murph. 'I was! You can't leave me alone for a minute . . . '

Edie pulled open the door a fraction, and as she slipped through it, she paused and turned back. 'Oh — and please keep that to yourself, OK?'

Murph watched her hand slide down the door and disappear as it closed behind her.

★ ★ ★

Helen lay in bed, with an upturned book on her chest, staring at the ceiling.

There was a knock on the door. 'Helen! Helen! Are you awake? It's Murph!'

She turned towards the door. 'Yes. I'm in bed. But come in!'

He pushed the door open. 'It didn't feel right. The birthday girl. Are you lonesome?' He paused. 'Or were you dying to get away from us?'

Helen laughed. 'I was . . . I actually was lonesome.'

'Well, that's shite.' He looked around the room. 'This is fabulous.' He looked down at her. 'Can I come in for a cuddle?'

Helen laughed. 'You're mental. Of course you can.'

He hopped on to the bed beside her, and

167

shifted over. He put his arm around her, and she put her head against his shoulder. He gave her a squeeze.

'What are you doing down here?' said Helen. 'I hope I didn't break up the party.'

'Well, I hope you're not here thinking shite stuff about yourself. Seriously. It's *Happy* Birthday. Why wouldn't I be down here? Because you're in a wheelchair?' He looked over at it. 'Do you want to go for a spin for the craic? In your nightie.'

She laughed. 'Murph, I love you.'

'Good! Because I love you too!' He kissed the top of her head and put his hand against her cheek. 'Hey,' he said, 'what's this? Not tears.'

Helen let out a shaky sigh. 'I'm sorry.'

'Don't apologize to me,' said Murph.

'Look at this place,' she said.

'I know!' said Murph. 'All down to you.'

She laughed. 'Not all down.'

'All the important bits,' said Murph. 'All the award-winning bits.'

'I . . . I . . . ' She started to cry. 'I don't want to be an expert in this.'

Murph, his head against hers, closed his eyes at the words and held her a little tighter. 'I know, pet. I know.'

'I was an expert in adolescent psychiatry,' said Helen. 'I was a director of nursing, I gave talks to hundreds of people on psychiatric nursing, my staff came to me for advice.' Murph handed her a tissue, and she blew her nose. Then she sat up a little straighter. 'I'm still an expert in adolescent psychiatry!'

'Exactly!' said Murph. 'You can spot young

168

mentallers from a hundred feet.'

Helen sniffled and laughed. 'The others were all talking about kids and anxiety earlier and no one asked me a thing.'

'Ah, but that wouldn't have been on purpose.'

'No — I know,' said Helen, 'I do. And I'm not offended. Seriously. But sometimes it feels like . . . my slate is wiped clean. The wheelchair comes in, and steamrollers over everything. I am now the Woman in the Wheelchair. If someone wanted to narrow me down, that's who I am. Do you know Helen? You see her around town. She's the Woman in the Wheelchair. It doesn't matter who I am or what I did. I was strong, I was fit. Now I'm Poor Helen and God love her and the Woman in the Wheelchair.'

'You could go over there and be the woman in the wheelchair in the window and we could write a book about you.'

Helen laughed. They fell into silence. Murph kissed her head a few times. 'I'm doing this for the view.'

Helen slapped him, and adjusted her nightdress.

'Stop wrecking my night!' said Murph, pulling her hand away.

'Oh, Murph, I wish you were around more,' said Helen. 'I miss the craic. I'm so . . . I'm just at home all day, all night . . . doing what exactly? What's the point of me? If I was gone, what difference would it make? You know when you read obituaries and they say 'died surrounded by family'? What am I going to have? 'Died surrounded by . . . eggshells'.'

'That's a good line,' said Murph. 'I'll put that

169

in the woman-in-the-wheelchair book.'

Helen laughed.

'Listen — you're not dying, and unless you fall out of that while you're making your breakfast, there'll be no eggshells involved. And if that does happen, you'll die knowing you'll have given me a brilliant story for the funeral.' He paused. 'Do you want me to do the eulogy?'

'Oh God — do,' said Helen. 'Please do.'

'Helen — or the Woman in the Wheelchair as she was known to most — made her last omelette this week. The Woman in the Wheelchair in the Kitchen with the Eggshells . . . ' He paused. 'Speaking of which . . . I realized earlier: you know what Edie and Johnny could do? They've got a study, a kitchen, a conservatory, a Billiard Room, a library, a dining room . . . they could do those swanky sex parties . . . with a Cluedo theme. Lewd-o.'

'You could be the spanner,' said Helen.

'That's my girl!' said Murph. He laughed. 'Right — I better get back to the others.' He slid his arm out from under her, and knelt up on the bed. 'But I do want to say one thing before I go: most beautiful girl in the room tonight.'

Helen smiled. 'Aw, thank you.'

'My pleasure.' He looked around. 'Jesus, I could stay here now, happy out for the night.'

'Why don't you?' said Helen.

Murph stood up. 'Because you're in a wheel-chair.'

Helen burst out laughing. Murph danced across the room, then blew her a kiss from the door.

23

MURPH

Castletownbere, Beara
10 February 1984

Murph took the replica Aer Lingus plane from his bedside locker and flung it across the room. The only reason he had it was because his mam was dying, and his uncle had come back from America to say goodbye. Murph was delighted with the plane even though he was too old to play with it. But he didn't know then that you could look at a thing — a toy, or a game, or a pair of pyjamas, or a pillowcase, or a coat in a wardrobe — and it could upset you. He only found that out when his mam died. And then he lay there thinking about how sounds can even make you sad — like bracelets banging off each other when someone was giving you a hug. And then he thought about smells, and decided they were the worst and the best of all of them.

Today, he'd been sitting on a bench in the square, because his dad was in the pub, and the Sergeant's wife came up to him, Laura's mam, and she was a lovely, gentle lady. And she asked him how he was, and he said he was OK, but he

171

knew he looked sad, because he was sitting there, sticking his legs out in front of him, staring at his shoes. And she had crouched down in front of him, then, and said to him, 'I'll never forget what your father said once, years ago, before you were born. Did you know your parents waited ten years for you to come along? And your dad said to me: 'Wouldn't it be an awful shame if people thought myself and Nora weren't a family because we didn't have a child?' And well, that's what I think now, Liam — wouldn't it be an awful shame if people thought yourself and your dad, no matter what, weren't a family?'

And Murph realized later that 'no matter what' wasn't just because his mam had died, it meant 'no matter how drunk your father is' and 'no matter how many times you're spotted wandering around on your own' and 'no matter how many times people drive by the house and see one little shape on the sofa in front of the television'.

And he remembered that he was suddenly in Laura's mam's arms and it felt like it was an accident, as if you could slip off a bench and jump into someone's arms and after she hugged the life out of him, she put her cold hands to his cheeks, and he could smell flour and apple skins and margarine, and he wanted to cry more, but he wanted to be polite. He started to think about his mother with her hands covered in pastry, slicing apples so fast it was like a magic trick.

★ ★ ★

Three hours later, Murph woke to the sound of hammering on the front door. He sat up, his heart pounding. He waited for it to stop, but it didn't. He went to his door, and opened it quietly, and ran across to his father's room. He knocked on the door. There was no answer. He knocked harder. Then he opened it. His father's bed was empty. The hammering on the door wouldn't stop. Murph went to the landing, and hid behind the wall, and looked down at the front door. He could see a hand pushing through the letter box, and his legs started to shake.

'Liam! Liam! Is there a Liam here?'

Murph frowned. He didn't recognize the voice. But whoever it was, he knew his name.

'Liam! It's about your granddad! Open up!'

Murph thought his heart would explode from his chest. He ran down the stairs, slipping on some of them, then got to the front door, struggling with his shaking hands to open the latch. There was a man standing there — a stranger — and Murph was panicking now about opening the door to him.

'Don't worry, son — everything's going to be OK,' he said. 'Your granddad's taken a bit of a fall — '

'He's my dad!' said Murph. 'He's my dad! He's just old.'

'I'm sorry,' said the man. 'He's not making a lot of sense. He told me he lived the next house down, and he told me your name was Liam, that you were twelve and I — '

'Where is he?' said Murph, already running, in his bare feet and his pyjama bottoms, in the

173

direction the man had pointed.

'I was driving by, and the headlights caught him,' said the man, following Murph. 'He's back there a small bit — I can show you — '

'Dad!' Murph screamed. 'Dad!' He almost ran out on the road, then turned, and started running in the pitch dark. 'Dad!'

He stopped when he saw the top of his father's head, and the strips of his grey hair half across it, half falling down. He was lying curled on his side in the ditch, his black wool coat around him.

Murph rushed to him, and collapsed on the grass beside him. He took his head gently in his hands, and turned it up towards him.

'Daddy!' he cried when he saw the blood, and the grazes down his face. He could hear the fright in his voice and it frightened him more and he burst into tears. 'Are you alive? Dad! Are you alive?'

He put his ear to his father's mouth, and he could feel his breath against it, and he went dizzy with relief. He hugged his head, then his chest, and then he lay his head against it. He could feel his father's shoulder shift, and his arm fell down heavy across his back. Murph closed his eyes and hugged him tighter.

His father patted his back. 'Liam,' he said. 'Liam. Liam. Liam.'

'Yes,' said Murph.

His father let out a long sigh.

'You're OK,' said Murph. 'You're OK. We'll get you home to bed. You'll be right as rain in the morning.'

The man had come up behind Murph. 'Is he

174

all right, son? Is it bleeding much? The cut? He wouldn't let me call an ambulance. Will I call an ambulance?'

'No, thank you,' said Murph, looking at the man over his shoulder. 'Thanks all the same. He just wants to come home.' He turned back to his father.

The man looked away, pressed his fingers into the corners of his eyes. 'Let me help you with him, so.'

★   ★   ★

Murph sat by his father's bed. There was a roll of cotton wool and a small basin with water and Dettol on the bedside locker. He started to pick the black bits of gravel out of the cut. Jerry was drifting in and out. Murph tore off some cotton wool, dipped it in the basin, and squeezed it out.

'It might sting a small bit,' he said, pausing before he put it gently to his father's face.

Jerry winced, but then seemed to drift off. By the time Murph had cleaned the wound, his father was watching him with one eye and it made Murph smile.

'It looked worse than it was,' said Murph, patting his father's arm.

'You're a great man,' Jerry said. 'You're a great man.'

'Aren't you the same yourself?' said Murph.

It reminded Murph of what people used to say about his father: 'That's a man you can rely on', 'That's a man that'd never let you down.' But since his mam got sick, and then when she died, Murph heard different things about his father: Jerry Murphy was 'gone altogether', 'devastated altogether', 'in a heap altogether'.

'She took his heart with her to the grave,' he heard an old woman say outside Mass one Sunday. She didn't realize Murph was right beside her. He wanted to turn around and roar at her: 'My dad tells me the whole time he loves me! No one's dad does that! And you have to have a heart to love someone, so it's not in any grave! It's inside his chest! And Mam had the biggest heart in the world, and people with big hearts don't usually steal things in the first place, plus she's probably up there now handing out bits of it to the angels if they're stuck.'

Instead, he made his eyes look scared, turned to the old woman and said: 'I heard every Valentine's Day, it comes back to haunt him.'

Murph sat in silence for a moment, watching his father's chest move up and down. 'Is it I'm too much trouble for you?' he said. 'Without Mam here?' He waited for an answer, shoulders rigid, heart pounding. 'Because I've no problem . . . it's as easy to make two sets of sandwiches in the morning as it is to make one.' He remembered Laura's mam. Wouldn't it be an awful shame if people thought we weren't a family? Wouldn't it be an awful shame? Murph wiped his arm across his eyes, and under his nose.

'I miss Mam,' Murph said, then. He didn't mean to.

His father nodded, and he kept nodding, and

his head was loose on his neck. 'The auld
. . . bitch,' he said.

Murph's heart closed like a fist, then burst to
fill his chest and pound against it.

'Cuh . . . cuh, cuh . . . ' sobbed his dad.
'Consolata . . . '

Murph let out a breath.

'Telling everyone,' said his father. 'Telling
everyone . . . '

Murph felt his gut twist, because he didn't
want to know what Consolata was telling
everyone, because it can't have been good, and it
could travel so far.

'Saying . . . I'd done a bad job up above . . . '
said his father, 'that I couldn't be relied on, that
I was too . . . too . . . fond of the drink . . . that
. . . that . . . I was a wreck altogether . . . '

'What?' said Murph, because he knew that
when his dad was working, he worked hard, and
he didn't drink. He only drank with the
loneliness of the house around him.

His father nodded. 'Told people . . . I was . . . '
He shook his head. Then his forehead crumpled,
and he raised a limp hand to cover it. Murph's
heart started to pound again. His father let his
arm fall to his chest, and when he looked at
Murph, it was like he wasn't seeing him any
more, that he'd forgotten he was there, because
then he mentioned Rosco, and that was too
much at this stage.

'And . . . ' said his father, his head rolling away
from him. ' . . . Rosco.'

Murph wanted to run now, at the thought he
might hear something upsetting. Now his father

177

was gripping his hand, and looking at him again. He put his other hand to Murph's cheek. ' . . . gone,' he said. 'Gone.'

And then his chest seemed to collapse in on itself, and his shoulders shook, and he let out a terrible sob. ' . . . And the child,' he said, sobbing again ' . . . and the child without . . . ' His breath heaved. 'And the child . . . without a . . . '

Mam, Murph was thinking. Mam.

Rosco had been missing for five weeks. And every morning since, Murph woke up, thinking this was the day Rosco would come running up the drive and jump into his arms with the absolute confidence that he would always, always be caught.

But there was something about the way his father said 'gone' that told Murph tomorrow morning, things might be different.

24

Edie was standing in the window of the Billiard Room, her cheeks flushed, fanning her face with her hand. The rain was loud as it pounded on the windows, intermittently quietening when it was whipped in a different direction by powerful gusts. Edie looked at her reflection in the window and adjusted her hair. She went to the door and opened it gently, pausing on the threshold before going into the hallway and turning right. She walked down to the entrance hall, opened the door of the honesty bar and stuck her head in.

Laura was standing in front of Johnny's photo wall, holding a black-and-white photo of him in her hands. She looked up at Edie and laughed. 'It fell,' she said. She held up the torn string at the back of it.

Edie laughed. 'Well, I didn't think you were standing there admiring it.'

'Lucky it didn't break,' said Laura.

'I know,' said Edie. 'The symmetry would be all off.'

Laura handed it to her. Edie put it on the floor against the wall.

'Where's Murph?' said Laura.

'He was here last time I saw him,' said Edie. 'God knows.'

'Is Clare not with you?' said Laura.

'I left her in the library,' said Edie. 'I presume

she's still up there.'

Laura looked around the room. 'You did a fabulous job on the place.'

'Thank you,' said Edie. 'Are you OK for a drink?'

Laura tapped her glass. 'I helped myself.'

'I hope so,' said Edie. 'I don't feel like I'm being a very attentive hostess tonight.'

'Jesus — relax,' said Laura. 'We're happy out.'

'I have to find Johnny,' said Edie. 'What do you want to do? I feel bad leaving you here on your own.'

'Do you have any idea how rare it is for me to have a room to myself?' said Laura. 'I have the three of them following me around the place the whole time. None of them can make a decision by themselves. 'Mammy, can I?' whatever. 'Laura, can he?' whatever. 'Am I allowed?' this, that, and the other. It would do your head in.'

'I know,' said Edie. 'They're helpless.'

'I was watching this programme about people who go into cults and they have to be deprogrammed when they come out and I thought: Someone needs to set something like that up over here for men whose mammies did everything for them. Frank's mother made a balls of him.'

Edie laughed. 'Did you say that to her?'

'Probably at some wedding or other,' said Laura. 'Probably at our wedding.'

'Are you sure you'll be all right here?' said Edie.

'Yes!' said Laura. 'Go. I'll stay here admiring photos of Johnny.'

Edie laughed. 'As soon as I find him, I'll be back. I'm done now — all I want to do is sit back for the rest of the night.'

Patrick stuck his head in the door behind her. 'Ladies,' he said.

'Right,' said Edie, turning to Laura. 'I'll leave you in Patrick's capable hands.'

'Am I interrupting you?' said Patrick.

'Not at all,' said Edie.

'No,' said Laura. 'Get in here, stay quiet, and don't ask me any questions.'

⋆ ⋆ ⋆

Edie went out into the hall, then walked down to the conservatory. The double doors were open. She reached out for the handles to close them when a movement outside caught her eye. She walked across the room, and up to the glass. Outside, by a pallet of cinder blocks, a sheet of tarpaulin was inflating and deflating in the wind. As she watched, one strong gust blasted it up against the blocks. Edie squinted into the darkness. As the tarpaulin floated down, she could see hair, the top of a bloodied head, and a body that was very still. It was Terry Hyland.

Edie screamed and ran to get the others.

25

The rain had stopped, but the wind was wild, tearing at the trees, whipping water from the puddles. The narrow rope of the flagpole was slapping against it, the metal clasp sending a faint chime into the night.

Murph was the first to reach the body. He crouched, covered his hand with the sleeve of his rain jacket, and pulled back the tarpaulin, exposing Terry's head, his grey face, and the mess that had been made of the left side; through a gaping wound, the visible white of bone shone from the darkness of the pulped flesh around it.

Murph batted his hand behind him. 'Don't, lads. Get back t'fuck.'

He looked, wide-eyed, at Edie, lost inside a black rain jacket to her knees, holding her hood closed under her chin, bracing herself against the wind. Johnny stood, rooted, four feet to her left.

Clare walked towards the body.

'Clare — don't,' said Murph. 'Don't.'

'For God's sake — I'm a big girl,' said Clare. Still, as soon as her gaze lowered to Terry, she lurched to one side, stumbling in the mud before she righted herself.

Patrick walked towards the body, but stopped a foot short of it. He winced and turned away, bowing his head, making a swift sign of the cross, ignoring Johnny as he walked past him to Murph.

'Jesus Christ,' said Johnny. 'What the fuck happened here?'

Murph looked at him.

'What?' said Johnny. 'How the hell would I know?' He glanced up at the roof and back down at Terry. 'He must have slipped.' He put his hands on his hips. 'Fuck, fuck, fuck. He was half-cut when he got here.'

'What the fuck was he doing up there if he was pissed?' said Murph.

' 'Half-cut,' I said.'

'Well, whatever fraction cut he was,' said Murph. 'What? You thought he could — '

'Fix his own fuck-ups!' said Johnny.

'I get it,' said Murph, 'but what was the big rush? Could you not have — '

'It was while he was here!' said Johnny, 'I was thinking — there's a gale force fucking wind out there, we've friends staying, we've no electricity and I don't trust that something's not going to blow off somewhere and kill someone.'

'What makes you think he fell off the roof?' said Laura. 'How did he get up there? Is there a ladder anywhere? And even if there was — what? He fell off, landed neatly in the gap between two pallets and wrapped himself in tarpaulin?'

Johnny stared at her. Murph walked around the pallets and shook his head. 'Nothing.' He locked eyes with Johnny. 'Jesus.'

Johnny looked, panicked, at Laura. 'But . . . what . . . ? Couldn't he have . . . ' He glanced at the top of the blocks. He ran his fingers through his hair. 'Jesus Christ. What are you saying? You're not saying . . . '

Laura nodded. 'I am. I'm sorry, but . . . '

Murph crouched at Terry's head and studied the wounds. Then he nodded slowly and looked up at Johnny. 'I think she's right. I think someone . . . did this.'

'What? No way,' said Johnny. 'There's no way . . . Who, even? Why?' He looked around the group. 'Whoa. What the fuck is this? Why are you all looking at me? Jesus Christ — you're all looking at me.' His eyes were wide, his pupils huge. He stopped at Edie. Her hands were over her mouth, her fingers trembling, her eyes filled with tears.

'No,' said Johnny. 'Edie — no. Are you serious? Do you seriously think I did this?'

Edie took a few steps towards him. 'I don't — '

'Is that what you all think?' said Johnny. 'We're having a nice dinner, I go out and kill someone, come back in . . . ' He shrugged.

Clare held up her hands. 'Look — apart from there being no evidence of him being up on the roof, no one knows what happened here.'

'Somebody fucking does,' said Johnny.

Everyone went quiet.

'And it's not me!' said Johnny.

'We need to call the guards,' said Laura. She held out her hand, palm up. 'And it's raining. We need to cover him up properly.'

'It's already been raining,' said Johnny. 'What difference does it make at this stage?'

Laura stared at him. 'That's ridiculous. Apart

from anything, there could be something inside in that tarpaulin with him. Or if rain starts to pool in there . . . '

'This is fucked up,' said Johnny. 'What the fuck?'

'Whatever the fuck,' said Murph, 'we're getting soaked here.'

'And there's no point standing around talking about it,' said Laura, 'Can we just go inside, call the guards and at least get that over with?'

Johnny was staring into space.

'Johnny,' said Laura. 'The guards?'

He frowned. 'Yes. Yes.'

Edie turned round and started to walk back to the inn, her arms wrapped across her stomach, her shoulders hunched. She stopped when she got inside the door and let the others pass. 'Go ahead into the bar,' she said. 'I'll follow you in.'

Johnny was the last to come in. He stood in front of her, fear flickering in his eyes.

'What happened?' she said.

'You're asking me? I told you — how the fuck would I know?'

'But . . . you were the only one dealing with him,' said Edie. 'What happened?'

'Why do you keep asking me that?' said Johnny. 'I don't fucking know.'

'You seem . . . edgy.'

'So do you! Jesus Christ. Of course I'm fucking edgy. There's a dead body in our garden.' He paused. 'This is a nightmare. What the fuck are we supposed to do? I'm in deep shit — '

Edie's head snapped back. 'Why are you in deep shit?'

185

Johnny stared at her, open-mouthed. 'You mean apart from 'because my wife's looking at me like I just made a confession by accident'? I'm in deep shit, Edie, because I couldn't stand the prick, half the town knows it, and now he's lying dead outside our house. Who'd be your number one suspect?'

'You need to calm down, Johnny. Seriously. You look . . . I don't know — '

'What?' said Johnny. 'Tell me — how do I look?'

She stared at him. 'Unhinged.'

'Wow,' said Johnny.

'If there's anything you need to tell me,' said Edie.

Johnny opened his mouth. Edie waited, panic flickering in her eyes. The sound of footsteps echoed towards them from the hallway. Edie spun around. Laura was walking towards them, then stopped. She stood with her arms crossed, looking back and forth between them.

'We're coming — sorry,' said Edie. She turned to Johnny, flashing warning eyes at him before she walked away. Johnny reached out and grabbed her arm, pulling her around to him.

'What are you doing?' said Edie, her voice a low hiss, as she gently slid her arm from his grip.

'Just . . . ' He leaned in close to her. 'Stop looking at me like that.'

'Lads — come on,' said Laura.

Johnny looked up at her. 'Give us a minute, for fuck's sake.'

'What's going on?' said Laura. 'We need to — '

'Can you shut the fuck up for one minute?' said Johnny.

'Jesus, calm down,' said Laura.

'How am I meant to calm down when — '

'Johnny,' said Edie, drawing his attention back to her. She lowered her voice. 'You're not doing yourself any favours, here. I mean it: calm down.'

Johnny let out a long breath.

'And looking at you like what?' said Edie.

'Like . . . you're afraid of me.'

A frown flickered on Edie's face. 'I'm . . . not.' She turned and walked over to Laura. Johnny followed. When they got to the door of the bar, he stopped.

'Go ahead in. Give me five.'

'What?' said Edie. 'Where are you going?'

'The jacks.' He walked away.

Laura turned to Edie. 'OK — what's going on?'

Edie frowned. 'What?'

'Did he . . . do something?'

Edie stared at her. 'What? No. He has no idea what happened. We're the same as the rest of you.'

★   ★   ★

Johnny walked down the steps to the basement. He made his way to the wine cellar, loosened a panel at the bottom of one of the shelves, reached in, pulled out a tin, and prised off the lid. He looked inside. It was empty. He frowned, then stared up at the ceiling.

'Fuck,' he said. 'Fuck, fuck, fuck, fuck, fuck, fuck, fuck.'

★   ★   ★

187

Murph was standing in the bar by the confession box. There was a bottle of Jameson, a bottle of Hennessy XO and five glasses lined up in front of him. Clare was standing at the window, her arms crossed, looking out into the night. Laura was sitting at one of the tables close to her. Patrick was standing at the edge of the hearth. He reached down, took a log from the basket, and threw it on to the fire.

'Where's Johnny?' said Laura. She leaned back in her chair. 'Edie! Where's Johnny?'

Edie was standing by the wall with her arms folded.

'Here's Johnny,' said Johnny, walking in the door, his arms outstretched.

He walked over to Murph and squinted at the glasses, counting them with his finger. 'None for me?' he said.

Murph stared at him. 'Patrick doesn't drink?'

Johnny gave him an upward nod, and took the first glass of brandy.

Murph frowned. He pointed to a bottle of 7UP. 'Give Patrick that.'

Johnny handed Patrick his drink, and nodded to the armchair by the fire.

'Thanks,' said Patrick, sitting down.

Clare reached out and drew the curtains closed. She fixed them neatly across the window, then sat opposite Laura.

Johnny started to pace in front of the door, glass in hand. He stopped halfway to the corner and looked up at Edie.

'Sit down,' he said, pointing her to the chair opposite Patrick's. She did as he asked.

Johnny kept pacing, the colour rising in his face, sweat sinning on his brow. Everyone exchanged glances.

'Sure, why don't you sit down yourself?' said Murph.

Johnny, scowling, batted a hand at him.

'I think he's right,' said Patrick. 'You might want to sit down.'

Johnny stared at him, his pupils huge. 'I'm fine. This is just fucked up. It's totally fucked up.'

'I know,' said Patrick. 'But — '

'It had to have been an accident,' said Johnny. 'It had to have been.' He stopped and wiped the sweat from his hairline. 'Like — I don't know how he ended up in the tarp . . . ' He shook his head. 'But . . . '

'You're probably right,' said Murph, walking over to him. 'It probably was an accident.' He put a hand on Johnny's shoulder. 'But, either way, you've had a shock and it might be a good idea to — '

Johnny elbowed his way out of Murph's grip. 'I'm fucking fine!' He raised his hands. 'Just . . . get out of my face for a minute.'

Murph hovered, then walked over to the window and sat at the free table.

Laura leaned forward until she was in Edie's eyeline. 'Edie? If he's just going to stand there — or walk up and down there — can you do the honours? Make the call to the guards and at least get that out of the way'

There was a flash of movement by the door and everyone looked up. Johnny was standing with his back to them, a triangle of sweat soaked into his white shirt, his left hand high on the door, his right hand turning the key in it. The lock clicked.

Johnny turned around. 'We're not calling the guards.'

26

Everyone stared at Johnny.

'What the fuck is this?' said Murph.

'This . . . ' said Johnny. 'This is . . . hear me out, OK? Hear me out. I didn't do anything. But . . . whatever happened . . . if someone did . . . if someone else did . . . whatever it is, I'm fucked.'

'What are you on about?' said Laura. 'Why would you be fucked if you did nothing?'

'Just — can everyone listen, OK?' said Johnny. 'Thats all.'

'Well, we're not going anywhere, are we?' said Laura. She leaned out and looked at Edie, who was sitting utterly still, blank-faced.

Johnny was staring at the floor, running his hand over his head, over and over. 'It's . . . I'm not sure you're getting what I'm trying to say.'

Laura stood up, knocking the legs of the chair and table together. Patrick spun around and gave her a warning look. As she was about to walk past him, he lowered his arm in front of her to stop her. She glared at him. 'Get your — '

Patrick cut her off. 'Why don't we all sit down, and hear the man out, at least?'

Johnny was directly in Laura's eyeline. 'Please,' he mouthed.

Laura let out a breath and went back to her seat. 'Would you just tell us why exactly you think you're fucked?' she said.

'Jesus Christ,' said Johnny, 'I'm standing out there, and you're all looking at me like I did something, and you're my friends, and . . . ' He turned to Edie. She was staring at him, panic flickering in her eyes. Johnny threw his hands up. 'So how do you think the guards are going to look at it?'

Edie started to stand. 'Honey, stop — '

'No!' said Johnny, batting her back down. 'No. Just stay where — '

'Johnny,' said Patrick. 'There's no need for that.' He grabbed the armrests and started to shift his chair back.

'You can stay the fuck where you are too,' said Johnny, 'and just hear me fucking out.'

'OK,' said Patrick, nodding, 'OK.'

'I did not lay a finger on that man,' said Johnny. 'I don't know what happened to him. But whatever it was, it's going to look like I did it. There's stuff you don't know, but trust me, Terry and I have a history, and it's not good. We've had rip-roaring rows. He'll bang on about me to whoever'll listen, and, well, I do the same myself.'

'You're the one keeps hiring him,' said Murph. 'What — '

'Jesus! Shut the fuck up about me hiring him,' said Johnny. 'The point is, as soon as the guards start going 'Who had a reason to kill Terry Hyland?' — '

'They'll say 'half the fucking town'!' said Murph.

'But only one of them has his fucking body lying in their garden,' said Johnny. 'You don't get

192

it. Everyone knows I can't stand Terry. I . . . I held back some of the money I owe him, and he wasn't happy. But he hadn't finished the jobs, and it was the only way I could get him to come back.' He turned to Murph. 'And I hired him because he's cheap, OK?'

Everyone went quiet. Edie stared at the floor.

'This is our lives,' said Johnny. He gestured over to Edie. 'And Dylan — heading to college in a couple of years. This is it. The inn is it. And, even if I didn't do anything . . . ' He paused. ' . . . which I didn't! Jesus. Stop looking at me, all of you. What I'm saying is, it doesn't matter who did this. Even with the simple fact that a dead body is found on our property — forever more, google The Inn at Pilgrim Point and that's what you'll see. And that's it — we're done.'

'You're not done,' said Laura. 'Don't be so dramatic'

'It is exactly the type of thing that could ruin a business like ours,' said Edie.

'Do none of ye care that a man's been killed?' said Laura.

'Look, we don't know what happened to him,' said Murph. 'Maybe it was an accident that someone tried to cover up — '

'Do you know who will know what happened to him?' said Laura. 'The State Pathologist. Then we'll have our answer, instead of sitting around here talking about it. Just open the door.' She started to stand up.

'No!' said Johnny. 'No! I'm not opening it. Sorry.'

Laura glanced over at Murph and looked set

193

to stand until he flicked his eyes at her chair. Johnny was pacing from one corner to the other, one foot out from the door.

'Look,' said Patrick, his voice calm, his eyes on Johnny. 'You've locked us in here. At least spell it out for us. What is it you want us to do, exactly? Agree to not going to the guards? And then what?'

'I don't know!' said Johnny. 'I don't know.' He lowered himself to the ground, and sat with his back to the wall, his forearms resting on his knees, his head bowed between them.

'If we come forward now,' said Patrick, 'we're normal, good people — which I'd like to think we are. But say we did agree not to go to the guards — how would any of us know how we'd feel about it in the cold light of day?'

'Yes!' said Laura.

'I don't think anyone's getting what I'm trying to say,' said Johnny.

'Oh my God,' said Laura. 'It's pretty fucking clear — '

'I mean *why* I'm saying it,' said Johnny. 'Like — how important this is.'

'We do!' said Laura. 'But that still doesn't mean we're going to cover up a crime! Jesus.'

Murph looked at Johnny. 'Because what's the plan? If we went along with you?'

Laura nodded. 'Yeah — like, what are you going to do with Terry? Bury him out there, keep your head down and hope no one comes looking for him? Throw him in a ditch and hope it'll look like a hit and run?' She paused. 'Jesus — Johnny's looking at me like 'that's not a bad

194

idea'.' She turned to Edie. 'Can you please just call the guards? This is madness.'

'No!' said Johnny. 'No! I told you. That's not happening.'

'I think you'll feel differently in the morning,' said Laura. 'I think you'll be glad we talked sense into you — '

Johnny exploded. 'I won't! I won't feel fucking different. I won't. I'm not watching my life go up in smoke because of that prick. I can't. I'm sorry.' He paused. 'He could . . . go into the water. If he went into the water, then . . . '

'Oh my God,' said Laura. 'This is — '

'It could look like an accidental drowning,' said Johnny.

'It wouldn't,' said Clare.

'Why not?' said Johnny.

'There would be no water in his lungs,' said Clare.

'Am I even hearing this shit?' said Laura.

'But he could have had a fall that knocked him out,' said Johnny. 'And that would explain the bang on the head, and then he could have fallen into the water.'

Murph nodded. 'Yeah — one minute, he was working away — hundreds of feet from the edge of the cliff — next minute he went flying.'

' 'The bang on the head'?' said Laura. 'Fuck me.'

'Not if he was down on the jetty,' said Johnny. 'He could have slipped on the jetty, cracked his head, and fallen into the water — '

'Seriously,' said Laura. 'I can't believe I'm listening to this shit.' She let her head fall back and stared up at the ceiling. 'As if he'd be down on the jetty on a night like tonight.' She sat up. 'Is it because you're drunk or what?

'It's not shit!' said Johnny.

Murph turned to him. 'Look — nobody wants to be in this situation, we get it. But I'm not sure you're the right person to be taking the lead, here.'

'I own the fucking place!' said Johnny. 'Who else is going to — '

'God forbid Edie might have a — ' said Laura.

'Stop it!' said Edie. 'Stop it — all of you.'

'But — what does he think's going to happen, here?' said Laura. 'He keeps us here for the night, and wears us all down? We promise to say nothing, then we head off, and he hopes no one cracks?'

'Just . . . just let me think,' said Johnny.

'Hmm . . . not sure your thinking's a hundred per cent,' said Murph.

Johnny clambered to his feet and strode towards him. Murph jumped up from his chair, knocking it over. 'Whoa, whoa, whoa. Fairly fucking aggressive, there.'

'Fuck you,' said Johnny, stabbing a finger at him.

Murph looked at him, wide-eyed.

'What?' said Johnny. 'What?'

'I don't know,' said Murph. 'You tell me.'

'What are you getting at?' said Johnny.

'What am I getting at?' said Murph. 'Was 'fairly fucking aggressive' not clear enough? But, OK — if you want me to spell it out . . . you're an angry bollocks who's just made a lunge for

196

one of your mates. So, the state you're in, it's not a big leap to think Terry Hyland pushed you over the fucking edge. And that maybe you pushed back just that little bit harder.'

27

Johnny stared at Murph, then broke away, shaking his head slowly. He took a few steps backwards.

'Look,' said Murph. 'Why don't you just hold up your hands and say, 'Lads, I fucked up, and I need your help.''

'Because,' said Johnny. 'I did not do fucking ANYTHING.' He slammed his fist hard against the side of the confession box. Everybody jumped.

Laura knocked over her drink. 'Jesus Christ!' Johnny handed her a pile of napkins from the shelf behind him. Laura grabbed them out of his hand and held them to the trickle flowing down the side of the table. 'He's lost the plot altogether.' She turned to Edie. 'Is he on drugs, or has he stopped taking whatever he's supposed to be taking?'

'Laura,' said Patrick.

'I'm serious,' said Laura, throwing the balled-up napkins on to the table. 'He's expecting everyone here to take this massive hit for him, when he's in a total state of — I don't know what. Madness? Paranoia? And we've all got a lot of alcohol in our systems. Bar you,' she said, looking at Patrick. 'Does any of this seem sane to you? Honest to God, it's like a load of psychiatrists nodding away, going along with whatever nonsense the mentallers are telling them.' She let her arms flop out over the chair. 'Jesus. CHRIST. CALL THE GUARDS.'

'Fine — we call the guards,' said Johnny. 'And here's what'll happen: we wait an hour or more for them to get here from Bantry. Then we sit around all night, while they take our statements, and then it's the morning, and the State Pathologist's here in her white suit, with the CSI guys in tow, and what happens if a post mortem is inconclusive? I get to walk around town like Kevin fucking Crossan for the rest of my life? Jesus Christ.' He looked over at Edie. 'Imagine that? And, of course, you'll have the journalists and the photographers making sure they've got a good shot for the front page of the *Sunday World*. 'Murder at Luxury Inn' has a nice ring to it. Or 'Mysterious Death' even better. You'd read it, wouldn't you?'

''Mysterious' has too many letters for a headline,' said Murph.

'Shut up, Murph,' said Laura.

'But this isn't about 'God love us, we'll end up in the papers',' said Patrick.

Laura turned to him. 'Thank you,' she said. 'Thank you. Someone's talking sense. Plenty of innocent people are involved in dodgy situations, or they've witnessed a crime, they do the right thing, they might be in the papers for a week, and that's that.'

'And none of us knows the ins and outs of Terry's life,' said Patrick. 'He could have been involved in a lot of shady dealings, which could lead the guards directly to whoever's responsible for this.'

199

'Except there are no guarantees that they will!' said Johnny.

Laura turned to Edie. 'What's your story? Are you going to go along with this madness?'

Edie said nothing.

'Wow,' said Laura.

'Jesus,' said Johnny, looking over at her, 'I forgot what a pain in the hole you are.'

'And I forgot what a self-centred prick you are,' said Laura.

'It's not just me!' said Johnny. 'It's Edie, it's Dylan.'

'It's my fucking life too!' said Laura. 'Everyone else's here too and you're expecting us all to lie to the guards, lie in court if it came to it.' She looked across at Clare. 'I'm sure you'd love that, wouldn't you?' She turned back to Johnny. 'Have a think about that. And then you're expecting us all to sleep at night for the rest of our lives?'

'I care about your lives too,' said Johnny.

'You do in your hole,' said Laura. 'You had to guess how many kids I have! Did you go visit Murph's dad when he was up above in the hospital? Do you know Clare's kids' names? Do you know — '

Clare's hand went down on Laura's arm, and she squeezed tight.

'Look — I'm sorry I'm not as stuck into everyone's lives as you all are,' said Johnny, 'but that's just . . . me. It doesn't mean I don't give a shit. I — '

Patrick got up from his chair and stood at the edge of the mantelpiece.

'Right,' he said. 'Show of hands.'

'Show of hands?' said Laura. 'Are you joking?'

'And if the majority wants to go the guards, then that's what we do,' said Patrick. 'What's the alternative? Stay here all night looking at each other?'

'And, sorry, lads,' said Murph, 'but anyone could come looking for Terry in the meantime.'

'I can't stay, either way,' said Clare. 'So you'll have to let me go.'

'I can't stay either, then,' said Laura. 'I have to go too.' She shrugged at Johnny, then turned to Patrick. 'Right, so, Patrick. Show of hands and we can all get the fuck out of here — '

'Well, you won't be getting out of here if we go to the guards,' said Johnny. 'You'll have to hang around.'

'At least they won't lock us in,' said Laura.

'Right,' said Patrick. 'Raise your hand if — '

'Not a show of hands,' said Clare. 'Pen and paper. Let's keep this anonymous.'

'But we're all friends here, aren't we?' said Laura.

28

Clare gestured to Patrick. 'Patrick's the sober one. Does anyone have any objection to him doing the honours?'

'I can't believe you gave that job away,' said Laura.

'What — counting to six?' said Clare.

'No — being in charge,' said Laura.

Clare exchanged glances with Edie.

Johnny tore out a chunk of pages from the back of the notepad by the drinks and handed them around. Edie handed out pens from the cabinet drawer.

'Straightforward vote,' said Patrick. 'YES — we call the guards. NO — we don't.'

Everyone wrote their answer, and folded it over. Patrick collected the pages, walked back to his table and unfolded them. He looked up at everyone. 'The results are four for YES — we call the guards. And two NOs.'

Johnny slumped against the wall, and let his weight take him down to the floor, where he sat with his head in his hands.

'Jesus, what did you expect?' said Murph. 'Obviously, yourself and Edie are the 'Nos' — because you're the ones with the most to lose.'

Edie's head shot up.

'I don't think Edie was a 'No',' said Laura.

202

Edie turned to her, a flash of anger in her eyes. 'Why do you say that?'

Johnny turned to Edie, his eyes wide. 'You voted 'Yes' to the guards?'

'Because I know you didn't do this,' she said.

'So do I!' said Johnny. 'That's not the point! Jesus, Edie. Were you listening to anything I said?'

Edie's hands trembled. She glanced at Laura, who was staring ahead, jaw set, lips pouting, gaze unwavering.

'So,' said Laura, 'if Edie voted 'Yes' — who was the other 'No'?'

'Laura,' said Patrick. 'Come on.'

Murph started to count on his fingers. 'It's not me, it's not Clare, obviously. It's not Patrick.' He frowned.

'Murph,' said Patrick. 'This isn't helping.'

'So it was you, then,' said Murph. 'That raised hand was a ruse.'

'Oh, for God's sake,' said Clare. 'It was me. I voted 'No'.'

Everyone's heads whipped around to her.

'You?' said Laura, straightening in her seat.

'Yes,' said Clare.

'I've seen it all now,' said Laura.

'I can understand Johnny's concerns,' said Clare.

Johnny sat up. 'Thank you!' he said. 'Thank you.'

Laura looked at Clare. 'Are you joking me?'

'Johnny is right,' said Clare. 'If he didn't do this, like he says, that doesn't mean the guards won't come to a different conclusion.'

'This is an irreversible decision,' said Patrick. 'I'm not sure everyone gets that — '

'Of course we get that,' said Clare. 'Don't be ridiculous! Sorry but think of the regrets we might have if it all goes horribly wrong for Johnny and Edie? Or if our lives end up — '

'Nothing's going to happen to your life,' said Laura. 'Don't be so dramatic.'

'It's all very honourable to want to go to the guards,' said Clare, 'but you need to know that what happens after that will be completely out of your control. Once the genie is out of the bottle — '

'There is never just one genie, though, is there?' said Patrick. 'What about bottle number two, genie number two? The one that appears a year or two down the line? And then we'll all be hitting the headlines for covering up a murder. How is that going to play out? How can we justify that? Because, in that case — every, single one of us is guilty. It will be obvious that we all agreed to this, that we spoke about it, that we voted on it, and that there was consensus. Otherwise, obviously, someone would have come forward. It means six people made a clinical decision — '

'It's hardly clinical,' said Clare.

'Well, I'm not seeing a lot of emotion from you,' said Laura.

'Excuse me?' said Clare.

'Lads, lads, lads,' said Murph.

They fell into silence.

'How did he get here?' said Murph. 'Terry. Is his van here? He'd hardly have been out walking

— a night like tonight.'

'I didn't see it,' said Johnny, 'but that doesn't mean it's not somewhere.'

'Someone could have seen him drive up,' said Laura.

'Of course,' said Murph, 'because it's a busy thoroughfare.'

'Well, he could easily have texted someone he was heading this way or he'd be held up because he had to stop by the inn.' Laura paused. 'Look how that good deed turned out for him.'

'Everyone knows they don't go unpunished,' said Murph. 'It's his own tough.'

'Stop,' said Laura. 'And he easily could have texted someone since he got here.'

'If he had any coverage,' said Clare. She looked at Johnny. 'Did he have a mobile with him? Because they'll be able to trace him pretty accurately with that.'

'I don't know,' said Johnny.

'Well, does he usually have one?' said Murph.

'Why are you all acting like you're figuring out how to cover up a fucking murder?' said Laura. 'What was the point of the vote, so?'

'Not always,' said Johnny, ignoring her, answering Murph. 'There's fuck-all coverage, so we use the walkie-talkies when he's here. We've Wi-Fi in the house, so he might have WhatsApp, but that's not going to work outside. And it obviously wouldn't have worked tonight anyway.'

'The thing about the phone, if we had it,' said Murph, 'is that it might have something on it, a text or whatever, that might prove to you' — he looked at Johnny — 'that you have nothing to

205

worry about, and we can call the guards and be done with it. Terry could have been in the shit somewhere else and it has nothing to do with you.'

'Well, I know it has nothing to do with me,' said Johnny. 'That's the whole point.'

Edie stood up. 'Sorry. I need to breathe.'

Everyone looked at her. 'If you don't mind, I'd like my husband to excuse me. Because there is one place I can think of to check for Terry's phone.'

Laura looked at Edie. 'You do what you want, girl. It's your house. And your husband.'

Edie walked over to Johnny. He took the key from his pocket, and unlocked the door. 'Where are you going?' he said, quietly.

'Just . . . checking something,' said Edie. 'I'll be right back.'

Johnny locked the door after her.

'This is a joke,' said Laura.

★ ★ ★

Edie took the stairs down to the basement. She was guided to the boot room by the glow from the emergency wall lights. She threw her heels into one of the slots, pulled on black rain boots, and grabbed a guest raincoat that went down to her knees. She ran into the utility room, and unhooked a set of keys from the rack. She pulled up her hood and paused at the door to look out through the small glass panel. The rain was striking the ground like spears.

She braced herself, opened the door, and went

out into the wild night. The wind took her breath away. She paused, her hand to her chest, then ran up the slope towards the front of the inn, struggling to walk in the shifting, rain-soaked gravel.

She glanced into the car park, and saw three cars: hers, Johnny's, and Patrick's. She kept walking towards the chapel, nestled in a wishbone gravel path, and took the rear one to the chapel gate. She unlocked it and stepped out on to the narrow side road. She looked right and saw Terry's van, parked up against the ditch, under a canopy of trees.

★   ★   ★

Clare shifted in her seat. 'Johnny's right about the attention this would bring, not just on the inn, but on all of us personally,' she said. She stood up. 'And I don't know if you can see how we all look, but, to the outside world, we're going to look like a group of drunk, entitled rich people, partying in a luxury hotel. Definitely drinking, possibly drugs. Some local inconsequential perhaps stumbled on to a secret, something our privileged world didn't want revealed.'

'But we're not 'rich people',' said Laura.

'I'm not talking about how we see ourselves,' said Clare. 'I'm talking about optics.'

'What the hell is 'optics'?' said Laura.

'How this will look to the outside world,' said Clare. 'How, for example, you could view tonight, versus how a newspaper would view it based on how their readers would like to see it. The facts:

we're in a luxury inn, recently featured in Condé Nast Traveller — insert quotes from that — owned by a local rugby legend and his glamorous wife, the daughter of wealthy English blow-ins. 'Among the guests' were a multi-millionaire hedge fund manager, the former director of nursing of the local hospital, the former sergeant's daughter, a district court judge, and . . . ' she turned to Murph.

'The newly appointed principal of the local secondary school.'

Everyone stared at him.

'I know,' said Murph. 'And you thought the night couldn't get any more fucked up.'

'Congratulations?' said Clare. 'And so, off the top of my head — the spin on those facts. 'Mystery Death at Luxury Inn. Body of fifty-something-year-old male discovered late last night on grounds of luxury inn, luxury, luxury, eye-watering room rates, drunken revellers, former convent, sacrilege, sacrilege, delay in reporting, blunt-force trauma, possible motive, unnamed sources, fractious relationship with owner. Ha, ha, 'for all their money', ha, ha, — misery, misery, entitled, entitled.'

'But we're . . . us,' said Laura. 'Everyone around here knows us.'

Clare looked at her. 'Not any more, they don't.'

29

Patrick reached down and threw a log on to the fire. He tapped on the bar. 'Clare's right about how this could look to the rest of the world — '

'Do you think the 'rest of the world' gives a shite about us?' said Laura. 'And if they did, I sure as fuck wouldn't give a shite what they thought about me. I know who I am. And I'm happy out with it. I know I'm someone who does the right thing. And another thing I am is a guard's daughter. Look at my entire family. My father and his father and his father before him — '

'All loved the taste of Kerrygold,' said Murph.

'It's not funny!' said Laura. 'I'm not buying your dark funny bullshit — '

'I'm not selling it,' said Murph. He spread out his arms. 'Joke like nobody's laughing.'

'Shut up,' said Laura. 'I'm serious — all of them, respected guards. Sergeants! But I suppose ye all think the guards are thick shits!'

'This isn't about your dad,' said Clare. 'If he was still the Sergeant, I might feel differently — '

'Jesus, if Colm was still Sergeant, I'd definitely be fucked,' said Johnny.

'He's not wrong,' said Murph.

'I'm not sitting here listening to everyone talk shit about my dad,' said Laura. 'You couldn't meet a more decent, hardworking, honest man.

209

He never left a stone unturned — '

Murph raised his eyebrows.

'What was that in aid of?' said Laura.

'Nothing,' said Murph. 'Sorry. Low blow.'

'What do you mean low blow?' said Laura.

'Just,' he shrugged. 'This has nothing to do with Jessie.'

The room went very still.

'Jessie?' said Laura.

Murph's face started to redden.

'Is that what you all think?' said Laura. 'That my dad fucked up there? My dad worked his — '

'No,' said Clare, 'we do not think that.'

'Lads,' said Murph. 'We're getting off the point. We're talking about thirty-odd years ago, and a sergeant who's retired.'

'Yes,' said Clare. 'Can we all agree that this has nothing to do with Laura's father?'

'Well, it does if it's affecting how she's voting,' said Johnny.

'My morals are affecting how I'm voting,' said Laura.

Johnny's eyes widened.

'Go fuck yourself,' said Laura.

'Jesus, do we like each other at all, lads?' said Murph.

'All I'm saying,' said Laura, 'is I'm not going to ruin my family's name — '

'Too late!' said Murph.

Laura slammed her hand on the table. 'Stop!'

'This isn't about your dad,' said Clare. 'Don't personalize this.'

'Are you fucking joking me?' said Laura. 'So 'don't personalize' this, but then I'm supposed to think about Johnny's personal life before I go around having the cheek to do what's right?' Laura looked around the room. 'Whatever you thought of him personally, there's a man out there whose life has been taken, who — if you had your way, by the sound of it — would be robbed of the right to a decent burial, whose family might never know what happened to him. What is wrong with ye? Have ye a conscience at all between you?'

'But,' said Clare, 'you're talking about — '

'Breaking the law!' said Laura, throwing up her hands. 'Breaking the fucking law! Surely, I don't need to explain that to you, Your Honour.'

Clare stared at her. 'Will you be at that for the night: 'Your Honour'?'

'Not at the rate you're going,' said Laura.

'God, you are one angry woman,' said Clare.

Laura's mouth opened.

'Lads, can we keep this a bit civilized?' said Murph.

Johnny laughed. 'You know you're fucked when Murph's the one calling for civil . . . '

'Civility,' said Clare.

'God — you're one arrogant woman,' said Laura.

Clare's eyes sparked with anger.

'Can we scrap all the talking?' said Laura. 'I'm not going along with this. There is literally nothing any of you can say that's going to make me change my mind.'

'How can you possibly know that?' said Clare.

'For exactly the reasons I just mentioned,' said Laura. So we can go back and forth the whole

211

night, you can vote whatever way you like, but I'm not going to go along with it. You're still going to get the same answer from me: we do the honourable thing. We call the guards. End of.'

Clare sprung to her feet, startling her, startling everyone. She slapped two fists down on the table and leaned across to Laura. 'You know something?'

Laura drew her head back. Clare leaned in closer and stabbed a finger at her. 'FUCK honour. Fuck it.'

30

Clare's eyes bored into Laura's. 'Sorry, but I can't. I can't listen to one more word about your father and honour.'

Laura's eyes widened.

'Hold on a second now,' said Murph.

'No!' said Clare, batting him back without looking at him, her gaze steady on Laura. 'I can have this conversation with you here in front of everyone or we can take it somewhere private.'

Laura laughed. 'Oh, get it all out, girl,' she said, spreading her arms wide. 'Get it all out.'

'Are you sure?' said Clare.

'We don't have to hear any of this, Laura,' said Murph. 'Why don't you and Clare — '

'No,' said Laura. 'No. We've no secrets here — isn't that right?'

Clare paused. A nervousness flickered in her eyes.

'What?' said Laura. 'Is it that bad?' She tried to laugh.

Clare let out a breath.

'I just think you might feel differently when I tell you what it is.'

'I won't,' said Laura. 'Just fucking tell me.'

Clare shrugged. 'Jessie's dad — Kevin. Do you remember he used to work for my dad?'

Laura frowned. 'Vaguely. Why?'

'You know Kevin had a terrible time after the

rape — people thinking he did it, looking at him sideways, telling their kids not to set foot inside their door? Well, Mam and Dad used to have him over for dinner. Quite a lot. Things weren't going well between him and Teresa, so it was him on his own, maybe after work or on the odd Sunday evening. If you think about it — there were three young girls in our house, but my parents still invited him up all the time. They didn't seem to have any issue with him, didn't tell us not to be alone with him, nothing.'

Laura shrugged. 'So they believed him — so what? Loads of people did.'

Clare shook her head. 'No — it wasn't just that. Mam told me — years later — that it was because they knew, categorically, that Kevin did not rape Jessie.'

'How could your parents know 'categorically' when Dad didn't? And he was the Sergeant,' said Laura.

'That's my point,' said Clare. 'Your father did know.'

Laura stared at her. Clare didn't drop eye contact. There wasn't a sound in the room.

'Are you sure that you want to hear the rest of this in front of everyone?' said Clare.

'Yes!' said Laura. 'I do'

'Did you know,' said Clare, 'that at the time of the rape, your mother was having an affair with Kevin?'

Laura looked at her like she had lost her mind. 'Kevin. And my mam. What — in between baking? Jesus — Mam'd get up and turn off *Dallas* if there was a sex scene. We used to say

214

she only had sex three times — to have us.'

No one spoke.

'Sure, she'd push Dad away if he came up behind her when she was making the dinner,' said Laura.

Clare waited.

'Ah, get lost,' said Laura. 'Everyone's mam was like that. That doesn't mean anything.'

'I can tell you the rest,' said Clare, 'but I don't want to upset you.'

Laura laughed. 'You couldn't give a shit. Obviously.'

'In fairness to Clare,' said Murph, 'you're the one who told her she could say it in front of all of us.'

'That's not what I'm talking about,' said Laura. 'I'm saying . . . in general.'

'Ah, come on,' said Murph.

Laura looked at Clare. 'Go on, so.'

'Your mam and Kevin . . . that was going on when we were in sixth class,' said Clare. 'The night Jessie was raped, Kevin had left her on her own to go meet your mother — '

'Whoa — what?' said Murph.

'Laura — your dad was on duty the night of the rape,' said Clare, 'but he had his suspicions about your mam, so he kept an eye on your place, and when she came out, he followed her to the graveyard. Kevin was picking her up in the van.'

'And where's all this coming from?' said Laura. 'How come you 'know' all this?'

'I do know,' said Clare. 'Kevin told my parents. They were the only people he told,

215

apparently. But, basically what happened on the night was that your dad stayed following them, and when they went their separate ways, he followed Kevin home.'

Everyone exchanged glances.

'And . . . ?' said Laura, looking at Clare.

Clare waited.

'What?' said Laura. 'What am I supposed to be getting here?'

'Fuck's sake,' said Murph. 'It obviously means — '

'Shut up,' said Laura. 'I'm not asking you.'

'It means,' said Clare, 'that your dad knew exactly what time Kevin got home. And if Kevin called the guards as soon as he found Jessie, which he did, then your dad would have known for a fact that Kevin wasn't the rapist — he wouldn't have had the time.'

'Jesus Christ,' said Murph. 'Literally, Kevin could have had a sergeant as his fucking alibi — '

Clare nodded. 'And how would your dad have been able to explain that?'

'That poor prick — Kevin,' said Murph. 'And there wasn't a thing he could do about it.'

'No one wanted the affair to get out — it wasn't in anyone's interest,' said Clare. 'Colm would have looked like a fool in front of his colleagues, Teresa was away at a pilgrimage in Knock and had left Kevin in charge of Jessie, and if she found out that he left her alone to go off and meet his . . . '

'Fancy woman?' said Laura.

'That wasn't what I was going to say,' said Clare. 'But — out he goes and we know what

216

happened next. He said he locked the door, though, he thought she was safe.'

'Well, of course he was going to say that,' said Laura.

'So,' said Clare, 'he and your parents agreed that they would all go with the story that he had the television up loud, and he didn't hear anyone come in.'

'Didn't I tell you?' said Murph. 'I knew that was weird.'

Laura stared into space. 'But Dad could still have stopped the rumour about Kevin before it started. He could have made it very clear 'there's no way that that man would ever lay a finger on that child' or whatever and everyone would have believed him. Everyone trusts Dad.'

No one spoke.

'Dad wasn't . . . ' said Laura. 'He wouldn't have . . . he's not a spiteful man. He wouldn't have let that to happen . . . deliberately . . . ' She looked around at everyone. 'Would he?'

'Maybe not deliberately,' said Clare.

'But . . . he didn't really go out of his way, did he?' said Laura. 'Dad. To find out who did it.' She looked at Murph. 'That's what you were getting at earlier.'

'No, it wasn't,' said Murph. 'That was a general . . . I don't know what it was. A dig at the guards, maybe.'

Clare looked at Laura. 'You said yourself, earlier, that your dad left no stone unturned.'

'Yeah, well it's looking a little different now, isn't it?' said Laura. 'I mean, Kevin's whole life went to shit. If Dad had caught the bastard who

217

raped her, then none of that might have happened.' She paused. 'I mean — the fire would have, but . . . ' She glanced at Murph.

'Laura,' said Clare, 'there's no way your dad would have done something as awful as not tracking down the rapist, just to spite Kevin. Don't forget — you were eleven too. We all were. Miriam was — what? Same age as Johnny — sixteen?'

Johnny nodded.

'Do you really think your dad wouldn't have done everything he could to find the guy?' said Clare. 'He mightn't have gone out of his way to clear Kevin's name, but he wasn't arresting him either.'

Laura let out a breath.

'And it was Regatta,' said Murph. 'Town was crazy. Especially back then. There was no way they could have tracked down everyone. Plus all the boats that were in, the crews, the people working the merries.'

'And it wasn't like they have the technology they have today,' said Patrick.

'Thanks, lads,' said Laura, 'but he still sat back and let a man's life be destroyed.' She paused. 'I know he's my dad and I love him . . . but . . . '

Clare looked at Laura. 'I'm so sorry I had to tell you all that.'

'No, you aren't,' said Laura. 'And, no you didn't, did you?' She gave Clare a slow tight smile. 'But the message is — I'm being very loyal to a man who doesn't deserve it.'

'I wouldn't have put it quite like that,' said Clare. 'And you don't have to defend a daughter's loyalty to anyone here.'

Laura sat back and folded her arms. 'Well, if what you're saying is true, surely, if there's anything to be learned from it, it's that lying — or lying by omission or covering shit up — can ruin people's lives.'

'There are lots of ways to ruin people's lives,' said Clare, glancing at Johnny.

'But if people told the truth from the get-go,' said Laura. 'Then — '

'Oh, good God,' said Clare. 'Coming from the prison officer?' She laughed.

'What?' said Laura. 'I'm now. supposed to believe the inmates that say they're innocent? They told the truth, and look what happened to them?' She laughed back at Clare.

'There are five people in this room,' said Clare, 'who are part of five families, and who all have multiple responsibilities. This is not just about you, and your world. You said it yourself — your world is tiny: prison for work, prison at home, and inmate in a maximum security Micra in between.'

'I was being funny,' said Laura.

'I know,' said Clare. 'Because you are funny, and you have a way of summing things up that none of the rest of us have.'

Murph nodded. 'Yeah — you don't give a fuck.'

'Well, I give a fuck now!' said Laura. 'And ye can't handle it. Or do I have to not give a fuck about a human life to be friends with ye all now?'

Everyone went quiet.

Laura folded her arms. 'I'm disgusted with ye, lads.'

'Give it a rest, Laura, for fuck's sake!' said Murph. 'We came here tonight because it was Helen's birthday, we'd be happy to fucking see each other, and we wanted to have the craic. And we did! Until . . . this — '

'"THIS",' said Laura, 'is a fucking murder, Murph. Can you say it? Or is it too much for your sensitive soul?'

'You're acting like we're all savages,' said Murph. 'What do you think happened? We all fucked off over the years, going about our business, turning into monsters? Meanwhile, you're in the slums of Limerick, turning into Mother Teresa? Are you telling me you were sitting here earlier, thinking: Jesus, I'm getting a funny fucking vibe off Murph? Or: Christ, Clare's turned into an awful heartless bitch?' He took a breath. 'We were handed a shit sandwich . . . and all we can do at this stage is scrape off the shit, and stomach the rest.'

'Well,' said Laura. 'I hope you all fucking choke on it.'

As she turned away, she caught Clare staring at her, shaking her head.

'What?' said Laura. 'What's wrong with you now?'

Clare's eyes were lit with anger. 'Is everything an absolute with you? The black and white, the 'surely' this, the 'I'm on the moral high ground, you're all a disgrace'.'

'I didn't say anything about the moral high ground,' said Laura. 'But sorry if you're all so

220

fucking offended by the fact I thought you'd do the right thing. That's actually a compliment, if you think about it.'

'Yes,' said Clare, 'if your definition of 'the right thing' is the only one anyone can have.'

Laura looked away.

'OK,' said Clare. 'Let's be very clear about what this 'truth' is that you're so determined to get off your chest to the guards.'

Laura turned back to her.

'The truth is,' said Clare, 'that before we did get around to calling them, we all sat back and had a brandy by the fire while we discussed whether or not we actually would.'

'That wasn't my fault!' said Laura, pointing at Johnny. 'He locked — '

'We even had a vote!' said Clare.

'He locked us fucking in!' said Laura.

'Oh, for God's sake,' said Clare. 'If you really wanted to get out . . . what did you think he was going to do?'

'Then why are you still sitting here if you think you could have left?' said Laura.

'Because we are friends,' said Clare. She looked around the room. 'And if our friends are in trouble — '

'We cover up for them and shit ourselves for the rest of our lives that we'll get found out?' said Laura. 'Hear on the news a body's been found off the coast of wherever the fuck and wonder if it's Terry Hyland's?' She stood up. 'If I'm free to go, then I'm not sitting around listening to this shit.'

'You might want to hear me out,' said Clare.

'About the truth?' said Laura. 'The truth is the truth.'

'That's my point,' said Clare. 'So let me tell you the last of it. The guards are asking you how this whole voting thing went so they can get a good handle on who might have had something to hide and you're telling them and they're asking who seemed particularly wound up. And you say Clare! And she's a District Court Judge! She even said 'Fuck Honour!' That's how bad it was! And why did she say that, Mrs Hurley? That's what I asked her! And what did she say? Oh, she told a terrible story about how a former sergeant in the same small town mistreated the father of a little girl who was raped in her bed and left for dead . . . all because of a personal grudge he held against the man, who was having an affair with the Sergeant's wife at the time! And did she say who that sergeant was, Mrs Hurley?'

Everybody went very still.

Laura stared at her. 'Wow.' She looked around the room. She waited. 'Is no one going to say anything?' She turned to Clare. 'Am I the only one you're blackmailing? Or are you just assuming none of our 'friends' will go to the guards either to protect Dad's reputation?' She turned to Patrick. 'Are you OK with this, all of a sudden — not going to the guards? Murph? Or has Clare ruled and 'case dismissed'?' She looked at Johnny. 'I think you at least owe her a big thank you.'

'Shhh,' said Johnny, raising his hand.

'Don't fucking shush me,' said Laura.

222

'Seriously,' hissed Johnny. 'Stop. Did anyone hear that?'

'What?' said Patrick.

'Knocking,' said Johnny. 'On the window.'

'Oh, fuck off,' said Laura.

Clare sat up straight, her eyes wide. She nodded. They all went quiet.

'Such bullshit,' said Laura. 'There's a gale blowing, Clare hasn't stopped talking for the past ten minutes — how could anyone hear a thing?' She reached for the pull cord on the curtains and yanked it down. The curtains swept open as the hammering on the window struck up again. A figure in a dark hooded jacket was standing outside, shoulders hunched against the wind and rain, fist raised.

Johnny squinted into the darkness, then started to walk towards the window. His eyes went wide. 'Oh, Jesus,' he said, then rushed in a smile. 'Val!' He pointed to his left and mouthed. 'Front door.'

Val gave him a thumbs up, then disappeared from view. Johnny's legs went weak and he grabbed on to the back of Clare's chair to steady himself.

'Who the fuck was that?' said Murph. 'What's wrong with her face?'

Johnny's knuckles were white, his head hanging. 'We're fucked, lads.' He raised his head slowly. 'Fucked.'

'Why?' said Clare. 'Who was that?'

'Our neighbour,' said Johnny. 'The Sergeant.'

31

Edie sat in the driver's seat of Terry's van, her head bowed against the steering wheel. Her heart flipped with the guilt of not telling Johnny where she was going, or how she had known where the van might be — her own fears about the anger that Terry brought out in him. At first, she had asked Terry not to park outside the inn because they didn't want guests to feel like they were arriving into a construction site. Then he had parked at the side of their house, out of sight of the guests. But as things worsened between him and Johnny, she had decided it was better for everyone if she kept them as far apart as possible, so she cut an extra key to the chapel gate, and had given it to Terry earlier in the week — he could park along the ditch outside, and come and go in a way that limited the risk of running into Johnny.

She looked around the car for Terry's phone. It wasn't in the holder on the dashboard, it wasn't in any of the compartments. She leaned across the passenger seat and popped open the glove box. It wasn't there. She saw the new key to the chapel and put that in her pocket. Then she remembered there was storage underneath the seat and she popped it open. She was hit with the faint smell of paint. She saw a can of red spray paint, a pair of black gloves streaked with red, and a white mask with traces of a fine spray in the same shade. She set them on the floor of the van and started rifling through everything else. Wedged behind some small, sample wood panels was a thick plastic bag. She pulled it out. It was folded tightly around something rectangular. There was a notebook inside; a cheap, black A5 hardback. She opened it, expecting to see job lists or price lists or floor plans. But when she started to flick through it, she realized it was something else entirely. Her heart started to pound. A blur of vile, angry words, in red and black ink, hopped off every page.

Then she started to see drawings like the ones she had found on the dining-room floor — with the same punctures in the pages from the same heavy hand. Like the ones she had found, the drawings of the faces were on the right-hand page. The facing pages were covered in single words or sentences or phrases, in all different sizes of writing, some of it almost illegibly small, one word always bigger than the others.

I loved you.

We're the broken halves of the one child you said.

And I loved you even more.

I don't mind being your secret. I like it.

WILL DADDY COME UPON YOU?

YOU'LL BE IN SO MUCH TROUBLE!

WILL HE FORGIVE YOU YOUR TRESPASSES?

STICKS AND STONES WILL BREAK MY
  BONES
YOU'RE THE UGLY STICK
AND IT'S YOUR TURN TO BE BEATEN.

YOU WILL NEVER BE ABLE TO CARE ENOUGH
ABOUT ENOUGH PEOPLE
TO CHANGE THE NIGHT
YOU ONLY CARED ABOUT YOURSELF

YOU CAN HAVE AN ICY DEATH!
YOU CAN DROWN IN THE SEA!
SEA, SEA, SEA HOW YOU LIKE IT!

ONCE UPON A TIME
THERE WAS A BOY
WHO DIED LAUGHING.

THE END

Edie closed the notebook. What was wrong with him? And why had she never suspected that anything was? But had Johnny? Her stomach flipped. She got a flash of Johnny on a witness stand. She wondered how he would come across to a jury.

32

Clare looked across the room at Johnny. 'She didn't see me behind the curtain. Can I go . . . until she's gone?'

Laura shook her head. 'Jesus, do you give a fuck about anyone but yourself?'

'But,' said Clare, 'I'm a . . . ' She trailed off under the heat of Laura's glare.

Johnny was standing, paralysed, in the middle of the room. 'She's going to be here any second. What'll I do? What the fuck will I do? Jesus Christ. What the fuck does she want? Like, it's one in the morning — '

'Hurry the fuck out to her, either way,' said Murph, 'or it'll be even weirder. She'll be in on top of us.'

'It's fine,' said Johnny, batting a hand at him. 'The door's locked. I have to know what I'm saying — '

'You can't leave her standing out there in the rain,' said Clare.

'Shut the fuck up!' said Johnny, wild-eyed again. Glances fired around the room between the others.

Laura stood up. 'I'll go.'

'And have the Sergeant all to yourself?' said Johnny.

Laura raised her hands. 'Well, I'm hardly going to do anything now, am I?' She tilted her head towards Clare. Clare crossed her legs, angling her body away from her.

'Look — I'm in now,' said Laura. 'I might as well help you out on this. I am — after all — a sergeant's daughter. And they look after their own.'

Johnny looked at Murph and Patrick.

Patrick nodded. 'It's not a bad idea.'

'Fair play,' said Murph.

'OK,' said Johnny. 'Go. Thanks. We'll come up with something. Just keep her in the hall as long as you can.' He paused. 'Act normal.'

'Title of your sex tape,' said Murph.

Everyone broke into nervous laughter.

'Go,' said Johnny.

She started to walk past him.

'Cut to: Laura confesses,' said Murph.

They laughed again. The doorknob started to rattle back and forth. 'Jesus, it sounds like great craic altogether in there!'

Murph pointed towards it, hissing at Johnny. 'The fucking key!'

'Shit,' mouthed Johnny. 'Val — Jesus — you were quick!' he said, lunging for it, fumbling with it. 'Hold on!' He opened the door.

'Is it a lock-in altogether?' said Val, walking in. Everyone laughed.

She stood between Johnny and Murph, filling the space between them — almost as tall as them, broad-shouldered with thick sandy hair pulled into a low ponytail.

'It's not a lock-in until a guard's got a drink in his hand,' said Murph. 'Her hand. A sergeant. What are you having?'

'I won't, no,' said Val.

'You will,' said Murph.

'Oh, go on, so — a small Jameson.' She turned to Johnny. 'Front door wide open, honesty bar locked. Who are these savages that you have to secure them?'

'There's a problem with the draw on the fire,' said Johnny, 'and with the wind tonight, the door was rattling.'

Val looked at the door. 'Solid mahogany? I'd get my money back.' She looked at everyone. 'Don't mind the face,' she said, pointing to it. 'I'm a unicorn, in case you're wondering.' Her face was pink with glitter sprinkled across the sides and diamantés glued beside her eyes. 'The youngest was at a party earlier and, sure, we all got roped in.' She unzipped her jacket.

'So,' said Johnny. 'These savages . . . we were in school together. I mean . . . apart from me. It's . . . Helen's birthday.' He looked around the room. 'Oh.' He paused. 'Helen's in bed, of course.'

Val shot him a bemused look.

'So,' said Johnny, 'that's Patrick by the fire, Laura in the corner, Clare . . . and this eejit.' He tilted his head towards Murph.

'The eejit with the drink,' said Murph, handing it to Val. 'Isn't it some night?'

'Shocking,' said Val.

'What's brought you out in it?' said Murph.

'I'm on my way to pick my son up from town and I was swinging by to have a word with Edie . . . or Johnny.' She looked around the room. Murph followed her gaze to Laura — her hair

229

was flat against her scalp and there were watery trails of black mascara down her face and blotches of eyeshadow in the sockets. Opposite her, Clare was red-cheeked and red-nosed, her dark hair frizzy, dark smudges under her eyes. She was still wearing her rain boots.

'I had the girls in an awful state,' said Murph in a boom that drew everyone his way. 'With a rousing rendition of that song about the little boy — heartbreaking. Patrick's up next. 'Green Fields of France'.'

Patrick stood up. He smiled. 'I don't think so.'

'But the girls haven't cried all their make-up off yet,' said Murph.

Patrick gestured towards the fire and looked at Val. 'Murph and I were about to go out for logs.'

Murph shook his head. 'I fucking hate the sober people.'

'Well, I hope I'm not breaking up the party,' said Val.

'Not at all,' said Murph. 'Patrick's pulling a Langer on the whole thing.'

Everyone looked at him.

'Langer!' said Murph, gesturing towards Patrick. 'I was in New York — God, years back — and I looked Patrick up and we were out in some Irish bar in Manhattan 'til all hours, and one of Patrick's mates arrives in — Langer. I shit you not. That's how he introduces himself. Hand out — 'Langer'. And I basically told him langer was Cork for dick. And he wasn't a bit happy with that. Bit of a dry shite, no offence. What was his name? Langersomething. Langer . . . Langerwell! That was it. Because, of course, I told him

230

that was like being very good at being a dick, and, anyway, the point is, he was so pissed off with the whole thing, that when I tried to get him to give us a song later, he gets up, and walks out. Literally — stands up, leaves, doesn't say a word.'

Everyone looked at Patrick. 'At least I explained myself,' he said. 'My job is to keep the fire going.'

Murph nodded. 'I'll be on TripAdvisor first thing,' he said. 'The Inn at Pilgrim Point: one star. Sub-zero stars.'

'And I was thinking,' said Val, 'how are you not all passed out in here? The heat.'

Murph looked at Patrick. 'Come on, so, langer.' He squeezed past Val and walked out the door. Patrick followed him and closed it behind him.

Murph raised his arm, smelled his armpit, and recoiled. 'Jesus. She could use that as evidence. 'The smell of fear was the first thing I noticed on entering the premises.''

Patrick stifled a laugh.

'Fuck, though,' said Murph. 'That was a great move.'

Patrick bowed.

'Now, what are we doing here, exactly?'

'Well,' said Patrick, 'we don't know why she's here — '

'You're the one who hopped up — '

'She was hardly going to explain herself over the singing, either way.'

Murph pursed his lips. 'The deafening silence at the end would have given her a moment.'

'My point is — she could be here because her dog's gone missing and she wants to search the grounds — '

'Oh,' said Murph. 'Shit.'

'Or she might need to borrow tools or timber because the storm's blown something down,' said Patrick.

'She'd have sent the husband over for that,' said Murph. 'A night like tonight. Would you be arsed?' He paused. 'I didn't even notice where all Terry's shit is — did you? Could she have spotted his van? No. She wouldn't have, would she? She's coming from the other direction. But who knows?'

'And what was your sing-song plan?' said Patrick.

'I swear to God I thought a few bars of 'Green Fields of France' from you would have been the quickest way to get rid of her.' He paused. 'Jesus — you know what we *could* do? Have Val be the one to find the body.'

Patrick looked at him.

'I'm serious,' said Murph. 'If we move the fucker . . . Terry, his body, Jesus it's fucked up . . . out by her car where she can't miss it and she'll know it wasn't there when she arrived . . . well, we'll all have been inside — with a guard! — when it all went down. It'll be like what Colm didn't do for Kevin Crossan. We could literally have a Sergeant as our alibi.'

Patrick stared at him. 'No.'

'Just no?'

'Just no.'

'I'm a bit too pissed to be reliable here, in

fairness,' said Murph. 'but I'd fucking hate to be you. At least I've some hope of forgetting the whole night. Or it'll just stay feeling like the fucking nightmare it is now.'

'All we need to do,' said Patrick, 'is get the body out of sight. Preferably somewhere we can lock. Would Johnny have keys downstairs labelled?'

'Would that not be a stupid move?' said Murph. 'So, probably — yes. And if not, we can just cover it up properly t'fuck, put it behind the pallets and hope to fuck she hasn't lost her dog. And that it's not a cadaver dog.'

They walked towards the stairs to the basement.

'We better be quick too,' said Murph, 'or she'll be wondering what's kept us. We could tell her we had to chop some trees. Though, in fairness, we could have said 'fuck it' and gone to the bar for a drink.'

Patrick looked at him.

Murph nodded. 'There's nothing worse than being the sober one. She's in the bar. I get it.' He paused. 'We could have diarrhoea.'

Patrick stopped walking. 'I think we've made a mistake.'

'What?' said Murph. 'Why?'

'Leaving Johnny in there, the state he's in.'

⋆   ⋆   ⋆

Johnny walked over to the bar and poured himself a brandy. 'Everyone OK for drinks?'

'I'll have a vodka and tonic,' said Laura.

'There's no ice — is that OK?' said Johnny.

233

'No,' said Laura.

Johnny locked eyes with her. 'You're not going to make me go down and get ice, are you?'

Laura shrugged. 'Depends on whether we're getting less-special treatment than your fancy guests.'

Johnny let out a breath. He looked at Val. 'This is what you're dealing with.'

'Langerwell,' said Val.

Everyone looked at her. 'That name's familiar.' She paused. 'I don't know.'

'Maybe he was over here with Patrick at some stage,' said Johnny.

'Caught fleeing the scene of a sing-song,' said Val. 'Anyway . . . it'll come to me, I'm sure.'

There was a knock on the door. 'Open up! It's me!'

Val frowned. 'Is that Edie?'

'Edie!' said Johnny. 'It's open! Val's — '

Edie pushed in the door, holding up the notebook. 'This is so fuh — ' She stopped. 'Val! Is everything OK?' She lowered the notebook.

'Yes, yes,' said Val. 'I was coming over to see if Dylan could stay for the night. I tried calling.'

'Oh, thank God,' said Edie. 'I thought he'd a had a melt-down or something.'

'No, no — they're happy out,' said Val.

Edie sat down on the arm of the chair opposite her, holding the notebook on her lap with both hands. 'Isn't it terrible how your mind goes to 'something's wrong'? What age does that start happening?'

'Birth, if you've an Irish Mammy,' said Val. Everyone laughed.

Val glanced at the notebook. Edie's hands spasmed. 'So . . . they're not causing you any trouble over there,' said Edie.

'Not at all,' said Val. She looked at Johnny. 'So, what are you going to do about the electricity?'

'For now,' said Johnny, 'absolutely nothing. We've got the fire, the candles, the bar. And I'd say we'll all be passing out fairly shortly. By the time everyone's up in the morning, I'll have it sorted.'

'Who'll you get, now, to do that?' said Val. 'Would Terry Hyland get up out of the bed on a Sunday morning?'

Johnny laughed. 'You'd never know with Terry, all right. But I do have something I need him to look at down on the jetty too.'

33

Val glanced towards the window. 'I'm not sure how good the forecast is for tomorrow.'

'Not great, apparently,' said Laura. She looked at Johnny. 'I wouldn't go near the jetty, if I was you.'

'Speaking of Terry,' said Val. 'Mally was telling me about the chapel windows. What's the story there? And Terry trying to say Dylan did it. What was that about?'

'Don't mind him,' said Johnny.

'Mally was disgusted,' said Val. 'Said Terry saw someone in a hoodie and jeans running away and decided it was Dylan. And you know Mally: 'Sure, that covers half the lads in town.' But what interests me is that there've been a few reports of property damage about the place.'

'Really?' said Edie.

'What do you know about the Britten lad? 'Finno'.'

'Who?' said Johnny.

Edie frowned at him. 'The Brittens, Johnny! The wood people.' She rolled her eyes at Val. 'They only made all the signs for the grounds . . . and the fairy houses, and — '

'Sorry,' said Johnny. 'Of course. What about him?'

'There's a few rumours flying around about him,' said Val.

Edie nodded. 'I heard that, all right.'

Johnny looked at her. She looked at Val. 'He's dealing,' said Val.

'His poor parents,' said Edie.

'Apparently, if people aren't paying up, he's retaliating in some way,' said Val. 'Nothing physical — property damage. That's why it occurred to me.'

Edie laughed, and glanced at Johnny. 'Did we pay them for the toadstools?'

Johnny laughed.

'Well, if you hear anything,' said Val. 'Or if Dylan says anything. You know kids. They won't say anything to me.'

'Of course,' said Edie.

'So,' said Val, 'is there anything I can do?' She looked at Edie. 'The electricity. Anything you need?'

'No, no,' said Edie. 'Not at this hour. We're headed to bed.'

'Right so,' said Val. She looked up at the clock. 'I better get a move on.'

The door pushed open, and Murph and Patrick arrived back in, red-faced, with a basket of logs.

'Mission accomplished,' said Murph.

Val stood up.

'Are you off?' said Murph.

She nodded. 'I am. Settle in there by the fire, lads. Warm yourselves up.'

Edie stood. 'Let me walk you out.'

'Stay where you are,' said Val.

'Oh, she won't have that!' said Murph.

Edie laughed. She held the door open for Val.

237

Val paused in the doorway. 'Goodnight, now,' she said.

'Goodnight!' said Murph. 'Safe home.'

★ ★ ★

Murph slumped down in a chair by the fire and whispered, 'What the fuck was that about?'

Laura hissed a shush at him.

'I need to know,' said Murph, 'there's no dog involved . . . '

'No,' said Johnny. 'Dylan's staying over with them — that was all. She couldn't ring.'

'What did you do with . . . the . . . ' said Johnny.

'Propped him up in the squad car with a pair of shades,' said Murph. 'Weekend at Johnny's.' He sat forward, stabbed a finger at them, and spoke in a loud whisper. 'Lads, you're going to have to unmute your fucking laughter here. Because she's still in the hall, and unless it's a silent fucking retreat we're at, I think we've all gone a little too quiet.' Everyone exchanged glances.

''HOW DO YOU DO, YOUNG WILLY MCBRIDE?'' Murph started to sing as he rose from his seat and walked over to the fire. ''DO YOU MIND IF I SIT HERE DOWN BY YOUR GRAVESIDE?'' He mouthed, 'Too soon?'

They all started laughing.

''AND REST FOR A WHIIILE 'NEATH THE WARM SUMMER SUN . . . '' He mouthed, 'Is she still here?' 'I'VE BEEN WALKLN' ALL DAY AND I'M NEARLY DONE.''

★ ★ ★

Val stood at the front door. She tilted her head towards the room. 'Is that Patrick now? He got up in the end.'

Edie smiled. 'No — that's Murph. If someone refuses to sing, he gets up and sings their song.'

'No wonder no one sings,' said Val. 'He's got some voice.'

Edie laughed. 'I know. You don't expect it. He calls himself Murphé. Like Bublé.'

Val laughed. 'I'd say he's great craic.'

'He is,' said Edie.

Val looked at her. 'Is everything OK?'

'Yes!' said Edie. 'Of course! Why?' She paused. 'I mean — I've had a few too many, but . . . '

'And poor Helen couldn't last the distance,' said Val. 'We were in Mac's for an early birthday drink last week and she was fading by nine, the poor divil. What time did she head away?'

Edie went very still. 'Oh, no — she's here. She's staying over.'

'She'll hardly sleep through that racket,' said Val.

'No, no — she's . . . out in one of the suites.'

'She won't hear a thing out there,' said Val. She paused. 'And what would happen now if she had a fall — with the power cut?'

'Oh, a back-up battery kicks in for the emergency cord,' said Edie. 'Don't worry — we haven't abandoned her.'

Edie leaned an ear towards the room. 'Oh, God. Murph's on to 'Patricia the Stripper'.'

'That's my cue,' said Val.

'That's everybody's cue,' said Edie. She opened the front door and a wind whipped through. 'Well, thanks for having Dylan, and coming all the way out in this.'

'Not a bother,' said Val. 'Enjoy the rest of it!'

Edie closed the door and rested her forehead against it. The door to the bar opened, and Patrick came out into the hallway. Edie turned around and slumped back against the door. She let out a long breath.

'We could have done without that,' said Patrick.

'Honestly,' said Edie.

There was a hammering at the door behind her. She jumped, her eyes wide. Patrick made a face, pointed towards the men's room, and strode across the hall.

Edie turned around and pulled open the door.

'Sorry,' said Val. 'I remembered — Langerwell. Why it was familiar. There's a Langerwell the owner of the acre between our two places. I checked the land registry when I was buying ours.'

Edie frowned. 'What?'

Val nodded. 'There can't be too many of those about — a name like that. You should ask your friend — Patrick, is it?'

'I will,' said Edie. She closed the door after Val, started to walk towards the bar, then paused, and headed for the basement.

* * *

Murph was standing by the bar, pouring drinks. Clare stood at the window watching Val jog to her car. She drew the curtains across. Laura was

240

sitting on her own at a table beside her.

'You know something,' said Johnny, looking over at Laura, 'for all your talk of garda bonding, there was hardly a peep out of you.' His tone was teasing. Laura scowled over at him. Johnny raised his eyebrows, waiting for an answer.

'I don't think you're going to want to hear why,' said Laura.

Clare stood up. 'I'm going to the ladies.'

'She knows Laura is about to blow,' said Murph.

Clare flashed a confirmation glance at Murph as she walked past.

'She wants to stand outside splashing distance,' said Murph.

Johnny laughed.

Murph looked over at Laura. Her head was turned away. 'Well, whatever you're about to say, there's no point talking into the curtains. They're half the reason we're in this shit. Opening up like that . . . '

'I swear to fuck,' said Laura, stabbing a finger at him, 'I'll murder you myself if you keep cracking fucking jokes.'

'I'm nervous!' said Murph.

'Why can't you just shit yourself in peace like a normal person?'

'Because I don't find shitting myself very peaceful,' said Murph.

Johnny laughed.

'Right!' said Laura. 'Do you want to know why I didn't open my mouth?'

'It was surprising,' said Johnny, flashing a glance at Murph.

241

'You're a pair of pricks,' said Laura.

Murph zipped his lip. Johnny laughed.

Laura exploded. 'You thick fucks! The minute she walked in the door, she was clocking every fucking thing in the room. She was looking at the state of myself and Clare, she was looking at her in her fucking boots, she was looking at the pens on the table, the extra napkins, all the weird looks flying about the place . . . and no amount of shite out of you, Murph, was stopping her. And,' she said, turning to Johnny, 'she was looking at the size of your coked-up fucking eyeballs, wondering did you think she came down in the last shower — the one you would have left her standing outside in for the night if you weren't stupid enough to leave the fucking front door wide open.'

34

Edie went into the office, went to the safe, unlocked it, and took out the pages she had put in earlier, setting them on the desk in front of the notebook. She looked at the one with no name on it, the one with the crooked mouth, and the little line underneath it, and the gaping head wound. She opened the notebook, and started flicking through it to try to find a page with the matching tear. She found it.

YOU FUCKING BOARDING SCHOOL PRICK!

YOU THINK YOU'RE THE BIG MAN!

FUCK. YOU. MY DICK IS BIGGER.

Her heart leapt. The crooked mouth. The line underneath it. It was Johnny, her crooked-smiled charmer with the scar on his chin. She thought of Terry trying to bring his fantasy to life tonight and Johnny retaliating. She shook the thought away. But boarding school? Why would Terry care about that now? And 'click'?

She flicked through the notebook again and stopped, when she reached a page where ail the heads with Xs for eyes now had stick-figure bodies — six, all surrounded by flames. Her heart plunged when she reached the next page: it was a diagram of the old dormitory at the

243

convent: with the stick-figure people inside, and the containers of kerosene, and the title of the story Murph told that night: I Am the Ghost of the Manor. And underneath it, with arrows pointing to all the stick figures was:

I AM YOURS I AM YOURS I AM YOURS

She knew from the story that that meant manner of death and her stomach turned. Had Terry set the fire? How? Why?

She turned back to the pages with the disembodied heads, and, in a quick scan, she recognized Murph in one of them, Laura in another, Clare in another. She couldn't find Helen, she couldn't find Jessie, and she couldn't find herself. Maybe Terry didn't hate them. But she counted six stick figures in the dormitory, and there were six of them there on the night of the fire.

She locked the safe, then slid Patrick's and Johnny's pages into the notebook, and went upstairs with it. As she walked into the hallway, she bumped into Patrick.

'How did that all go?' he said. 'With Val.'

Edie let out a breath. 'OK — I think. But this is insane.' She held up the notebook. 'This is Terry's, and it's full of psychotic ramblings. Earlier — I didn't tell anyone — I found these notes on the dining-room floor. He had it in for Johnny, he had it in for you. He wanted to bash Johnny's head in, and he wanted to see you swinging from a rope.'

'What?' said Patrick.

Edie pulled the two loose pages from where

they were sticking out of the notebook, and handed them to him. His eyes widened.

'How well did you know Terry?' said Edie.

'Not well at all,' said Patrick. 'I mean — he did work on our house, but I took no notice.'

'I don't know what to do about this,' said Edie. 'I'm going to take another look at it, but . . . it's vile. The idea that someone who is in and out of your house, in your life, your business, knows so much about you — had all this going through their head is terrifying.'

Patrick levelled her with a look. 'Do not tell Johnny you have this. Don't tell anyone.'

'What?' said Edie. 'Why not?'

Patrick spoke gently. 'Don't take this the wrong way, but Johnny might already know about that notebook . . . '

Edie frowned. Patrick waited.

'Oh, God,' said Edie. 'You mean . . . he could have confronted Terry — '

'Well — maybe not,' said Patrick. 'Where did you find it?'

'In Terry's van,' said Edie. 'It's parked outside the chapel gate.'

'Is that where you went?' said Patrick.

Edie nodded.

'Why didn't you say that?' said Patrick.

'Because . . . '

'Because you were already worried about Johnny,' said Patrick.

Edie paused. 'I feel so guilty. Please don't say anything. I feel like . . . There's no way Johnny's capable of something like this. But you saw him tonight. He's . . . '

Patrick nodded. He put his hand on her arm. 'That's why I'm telling you not to tell him you have this, if there is concrete evidence out there that Terry had ill intentions towards him, whoever has that evidence . . . might be in danger.'

Edie's eyes widened. 'There's no way Johnny would lay a finger on me — '

'No, no,' said Patrick. 'That came out wrong. In a way. I'm speaking as . . . an observer, OK? An observer of his behaviour tonight, specifically. Under very stressful circumstances. He doesn't seem himself. You do agree with me on that.'

'Yes,' said Edie, 'but I still don't think — '

'I'm just looking out for you,' said Patrick. 'How many times do we read about people who snap? The nicest guy in the world and he snaps. A family man, a pillar of the community . . . everyone is shocked. I am not saying that Johnny is that man. We still don't know what happened tonight. But what I am saying is that I don't want to be watching the news tomorrow night, thinking: If only I'd said something — '

Edie stared at him. Tears welled in her eyes. 'Oh my God. He wouldn't. There's no way. I know him. I understand what you're saying — '

'Do you want me to take the notebook?' said Patrick. 'What I was also trying to say was that, if the guards got hold of it, it would look like evidence against Johnny — '

'Or you,' said Edie. 'When I saw these earlier, I nearly died. I was like, why you and Johnny? Just the two of you?'

The door to the conservatory opened and Johnny walked in. 'What's going on here?'

246

'Decompression,' said Edie. She lowered the notebook to her side.

Johnny looked at her. 'Are you OK?'

'Well — not really, obviously,' said Edie. 'After Val. Poor Patrick, getting landed with me.'

Johnny gave Patrick a wry smile. 'You must be regretting the day you ran into Helen Maguire.'

'Don't worry about me,' said Patrick. 'I'm just concerned that you're all right. At the end of the day, yourself and Edes are the ones left to deal with it. The rest of us are heading back to our lives tomorrow.' He paused. 'Albeit, taking our consciences with us.'

Johnny and Edie exchanged glances.

'Right,' said Johnny, 'well come on back in and we'll figure out what we're doing next.'

'Go ahead,' said Edie to both of them. 'I'll follow you in.'

Patrick hesitated. Edie flashed a look at him. 'OK,' he said.

'I'll be two minutes,' said Edie. 'I have to drop something to the office.'

She watched them leave, then walked a little way down the hallway, and opened the notebook again. She couldn't figure out how everyone else seemed to be described, except for her, Jessie, and Helen. Maybe Terry didn't hate them. He was kind to Helen for looking after his mother. And he still worked at the inn, even if he had a problem with Johnny.

She kept looking through the pages. And then she found out why there was no face drawn to represent her. It wasn't because he didn't hate her — it was because he hated her the most. And the pages were all stuck together. Bile rose in her throat as she cracked them apart.

Glued to the first page about her was a black-and-white clipping from the front page of the *Southern Star* — a photo of her standing on a stage in the square, waving to the crowd as the newly crowned Queen of the Sea. It was different to the one her mother kept framed on her sideboard — in this photo, Edie's eyes were burned through with a match. Most of her teeth had been coloured in with a biro — tiny, repeated, contained strokes blackening each tooth. Drawn all around the photo were flames in thick yellow, orange, and red felt-tip pen. The caption had been cut off and glued above her photo:

EDIE KERR, 15,
Queen of the Sea at Beara's
Festival of the Sea, 1988

And underneath the photo:

KERR-O-SENE KERR-O-SENE
KERR-O-SENE KERR-O-SENE

No one had ever mentioned anything sinister about Terry when they were growing up, no one had ever felt threatened by him. Edie didn't even remember noticing him.

The next page said:

I WILL FUCK YOUR FACE.

I WILL HOLD YOU DOWN.

I WILL CHOKE YOU.

AGAIN AND AGAIN AND AGAIN

UNTIL:

LIGHTS OUT.

A shiver ran up Edie's spine. Was this why the lights had gone out tonight? Was that his plan? Did Johnny figure it out? But she had been alone with Terry so many times at the inn — if he wanted to do something to her, wouldn't he have done it then?

She pulled Patrick's page out again — with his name on it and HA HA HA HA HA and the dead eyes and the noose around his neck. At the back of the notebook, she found its corresponding diagonal tear. She read the page beside it. Her head started to spin. Her throat and heart felt like they were attached to the same cable and it was in freefall. She slammed the notebook shut, squeezed her eyes tight, sending pinpricks of silver bursting in the darkness. She only realized she had stopped breathing when her lungs grabbed for a breath too huge for her shut-down chest, and she gasped with such anguish it startled her. She opened the notebook again and read to the same page again.

Smell the fire! Smell the smoke!

When you're choking on it, I'll watch you burn!

I'll watch you burn!

And I'll tie the rope around my neck and I'll tie the

end around the bough and I'll swing from it!
And I'll die listening to your screams!
And this is what will be left of me!
Can you see me now?

It wasn't Terry's notebook. It was Patrick's.

35

Laura was sitting with her elbows on the table and her face in her hands. Johnny and Murph were sitting by the fire. Patrick was standing beside Murph's chair.

'So, what's the plan?' said Murph. 'He's inside in the confession box in the chapel, and he's wrapped up . . . but . . . '

'Is that his decent burial, so?' said Laura.

No one replied.

'I love this,' said Laura. 'The men all sitting around like ye're the fucking Mafia and this is what ye do every weekend — have a drink and figure out where the next body's going to go.' She shook her head. 'And all I'll say is this — I've had to suck up not going to the guards about all this, but I won't be sucking up that man's family having a missing person on their hands for the rest of their lives — '

'If he was on their hands, though — ' said Murph.

'I'm fucking serious,' said Laura.

'Well, have you any suggestions?' said Johnny.

'Me?' said Laura. 'No. But if you want I can ask a few of the lads in the prison on Monday if they have any tips.'

'From their successful friends, though,' said Murph.

'And that's the other thing,' said Laura, 'I

don't know if it's the drink or what, but you've fierce confidence in your abilities to cover up a crime. Do you watch any television at all?'

'Patrick's sober,' said Murph.

'And do ye have a clue what Terry was hit with?' said Laura. 'Or could Val's dog be running around with it between his teeth in the morning?'

'Can we at least confirm,' said Murph, 'that Val has a dog, because it's been taking up a lot of head space that could be put to better use.'

'Val has a dog, but it's ancient, so it won't be coming near the place,' said Johnny.

'Thank you,' said Murph.

'Johnny turned to Laura. 'You don't have to be here for this.' He looked at Clare. 'Either of you.'

'So, we're just trusting you, so,' said Laura.

'Oh, for God's sake,' said Clare, 'what else can we do? Do you want to sit around and have another big discussion about it? Do you want to help haul the body yourself? We're no use to them at this point, and the less we know the better, to be quite honest.'

''Quite honest',' said Laura, 'that's our gold standard, now, for the rest of our lives.'

'You are unbelievable,' said Clare. 'This late-breaking morality.'

'I'm done with you, girl, at this stage,' said Laura. She turned to Johnny. 'Right — I'm going to bed, so. And, in case I haven't made myself crystal clear on this . . . I'm trusting ye. So ye can fucking respect it.'

Johnny and Murph nodded.

'So do you want to point me in the direction

of a room?' said Laura.

'Where's Edie, actually?' said Johnny. 'She said she was dropping something down to the office, and she'd follow us right in. She must be still down there. She'll have the keys. You're all out in the stables. Helen's in eight, so take seven, six, five, and four and decide among yourselves.'

'Not that it matters a fuck where we lay our heads at this stage,' said Laura.

Murph grabbed her hand as she walked past, giving it a squeeze.

'Do you want help with your bag?' said Patrick. 'If you want to come back up when you get the keys, I can walk you down.'

Laura frowned. 'You're fine out.' She stopped at the door and turned to them. 'You know something, lads — I've woken up to my fair share of strangers looking back at me on a Sunday morning. Just never from the mirror.'

36

Edie sat pale and hollow-eyed at the desk of the office, her hands resting on the notebook, her gaze fixed. She slid her hands on to her lap. Her shoulders slumped and she collapsed into sobs that wracked her entire body. She pulled open the desk drawers and rifled through all of them, eventually pulling out a red paper napkin. She gripped it in her hand as she waited for her sobbing to subside. Then she lunged for the same drawer, slid it open, pulled out a plastic bag, scrambled to untangle it, then vomited into it. She cried harder. She held the bag away from her, turning her head away, working hard to control her breathing. When she had finally calmed, she looked around the room, tied the bag in a knot and dropped it into the bin. She shuddered.

Then she stood up, grabbed the notebook and, clutching it, ran out the door.

'Jesus Christ Almighty — you scared the fucking shit out of me!' Laura was standing in front of her, booming into her face. Edie stepped back.

'Edie,' said Laura, putting a hand on her arm. 'I was looking for you.' She frowned. 'Are you OK?'

Edie nodded. 'Yes.' She smiled but it trembled so hard, it didn't last, 'Sorry, I'm . . . ' She let out a thin sing-song breath. 'I'm OK, 'I'm . . . It's . . . I . . . just . . . could you get me a bottle of water from the fridge?'

'If you'll sit down for me,' said Laura.

Edie nodded, then lowered herself on to the bench.

'Hang in there,' said Laura. 'I'll be back.'

As soon as the sound of her footsteps disappeared, Edie kicked off her shoes and put on a pair of rain boots. She grabbed a torch and a rain jacket, and went out the back door.

She ran across the grass towards the stables. Instead of going through the arch that led to the courtyard garden, she ran the length of the unfinished buildings, down to the end where the eight finished suites stood, overlooking the sea, with sliding French doors that opened on to a private terrace. She knocked on the glass of Helen's room. She knocked harder. Then she slipped the key in the lock, opened the door, and went inside.

'Helen! Are you awake? It's Edie!' She closed the door behind her.

'Come in, come in,' said Helen, rolling on to her back.

Edie went over to her bed and sat on the edge of it.

'What's up?' said Helen.

'Mind your eyes,' said Edie, turning on the torch.

Helen shielded her eyes with her hand. When she lowered it, she caught Edie's face in the light. 'Oh, my God — what is it?'

'I need you to look at something,' said Edie.

'And give me your professional opinion.'

'What?' said Helen.

'This notebook,' said Edie. 'It's Patrick Lynch's. From when he was sixteen. I found it tonight and it's . . . I don't know what it is. It was like . . . he hated all of us. He hated us — '

'Whoa, whoa, whoa,' said Helen. 'What?'

'I want you to look at it,' said Edie, 'I want you to tell me . . . ' She paused.

'Edie,' said Helen. 'Edie, breathe. Breathe. It's only an old notebook. What — '

Edie shook her head. 'No, no, no, it's — '

'Let me take a look at it, OK? Has he given you any reason otherwise tonight that he might be a threat in any way?'

Edie paused. 'No.'

Helen reached for her glasses from the bedside table, put them on, and opened the notebook. She pulled the torch a little closer, and started to read. Edie watched her, panic dancing in her eyes.

Helen looked up at her 'Where is he now?'

Edie's eyes widened. 'What do you mean?'

'Where is he?' said Helen.

'I don't know,' said Edie. 'In the bar?'

'How did you get this?' said Helen. 'Does he know you have it?'

'I found it. And then I walked right into him. And I told him how disturbing it was, but I didn't know it was his.'

'Whose did you think it was?' said Helen.

'Just — what do you think?' said Edie, looking down at the notebook. 'What do you think?'

Helen shook her head. 'This is not good, Edie. This is . . . alarming.'

256

'In what way?' said Edie.

'Like . . . ' she paused.

'But he was only sixteen, though. 'There's no way he feels the same way now. I mean — why would he have come here tonight if he did? Why would he have helped me?'

'He tried to burn us all alive,' said Helen, looking up at her,

'But he didn't,' said Edie. 'He saved us. He must have changed his mind when the whole thing became real. He changed his mind, so — '

'Reading this,' said Helen, 'I would be amazed if he'd changed his mind. I don't know what happened that night, but . . . this reads like someone who . . . ' She looked up at Edie. ' . . . won't stop.'

'What do you mean 'won't stop'?' said Edie.

'These are the writings of an extremely disturbed teenage boy,' said Helen, 'rage, violence, sexual violence . . . '

'I know, but . . . '

Helen frowned.

'I know, I know,' said Edie. 'I know. I know what you're saying. And you know about all this. And . . . I know . . . ' She glanced down at the notebook. 'But he was . . . sixteen. And look at his life . . . his mother . . . '

'This is not about his mother treating him mean,' said Helen.

'And his dad not being on the scene,' said Edie, 'and — '

'It's not as simple as that,' said Helen,

'But what is it?' said Edie. 'What are you saying?'

257

Helen gestured to the notebook. 'Something like this — this is beyond that. I don't have all the answers, I'm not a psychiatrist, I can't diagnose him, but . . . somebody like this . . . this level of rage, the detailed, violent fantasies. Someone like that doesn't change. This is — '

'But how do you know that for definite?' said Edie, her eyes wide. 'Lots of people change. They have to. I — '

'Edie,' said Helen, opening a page of the notebook. 'Listen to this: 'You pushed my face into a sink full of butter knives and every time, I used to imagine rising up out of it with the handle of a hunting knife between my teeth and taking it in my hand and turning to you and — '

'Stop!' said Edie. 'Stop!' She put her hands to her ears.

Helen looked at her.

'Obviously that was his mother doing that to him!' said Edie. 'That would mess anyone up.'

'And what I don't get is . . . ' She paused. 'Did you not think he was completely normal tonight?'

'He hardly spoke,' said Helen. 'He had to be drawn into every conversation.'

'But he's shy!' said Edie.

Helen looked at her. 'Why was that piece I read out 'obviously' his mother?'

Edie stared at her. 'What?'

'I think you're right, but'

'Maybe Jessie told me — I can't remember. It doesn't matter. The main thing is — '

Helen spoke softly. 'You showed up here in an awful state — I've never seen you like this.' She

258

put her hand on the notebook. 'And I've never read anything like this. It's so disturbing — '

'I know, I know,' said Edie, 'but . . . I just can't — '

'Why do I feel like you came to me so that I would tell you Patrick Lynch is OK now? It seems to matter to you beyond — '

'I know, I know, but it's my fault he's here, tonight — '

Helen nodded. 'Forget that — '

'And what if he's . . . what if . . . ' She bent over and started rocking.

Helen put her hand on Edie's back and rubbed it gently. 'Edie, pet . . . something's happened . . . hasn't it?'

Edie sobbed. She drew herself slowly upright.

'What is it?' said Helen.

'I think . . . I think he might have killed Terry Hyland. Terry's dead.'

Helen's eyes went wide. She sat up straight. 'What?'

Edie nodded. 'Terry was killed tonight, and it's all a mess and — '

'Oh my God,' said Helen. 'Are the guards here?'

'It's a mess!' said Edie. 'We've all been trying to figure out what to do and we haven't a clue, and . . . '

'And where does the notebook fit in?' said Helen. 'Where was it?'

'In Terry's van. I don't know how Terry got it, but . . . ' Her gaze couldn't settle anywhere.

Helen shook her head. 'Edie! What's going on? You're going to have to tell me. This is not about

Terry. This is about something else.'

Edie covered her face with her hands, and sobbed. 'Oh, Helen, I messed up, I messed up so bad, I messed up so bad.'

37

EDIE

Edie sat on the hotel bed, a firm pillow between her and the headboard, one long leg folded over the other. She was dressed in a black lace push-up bra and black lace Brazilian-cut knickers. The curtains were drawn. The warm light came from the bedside lamp. The searing white came from the reading light she had angled over her book. She heard the door click. She turned off the reading light, put the book down, and stood up. She walked around to the end of the bed, and stopped.

Patrick was standing in front of the door, dressed in a dark blue suit, and a white shirt with the top button open. Edie smiled. He smirked, then, ran his gaze slowly up her body at the same time he was lowering his zip. As she walked towards him, he was taking out his cock, and by the time she was on her knees, he was ready to push it into her mouth. She looked up at him as she took it all in, then watched his eyes close, and his head tilt back. He looked down, grabbed

261

her head with both hands, and pulled it towards him. He held it there, his fingers firm, and started moving his hips in short sharp thrusts.

'I love fucking your face.'

She looked up at him, her eyes sparkling. He stared down at her, his eyes dark, the smirk back. A shiver ran up her spine, a ripple of fear that she buried. He pulled her to her feet, reached behind her neck, and yanked her towards him, kissing her hard. Then he released her, and she stepped back as he got undressed, her eyes never leaving his cock. He walked towards her, reached out, and grabbed her wrist, pulling it up, then twisting her around, and pushing her, face down, on to the bed. He grabbed her knickers and yanked them off. He unhooked her bra, and waited for her to pull it off. He knelt against the end of the bed, between her legs, and slipped his arm under her waist, pulling her back against him, grabbing her breasts. He pushed inside her from behind, fucked her hard, then turned her on to her back. She moved up the bed, and he followed her, climbing on top of her, pushing inside her again. He held his hand over her mouth, and pressed down hard. Her eyes widened, and her shout against his closed palm was a muffled hum vibrating between them. His eyes were cold and dark, fixed on hers, and then they were over her head, and far away.

She lay under him watching the movement of his taut chest muscles, his arms, his neck. Then his eyes were on hers again, and she could see the challenge in them, then he looked away, and she could feel his hand slide a fraction higher so the edge of his little finger was covering her nostrils. She grunted, shifting under him, twisting sideways, aiming with her sharp hipbone to push him off her, digging her heels into the bed, trying to leverage her weight against him. He didn't stop. He looked down on her again. Her chest was heaving, her eyes wide. He shifted his hand a fraction to let her take in some air. She rocked against him again, threw him off balance, until he took his hand away from her mouth, grabbed her arms, and held them over her head. He smiled down at her, kissed her hard, fucked her harder. She closed her eyes, lifted her hips, let him grind against her, then gave him two sharp squeezes, and he released her so she could wrap her legs around his waist. He hooked his arm under the small of her back, and yanked her up towards him. She squeezed her legs tighter around him, grabbing his neck to pull her mouth up to his. He watched her face, listened to her breathing. Then he slid his arm out from under her and let her head fall back on the pillow and he held the palms of his hands to each side of her neck, and squeezed as he moved slower inside her, then tighter against her, grinding and slamming until he squeezed as tight as he could and she came hard, and he pressed his hand over her mouth and she cried into it.

As her body relaxed under him, he flipped her over, and fucked her from behind as she was still gasping for air.

He came, then fell back on to the bed beside her. He lay there, his chest heaving, one arm over his head. She turned towards him and smiled, and he straightened out his arm, and she lay her neck on to it, and he rolled her into him, her head on his chest, her leg over his. She slid her hand up the centre of his chest, and rested it there.

'Hey,' he said.

'Hey, yourself,' she said.

She kissed his chest, then moved her hand up to his face and held it there. He kissed her head and pulled her closer.

'I love you, Edie Kerr.'

'I love you, Patrick Lynch.'

★   ★   ★

It still blew her mind that after one meeting, after all these years here they were. If someone had told her when they were ten years old that there would be a time when she would be in love with Patrick Lynch, wrapped around him, wanting him, needing him . . .

'Can I show you my ideas for the spa?' she said.

'Yes!' said Patrick, sitting up. 'I'd love to see them.'

Edie hopped up, went to her overnight bag, and took out a notebook. As she walked back to him, he told her to stop.

'You are so beautiful,' he said.

She smiled. 'Thank you. And you're so handsome.' She climbed up the bed to him, and slipped under the covers, pulling them up around her chest. She opened the notebook and turned it sideways. 'Ignore my 'artwork'. Spa, lap

264

pool, gym,' she said, pointing.

Patrick studied the drawing. 'Detailed.'

'Well,' said Edie. 'I ticked every box on my wish list.'

'You ticked every box on my wish list too,' said Patrick.

Edie looked up at him. He wasn't looking at the drawing — he was looking at her.

She laughed. He looked back at the plans. 'Looks really impressive.'

Edie turned over the page. 'My rough drawing of the site.'

'Oh,' said Patrick. 'You've moved it.'

'Yes,' said Edie. 'I was worried about it being on the same side as the chapel — that there would be too much going on, but I had a chat with the architect, and he suggested a different design that creates this symmetry with it, and now has sea views from the gym, pool, and relaxation room. When you see the actual plans, it'll make more sense.'

Patrick frowned. 'Have you thought about the implications of the archaeological survey?'

Edie looked at him. 'What?'

'Well, it's a site of historical importance, and if you're going to go digging there you have to get an archaeological survey, and that has to go in with the planning application or they won't look at it.'

'Johnny's dealing with all that,' said Edie. 'Hopefully.'

'More than 'hopefully' . . . ' said Patrick. 'Because if they find anything under there, no works can go ahead, unless an archaeological

265

team goes in, and . . . ' He paused. 'I know people who have been held up months, even years. It can end up costing a fortune — and you'll have to bear that cost.'

Edie looked at him, horrified.

'Did Johnny mention anything to you?' said Patrick.

'No,' said Edie. 'No. But I'm sure he's got a pretty good handle on it.'

38

Patrick walked out of the honesty bar towards the bathroom, then crossed the hall in long, light strides, taking the stairs up to the first floor two at a time. He went into the library and over to the window. He stood with his hands in his pockets, scanning the grounds.

★   ★   ★

Laura stuck her head around the corner of the bar. 'Johnny? Can I have a word?' She tilted her head out the door. He got up slowly, and walked towards her.

'I don't want to freak you out,' said Laura, 'but I think there's something going on with Edie. I think she's lost the plot. I don't know what happened, but she came flying out of the office into me and she'd been bawling her eyes out. She was in an awful state. I got the fright of my life. She managed to get her shit together to ask me to get her water, but that was just to get me out of the way. I couldn't have been gone two minutes and she was out the gap.'

'Do you know where she went?' said Johnny.

'Out the back door!' said Laura. 'Her shoes were thrown in a heap in the middle of the floor in the boot room, there were jackets pulled off hooks. I went after her, but it's pitch dark out there, so I said I was better off getting you.'

'What the fuck?' said Johnny. 'I was only talking to her about ten minutes before she went down there. What the fuck could have happened in that space of time?' He frowned.

Laura shrugged.

'Could she have gone to the house?' said Johnny.

'I don't know,' said Laura. 'Like I said, she was gone by the time I got back. Do you want me to do anything? Do you want me to go check the house? What way do I go?'

'No, no,' said Johnny. 'Stay where you are.' He paused. 'Unless . . . did you get a key to the suite? Do you still want to go to bed?'

'No, no,' said Laura. 'Not until I know Edie's OK.'

★ ★ ★

Johnny ran into the house and called Edie's name. He searched every room. As he was coming out of their bedroom, he paused, and went back in again. He went over to the chest of drawers, crouched down and pulled open the bottom one. He reached into the back of it and pulled out two black long-sleeved polo shirts. He shook one of them out and held it up. It was a medium fit with a turned-down collar that sat high on the neck and three black buttons. A Brooks Brothers tag hung from the label. He folded it up roughly and shoved the shirts back in the drawer. He glanced down at his feet and saw a Brooks Brothers gift receipt. His hand

268

trembled as he picked it up. He paused, then went back over to the drawers, opening the bottom one wide enough to slip it inside.

He paused and looked at himself in the mirror. Then he ran down the stairs, out the back door, and down to the end of the garden. He unlocked the gate, then left. There was a small stand of trees with a path that ran around the edge of it and a signpost that pointed to the fairy garden.

39

Murph and Laura sat in silence by the fire in the bar. Clare was curled up on an armchair, an interiors magazine open on her lap, her eyes closed, her head lolling forward. The magazine slid to the floor. Murph and Laura looked over. Clare lifted her head, briefly, then settled herself again.

'Where did Patrick say he was going?' said Murph.

'Out to help Johnny look for Edie,' said Laura.

Murph raised his eyebrows. 'That's a bit . . . helpful, isn't it? Are we assholes?' He paused. 'You didn't tell Patrick she'd lost the plot, did you? I don't think she'd be into that.'

'No, I didn't,' said Laura. 'I just said that I thought the stress of the night might have got to her.' She shrugged. 'And, same as Johnny, he said she seemed fine when they were talking to her.'

'It probably hit her all of a sudden, God love her,' said Murph. 'Val showing up . . . and having to keep her shit together for that. And the drink's probably wearing off at this stage, which is no help.' He paused. 'Should we be doing something? Like, I'm here thinking: We'll get all kitted up, head out into that, meanwhile Edie arrives back from a long spell in the jacks while we're fluting around in the rain looking for her?'

270

Laura looked at him. 'Or is that just way easier than thinking there's some madman out there?'

★ ★ ★

Patrick was crouched on the path of the fairy garden, examining the underside of an ornamental rock. He put it back on the wood chips, next to a toadstool. He heard a shout behind him and turned to see the beam of a torch flickering through the trees, growing in intensity.

He stood up when he saw Johnny striding towards him.

'You fucking prick,' said Johnny, slamming his hands against Patrick's chest. 'Are you fucking my wife?'

Patrick stepped back from him, raised his hands, palms out. 'What?'

'You know — I was thinking about this all week,' said Johnny. 'Helen bumping into you in Cork, randomly inviting you here tonight, when no one's laid eyes on you in years. So I made a few enquiries. And I know that Helen hasn't been in Cork since the last time I brought her there, so what the — '

'I am not 'fucking your wife',' said Patrick.

'I heard you earlier, calling her Edes — where did you hear that?'

'What?' said Patrick. 'No, I didn't, did I? Maybe because you did. I didn't even realize — '

Johnny shoved him hard. Patrick didn't move. Johnny staggered backwards, then straightened.

Patrick looked at him. 'Please, don't,' he said. 'Don't . . . embarr — '

271

'You prick!' said Johnny, charging forward. He swung wide with his fist and the force sent him staggering sideways. He lost his footing, his hand briefly hitting the ground, before he pushed himself upright. He stood in front of Patrick, heaving for breath, wiping the back of his hand across his brow.

'Is that a nice Brooks Brothers shirt you have on you tonight, is it?' said Johnny.

Patrick frowned. 'No. It's Tom Ford.'

Johnny blinked, put his hands on his hips, let out a few breaths.

'Johnny,' said Patrick gently, lowering his hands. 'Your wife's gone missing. I'm out looking for her and you're . . . what? What are you doing?'

Johnny stared at him.

'Deciding I'm 'fucking' her?' said Patrick. 'Aren't you concerned for your *wife*? And her wellbeing? Or just your own? Someone has been killed here tonight. Nobody knows who did it. Edie has disappeared — '

'Disappeared,' said Johnny. 'She's hardly disappeared.'

'Well, she's been gone for the past half hour,' said Patrick. 'And you're here asking me am I fucking her? How do you think that looks?' He shrugged. 'How could I not think that Edie is having some kind of breakdown tonight because she thinks — or maybe she knows — that her husband killed a man?'

40

Johnny stepped towards Patrick, stabbing a finger at him. 'Edie knows damn fucking well I'm not capable of anything like that.'

Patrick raised his eyebrows. 'I wouldn't be so sure. Where has she gone, then? If she 'knows' you didn't do it, surely she'd 'know' that there's somebody out there who did. Would she run out into the night on her own if there was a killer on the loose?'

'Why the fuck are you out looking for her?' said Johnny. 'And why did you come here?'

'No,' said Patrick. 'She mentioned earlier she likes to come here when she's under pressure. And while I was here, I came across a curious thing. Terry told you that the power to the site wasn't cut because your fairy lights were still on, but your fairy lights are solar-powered. I'm just saying — if Terry installed them, then he was lying tonight. I don't know if that's a good or bad thing.'

Johnny frowned.

Patrick levelled him with a look. 'The reality is you're coked out of your mind.'

Johnny stared at him.

'You're paranoid,' said Patrick. 'It's been ramping up and ramping up all night, we all watched it happen, and there wasn't a thing we could do about it, except try not to provoke the beast — '

'Fuck you, you sanctimonious prick,' said Johnny.

'It's not sanctimony,' said Patrick. 'Whatever you're into. But, unfortunately, whatever you're into has thrown a grenade into the group, and sent your wife running for cover. There's no other explanation.'

'There are loads of other explanations,' said Johnny.

'Well, hold on to those,' said Patrick, 'because Edie is still out there and the clock is ticking. So whether we need to save your wife from a killer or from losing her mind, standing here staring at each other because you can't keep your nose out of — '

'You're acting like I'm some fucking — '

'OK — answer this, then. Did you do some more? Did you come out to your special fairy house, put your little key in the lock and pick up your supply? Unless the well's run dry. I heard what your neighbour was telling everyone about the dealer who's going around trashing places when people don't pay up. Is that what happened to your chapel windows? Did the penny drop when your neighbour was giving you that Neighbourhood Watch announcement? Were you thinking that when Terry Hyland's body showed up tonight? That your 'supplier' might have come back to teach you another lesson and Terry was in the wrong place at the wrong time? Or maybe it was you. Maybe we were too quick to dismiss your coked-up madness as coked-up madness and not a coked-up veneer over the blind panic of a man who's beaten another man

274

to death. Is that what sent Edie running for cover?'

'I didn't fucking touch Terry Hyland!' said Johnny.

Patrick stared at him, his eyes flat.

'Why are you still here, if that's what you think?' said Johnny. 'Why didn't you get in your car and fuck off out of here?'

Patrick shot out a laugh. 'Because it's too late now, Johnny, boy. Like all the rest of us, I've been sucked into the 'Bail Out Johnny' Show. So while you were squealing like a pig as the Big Bad Guard was huffing and puffing at your window, myself and Murph were trying to change the fucking ending. And while you were welcoming her in to sit by the fire, we were heading out into the dark night for you to throw a dead man into your ripped-out confession box. And while you were prancing around under the fairy lights, deciding I'm 'fucking your wife', I was actually out trying to find her. Because the only person fucking your wife, Johnny, is you.'

Johnny stared at him.

'Is there anything you won't fuck up?' said Patrick. 'Is there any plate you won't flip up into the air when there's something being handed to you on it? Do you like the sound when they break?' He paused. 'Do you know what you're like? You're like a man with a container of kerosene in his hand, and there's a hole in the bottom, and he's walking around in circles by the light of a flaming match, trying to figure out why he's in a ring of fire the whole time.'

41

Clare woke up and looked around the bar. Murph was asleep on the opposite sofa, his head back, his mouth open, two buttons popped on his shirt. Laura was asleep on his shoulder.

Clare got to her feet, and picked up her handbag off the floor. She pulled out a piece of paper and a pen and wrote:

GONE TO BED — TAKING SUITE 4. CLARE xx

She hung her bag on her shoulder, picked up her shoes, and left the note on the table in front of Laura and Murph.

★   ★   ★

Helen was sitting in bed with Patrick's notebook open in front of her. Tears streamed down her face. She was staring at two pages — another face with Xs for eyes, this one with a big semicircle smile. There was a drawing of a sailboat beside it, just like the one Clare designed for her father's company logo. There was a chain drawn from the top of the page to meet it. Underneath it was written:

YOU WILL NEVER BE ABLE TO CARE ENOUGH

ABOUT ENOUGH PEOPLE
TO CHANGE THE NIGHT
YOU ONLY CARED ABOUT YOURSELF

Edie walked out of the bathroom, her eyes swollen and vacant, her cheeks streaked with mascara. She walked over to Helen and sat down on the bed. Tears were streaming down Helen's face. Edie reached down and squeezed her hands, then slid the notebook out from under them, closed it, and pushed it to the other side of the bed.

Helen looked up at her, her eyes wide. 'You have to go,' she said. 'Go now — '

'I'm not leaving you!' said Edie. 'No way'

'Look at me,' said Helen. 'You have to. You have to get help. I'm so sorry, Edie, and I know you don't want to hear this, and it's unbearable, but . . . ' She paused. 'Let's think of Patrick as . . . a different person — '

'It doesn't matter,' said Edie. 'Say it. Say whatever you want to say. He's Patrick, and I loved him, and I fell in love with him, and oh, God. What have I done? What have I done? To all of us?' She held her hands to her face and wept into them.

'Edie — listen to me!' said Helen, her voice dropping to a low hiss. 'Listen to me! For God's sake!'

Edie, startled, looked up at her.

Helen's eyes were steely. 'The brutal truth is . . . you're not safe. That man wants to kill you.'

★ ★ ★

Johnny stood opposite Patrick, 'So . . . so . . . what . . . what do you think we should do about Terry?'

Patrick shook his head. 'You're asking me, now — '

Johnny nodded. 'You're . . . right. You're right about what you said. My head's fucked. It's fucked.'

'Well, I was going to suggest,' said Patrick, 'because of the power cut and the damaged cable in the chapel . . . that it's not beyond the bounds of possibility that a fire could have started. So . . . that's what we do. It doesn't have to burn for long — just long enough that it covers up his injuries.

'If Terry came up with some plan to screw up your night, Johnny, you better hope that he didn't share it with any of his drinking buddies, because that will come all the way back to you. That would push any man over the edge.' He glanced over his shoulder towards the cliff.

Johnny followed his gaze. Then they locked eyes.

'Do you think the two of us could manage it?' said Patrick.

'Of course we could,' said Johnny.

'It's fairly wild out there,' said Patrick.

'But there's a handrail,' said Johnny.

'A handrail and a high wind,' said Patrick.

'We only need to go down a few steps,' said Johnny. 'If he cracked his head open on the jetty, the blood would have been washed away by the rain anyway. It doesn't matter where he goes in.'

'Laura's going to be the problem,' said Patrick.

Johnny waited.

'So if we're doing this,' said Patrick. 'We're doing this alone.'

They started towards the chapel.

42

Murph jerked awake on the sofa, his body spasming. Laura woke up and pulled herself away from him.

'What the fuck is wrong with you?' she said.

'Sorry — Jesus,' he said. 'Nightmares.'

'All the time?'

'Not all the time, Laura — no,' he said. 'Just when I close my eyes.'

'No wonder you can't keep a woman.'

'Where's Clare?' said Murph, looking around.

'I couldn't give a fiddler's,' said Laura.

'Ah, pet,' said Murph, 'there's no need — '

'Yes, there is,' said Laura. 'Stupid bitch.'

'You can't be carrying around all that anger with you,' said Murph. 'That's like drinking a bottle of Ritz and expecting someone else to get drunk and puke on their shoes.'

They both sat up at the edge of the sofa.

'Mystery solved,' said Murph. He picked up the note, and handed it to Laura.

Laura threw it back down. 'Well, of course, she's just fucked off. She's unreal.'

'What will we do?' said Murph. 'You were looking for a key yourself!'

'That was before Edie went missing!'

'Well, we were still here, having a snooze.'

'That was an accident!' said Laura.

'Will we just go to bed ourselves? Like — is

Edie OK? Or has it all gone to shit and we're here like gobshites?'

'Well — we've two options,' said Laura. 'Go out and look for everyone or go to bed.'

'There's actually a third — both,' said Murph. 'Where was Edie going earlier — wasn't she going to check Terry's van for his mobile — did she find that?'

'I don't know,' said Laura. 'She came in with a notebook and looked like she was about to launch into some drama about that, but then Val was there.'

'And did she say anything to you about it when Val was gone?'

'I wasn't talking to her,' said Laura. 'She brought it into the hall when she was letting Val out.'

'So,' said Murph, 'in between Val leaving and Edie losing it, she was talking to Patrick and Johnny and they both said she seemed fine. They said nothing about the notebook and they didn't come in with it. So . . . the only thing that didn't change in all that time was: the notebook. Chances are that was the thing she told Johnny she was dropping down to the office.'

Laura was nodding at him, impressed.

Murph pointed to himself. 'Sure, locked. SHER . . . LOCKED.'

'I got it,' said Laura, 'but thanks.'

'You did not,' said Murph. He stood up. 'So, here's what we're going to do. Go to the office and get the keys to our rooms. If there's a notebook on the desk, we nose into it and if we lose our minds, we'll know that's what happened. If there's no notebook, then, let's face it, that means nothing, because she could have locked it in a drawer. Either way, we have our room keys. Then we walk to our suites — '

'Via the chapel?' said Laura. 'She could have gone there to — '

'Search a dead body for a phone?' said Murph. 'Edie?'

'I'd say set aside whatever notions you have of who Edie is right now,' said Laura, 'because whoever I bumped into in the hall was not Edie.'

★   ★   ★

Patrick stood at the top of the jetty steps, the wind whipping around him, rain pouring down. Behind him, weighted down by a rock, was a sheet of tarpaulin with the fold of a high-vis jacket sticking out of it. Terry's body was on the ground, his head at Patrick's boots, the rest lying down the top five steps of the jetty. Johnny was on the eighth step down, gripping the metal handrail with one hand, using the back of the other hand to wipe his mouth. His jacket and boots were flecked with vomit.

'Let's try that again,' said Patrick.

Johnny let out a breath, then nodded.

'Be. Careful,' said Patrick.

'Can we not just push him through the gap in the railing posts?' said Johnny.

'I told you,' said Patrick, 'there's no guarantee he'll fall clear. You don't want him sprawled on the rocks ten feet down while the coastguard helicopter is out searching for the kind of fuckwit who goes near exposed coastal areas in a fucking storm.' He smiled.

Johnny glanced down at the rocks.

'Right,' said Patrick. 'I've got the heavy end of him. All you need to do is grab his ankles. I'll lift my end, you do yours and as soon as we've got the handrail under him, wedge it up under your armpit, lean into it, get the boot down solid and we swing him out — job done.'

Johnny looked down at the steps and back up at Patrick, his eyes flickering with fear.

'Jesus — you're petrified,' said Patrick. 'Look, the only time you won't be holding on to that handrail is when you're holding on to his ankles. But I've got the rest of him, and I'm on solid ground up here. So picture Terry as the safety rope between us. Making himself useful.'

Johnny frowned.

Patrick glanced towards the inn, and back at Johnny. 'Come on.'

Johnny took a breath.

Patrick lifted his end of the body. Johnny reached down with his left hand and took Terry's left ankle. 'Good man,' said Patrick. 'I've got you.' He rolled his eyes as Johnny bent down, took his right hand off the handrail and grabbed Terry's other ankle. He let out a breath.

'On three — lift,' said Patrick. 'One . . . two . . . three.' They lifted the body. Johnny swayed back momentarily, locking his panicked eyes on Patrick's. Patrick shifted his arms up higher under Terry's armpits, gripped him tighter against his chest.

Johnny swayed sideways. 'Jesus Christ! Are we

fucking mad?' He swayed backwards again.

'To answer your question,' said Patrick. 'Yes.' He paused. 'I am fucking your wife.'

Johnny's eyes widened, his legs buckled. Patrick started to swing Terry's body from side to side. Then he dropped him. Johnny fell backwards, releasing his grip, cracking his head hard on the jetty steps, sliding down further, cracking it again, coming to a momentary stop, before Terry's body shunted him further again.

Patrick took a firm grip on the handrail and took solid, careful steps down to where Johnny lay, lifeless, a huge pool of blood under his head. His right arm was loose at his side, his palm up. Patrick glanced at the handrail.

'Not sure you had a pretty good handle on it,' said Patrick.

Terry's body had flipped on to Johnny's lower legs, and lay sideways across them. Patrick crouched down and pushed each body through the gap between the railing posts, watching, each time, as they plunged down the sheer cliff face into the sea.

★ ★ ★

Patrick jogged up to the top of the steps and looked up. Clare was looking away from him, her eyes wide, her hand over her mouth. She turned to run.

Patrick lunged.

43

Clare landed hard, the breath punched from her as her chest struck a mound in the grass. Patrick rolled her over and dragged her to her feet. He tried to yank her arms behind her back.

'They're too short,' he said. 'They're freakish.' He grabbed her, instead, by the upper arm and hauled her across the grass to the chapel as she struggled to breathe. He locked her into the pitch-black sacristy, then ran back to retrieve the tarpaulin. He picked up the rock on top of it, paused, then put it back, wrapping it up in the tarpaulin instead. When he walked back into the sacristy, he put it down on the floor, turned on the torch and shone it around the room until he found Clare, standing with her back to the wall, her hands flat against it.

'I suppose there wasn't much you could do,' said Patrick. 'The darkness is absolute.' He paused. 'I remember Father Owens saying to me once, in confession . . . I told him that sometimes I hear the voices of angels, and he said, 'Who are the angels that speak to you, Patrick?' And I said, 'The dark ones, Father. Only ever the dark ones.'' He smiled.

'And what did he say to that?' said Clare.

'You always have to know everything,' said Patrick. 'There is no bad time for Clare to have an unsatisfied curiosity. He said to me, 'Go way outta that, Patrick. Do you think I don't know what day it is today?' And we had a laugh about it.' Patrick flashed a smile, then levelled Clare with a dead stare. 'It was Hallowe'en,' he said.

Clare started to scramble towards the door.

'Stop!' He held up a hand. 'I'm thinking, here.' said Patrick. 'Nothing is decided. So sit down and relax.' He pointed to an upturned crate.

Clare kept edging along the wall towards the door.

Patrick gave her a patient look. 'Clare. I'm a foot taller than you, I take steroids, I work out every day. I'm fit. So . . . just let me think.'

Clare sat down on the crate. Patrick walked around, shining his torch across all the surfaces. 'I watched you tonight,' he said. 'Nailing everyone. You were vicious. Do you even know you're doing it? You're like one of those glow sticks that the kids have — you have a SNAP point and this anger comes out, like a poisonous gas. Do you know how angry you are?'

Clare stared straight ahead. 'I don't want to talk to you, Patrick. And I don't want to listen.'

Patrick laughed out loud. 'Brilliant!' He looked at her. 'You know everyone else. You pull out what's hidden in the folds of their shame and bring it under your glow-stick glow for all the world to see. Because if everyone's looking over there, then no one's looking over here.' He pointed to her.

'I didn't know you,' said Clare.

Patrick frowned.

'Tonight,' said Clare. 'I didn't know you.'

'You did,' said Patrick, 'but I'm the matching childhood shame you can't face. You erased my history of shame but, really what you were doing was erasing your own. You and me were in a silent agreement to see ourselves only as the wild adult successes we now are. But' — he held up a finger — 'by erasing my shame, you erased the thing that 'may' have caused some damage . . . that may have caused the unease? You did get a bad feeling about me, earlier. You can tell me now. Especially now that you know you were right.'

'Where is this going?' said Clare.

Patrick moved the beam of the torch in increasingly aimless swipes, then stopped. 'No one ever tells you . . . ' He let out a breath. 'I don't feel like killing you. You can be not in the mood for killing someone.' He shook his head. 'Where did you come out of, earlier?'

'I was going to my room,' said Clare. 'I saw you and Johnny carrying the body.'

'Were you coming over to say thank you? The less evidence, the less chance of your life imploding, and no further wrath of Laura if we took care of it. Or was it your usual? You couldn't not know. There's no loop Clare can be left out of.'

He looked down at the torch, twisted it, lowered the light. He walked over to Clare and set it down on the crate a few inches from her, the beam facing upwards, diffusing warm light.

'I know I gave you a terrible fright in the library,' said Patrick. 'And I am genuinely sorry about that.'

Clare frowned. 'You weren't in the library.'
'What?' said Patrick.
'You weren't in the library when I was there.'
'Not tonight.'
'When?' said Clare.
Patrick's eyes widened. 'You don't remember.'
'Remember what?' said Clare.
Patrick shook his head. 'I envy you.'
'I have no idea what you're talking about.'
'It was a seminal moment,' said Patrick.
Clare frowned.
'Not in a good way,' said Patrick. 'And you've . . . ' He mimed the flick of a switch.
'For God's sake,' said Clare, 'speak English.'
'You walked in on me . . . ' said Patrick. He shook his head. 'I can barely say it . . . but bear with me because I know what happened now — you walked in on me jerking off in the library. I came — by accident I have to say — and you promised you wouldn't tell on me.'

He studied Clare, her drifted gaze, her skin glowing red in the light.
'You look so young,' he said. 'You have almost no lines.' He paused. 'I'd say if you were turned inside out, though, the surface would be ravaged.' He tilted his head. 'And you meant it when you said you wouldn't tell.'
Clare nodded.
'Until Belle Mademoiselle Autin tumbled upon you and you saw your chance. To have her comforting arm around you. To rest your head against her, to be close enough to smell that lavender soap, maybe to accidentally feel your cheek against her chest, to see if you could raise

288

goosebumps on that exotic skin the way she rose them on the skin you wanted to jump out of.'

Clare didn't reply.

'No wonder you hate victims,' said Patrick. 'It wasn't what happened in the library that you wanted to block out — that was awkward, but the shame was all mine. You blocked out what happened in the library because it was all entwined in what happened next, because you chose to be a victim, because you broke a promise in the hope of a cheap thrill. And I don't know after that. Did it happen? Between you confessing to Mademoiselle Autin the horror of what Patrick Lynch did to you in the library and Mademoiselle running to Sister Consolata to tell her and Sister Consolata firing me — somewhere in there — did you get what you wanted?' He waited. 'I really want to know the answer. I hope you did. Because what Consolata said to me when she was firing me, what she told me about my father . . . it set me off on some downward spiral. And next thing you know, it's Hallowe'en. And we know what happened that night.'

Clare's head whipped around to him, her eyes wide.

'Fucking answer me!' said Patrick.

Clare gave a brief, short nod.

'As perfunctory as that?' said Patrick.

Clare didn't reply.

'It can't have been easy for you,' said Patrick. 'It was all going so well, your goody two shoes fit so perfectly — '

'I hate that expression,' said Clare.

'Well, I hated 'Smells'. Do you remember that?

289

Calling me Smells? 'Here's Smells!' like you were happy to see me.'

'No, I do not remember that,' said Clare, 'because we were children, which was a lifetime ago.'

Patrick nodded — long, slow nods. 'And there was so much of that to tamp down with your goody two shoes.'

Clare's eyes, briefly, narrowed.

'You're so irritated,' said Patrick, smiling. 'And do you know why? Because 'irritated' is the socially acceptable face of 'angry'. And do you know why you're angry?'

'Shut up, Patrick,' said Clare. 'Just shut up.'

'You are so angry,' said Patrick, 'because of all this sinning against — '

Clare slammed her fist down on the crate, 'I don't give a fuck about the Catholic Church!' she said, gesturing around the room.

'No, no,' said Patrick, walking to the door. He picked up the rock and grabbed a corner of the tarpaulin, dragging it behind him as he made his way slowly back to her. He crouched down, spread it out at his feet and looked up at her. 'Against the good girl your father wanted you to be. Against the good girl you promised him you would be. Against the good girl you thought you were. Against the good girl who died inside you and still festers there, stirring from her slumber every time her gut shifts, kicking out at every feeling like it's a warm blanket when all she wants to do is stay cold.'

44

CLARE

Castletownbere
24 October 1988

Vin Brogan sat at the kitchen table, his shirt sleeves rolled up over the elbow, tight on his muscular arms. He was holding Clare's home-work journal far enough away that he could read it.

Clare stood in front of him, her heart pounding, her cheeks burning. She could smell the sweat soaking into her school shirt and through to her jumper. Her father glanced up at her with sad eyes or disappointed eyes — she was never sure. All she knew was that she had only ever remembered them as bright and lively but they had been sad for years and it was all her fault.

She thought it started after what happened to Jessie, because he thought it could happen to Clare too, and the thought that it could happen to her frightened him and he loved her so much. But that didn't make sense when he grew more and more distant and it didn't seem to matter how many A's she got in her exams or how many awards or trophies or medals she won.

He used to compliment the fine head of hair that she used to fight with in the mirror, and the strong arms he had passed on to her that she used to wrap her hand around when she was on her own to see if her finger and thumb would ever meet and they never did. And then something changed and she thought it was because she was ugly now, that the changes that had happened to her body that she wasn't ready for had made her ugly now and there was no way of hiding them or stopping them and you had to get up in the morning and walk to school with your spots roaring, and your hairy face and your hairy legs and your chest bursting from your jumper and your sweat pouring into it and that was why her father could barely look at her. Until she realized maybe it was the other reason now. Because he could read her like a book. She knew her mother noticed how distant her father had got from all of them and even though she had never said anything, Clare knew her mother blamed her, she had to, but nobody was saying anything. Until now, Clare thought, her heart pounding. Until now.

Her father read aloud from the homework journal, 'Dear Mr & Mrs Brogan, Today's religion class was clearly not interesting enough to hold Clare's attention. I suggest she keep her mind on her books, instead of mooning after boys (see note) and disrupting the whole class in the process. Regards, Sister Consolata.'

Her father unfolded the note. 'I heart PATRICK,' he announced. He frowned up at

Clare. 'Patrick?' he said. 'Patrick Lynch?'

Clare's stomach turned. Tears welled in her eyes.

' 'Smells'?' said her father. 'Isn't that what you used to call him years ago that your mother gave out to you about?'

Clare nodded.

Her father's eyes narrowed and he looked down at the note again. She knew he was noticing that the first six letters were written in blue biro and the 'K' was written in black. Clare's heart was beating so fast, it frightened her, quickening the beat further.

'I had a word with a solicitor friend in Bantry,' said her father. 'And he's going to take you on a Wednesday afternoon after school to do some office work, filing and the like.'

Clare's eyes widened. 'What?'

'Pardon,' said her father.

'Pardon?' said Clare.

'Exactly that,' he said. He picked up the newspaper, folded on the table, and shook it out.

Clare stood, motionless.

'But what about my French grinds?'

'Your French is excellent, so I'm told.'

They locked eyes. Tears fell from Clare's and her father looked away.

'But . . . ' said Clare. 'I don't want to work in a solicitor's office — '

'It's not work,' said her father. 'It's something to keep you occupied.'

'I'm already occupied!' said Clare.

He raised the newspaper and started to read. 'I've already let the French one know.'

A stab of pain tore through Clare.

'What's this her name is?'

Clare's legs felt weak. 'Mademoiselle Autin.'

'Aren't you top of the class in French?' said her father. 'What more do you want?'

'Why do I always have to be better than everyone else?' said Clare. 'Why can't I just be an ordinary — '

'Clare — you will never be ordinary,' said her father. He lowered his newspaper and peered out over it. 'But you will not be different.'

Clare stood, heart pounding and breaking and yielding.

45

Edie lay slumped on Helen's bed.

'I'm sorry,' said Helen. 'I'm sorry. I know you didn't want to hear that. I know you don't want to leave me.'

Edie sat up suddenly. 'But, where is everyone? Where's Johnny? Why is no one . . . '

'I don't know,' said Helen. 'I've no idea what's going on over there. I don't even know how long we've been sitting here. All I know is you need to go and get help. If we're in danger, then we have a chance if you can do that. No one has a chance if you don't. No one knows this about Patrick except us. And Terry. And look how that worked out.'

Edie's eyes darted around the room.

'Edie!' said Helen. 'You have a guard living right next door, so pull yourself together, and go there. Go whatever way Patrick won't guess you'll go, if he is looking for you — he might not be! — but go.'

'I can't leave you,' said Edie. 'You would never leave me.'

'Yes, I would,' said Helen.

'Maybe he's gone!' said Edie. 'He could be gone.'

'Edie, Edie, Edie . . . you have Dylan,' said Helen. 'And I love that boy. And I don't want to — '

'Stop!' said Edie. 'Stop! Patrick wouldn't . . . I know what you said, I know, I get it, I get it, but . . . '

'Edie!' said Helen. 'He killed someone tonight. He killed someone.'

'But that was — '

'Edie!' said Helen. 'You need to hear this. You need to hear this. Patrick is a psy — '

'No,' sobbed Edie. 'No, no. Don't. Don't.'

★   ★   ★

Murph and Laura walked in silence down the path to the chapel, their heads down, their hands in their pockets.

'There's no way she's going to be in here,' said Murph.

'Look — we don't know,' said Laura. 'It's five minutes.'

'Then we're in our comfy bed,' said Murph.

Laura tipped her hood a fraction off her head, and looked up at him from under it. 'Yeah — those things we'll never be able to sleep in for the rest of our lives.'

They kept walking until they got to the chapel. 'Is it open?' said Laura.

'I have the key for the back door,' said Murph, 'from when we took it to put the . . . ' He reached under his jacket and put his hand in his jeans pockets. 'Shite,' he said. 'Shite. Maybe Patrick has it.'

'For fuck's sake,' said Laura.

'I was in shock,' said Murph. 'The whole thing's a blur.' He put his hand to his chest.

'Jesus. I did have the key, I think. Did I lock it? Or did I give Patrick that job because I knew better.' He stared at Laura, wide-eyed. 'Oh fuck . . . what if it's open and we've no key to lock it and the guards come looking for Terry? What if I was supposed to lock the fucking thing and I didn't? Or I left the key in it? Fuck.'

He grabbed Laura's wrist and started to run down the grassy slope. Laura slipped, and he hauled her up, and they ran on until they hit gravel. They stopped dead at the open door to the sacristy, and exchanged glances.

Murph shrugged. 'Will we go in?'

Laura rolled her eyes. 'Of course we'll fucking go in. That's why we fucking came here — to look for Edie.'

They walked up to the sacristy door, pushed it open wider, and stepped into the porch. They moved quietly through the doorway into the chapel. In front of the open door of the confession box, kneeling with his back to them was Patrick.

He looked at them over his shoulder, his eyes bright with fear. 'It was Johnny,' he said, as he rose from his knees. 'It was Johnny. He's lost it.'

46

Murph and Laura exchanged glances.

'What do you mean 'lost it?'' said Murph.

'He killed Terry,' said Patrick. 'And . . . there's no sign of Edie. And . . . ' He paused. 'Is Clare with you?' He tilted his head to look around them.

'No,' said Laura.

'She's gone to bed,' said Murph. 'But . . . where's Johnny now?'

Patrick held up his grazed hands. 'He attacked me, accused me of all kinds of things. I fell. I got away. And I came here because I knew it was open from earlier. He was like a mad man. I don't know what happened — was it the coke, the stress, the whole money situation — '

'And you don't know where Edie is,' said Murph.

Patrick shook his head. 'I don't think . . . I think she's gone . . . I think she's gone. He had . . . blood all over him.'

Laura looked up at Murph, her eyes filled with fear. 'He couldn't have. There's no way'

Patrick nodded. 'I'm afraid . . . I mean . . . I don't know for sure, but . . . '

'What are you doing in here?' said Laura.

'Getting away from Johnny,' said Patrick, 'and looking for these.' He held up Terry's keys. 'I just found them on him. We have to get out of here.

298

His van's around the corner. We can take that. Johnny could be waiting by my car if he thinks anyone's trying to get away'

'But what about Helen?' said Laura.

'I'm going to get Helen now,' said Patrick. He handed Murph and Laura the key to the front door of the chapel. 'Go around the front, lock yourselves in there. Johnny doesn't have a key for that. I'll get Helen. I'll come back and give three knocks and you can let me in.'

'I'll come with you,' said Murph.

Laura's face was white.

'No,' said Patrick. 'Keep her safe.'

'No — go,' said Laura, sobbing. 'Go to Helen. I'll be fine.'

Patrick shook his head at Murph. 'It won't take two of us,' he said. 'You stay here. Murph will look after you.' He gave Laura a half smile then turned and ran.

Murph and Laura ran around to the front door of the chapel, let themselves in, and locked the door behind them.

⋆　⋆　⋆

The moon was a sliver in the black sky. Patrick walked down the slope from the chapel, his head high, the rain like needles on his cheeks. His steps were deliberate, firm on the shifting ground. He crossed the grass to the shed. He slid back the bolt, and stepped inside. He shone the torch all around it. In a mottled mirror, propped against the countertop, he caught the smile on his face when he found what he was looking for.

Murph sat against the wall of the chapel, his arm wrapped around Laura, her head against his chest. There were three firm knocks on the door.

Murph tapped Laura's shoulder and she sat up. Murph got to his feet and went to the door.

'It's me,' said Patrick.

Murph unlocked the door and let him in.

'Right,' said Patrick. 'I don't know where Johnny is. I have Helen in the van — '

'What about Edie?' said Murph.

'I don't know!' said Patrick. 'All I can do is at least get the three of you somewhere safe.' He pointed at Laura. 'Hang on here — two minutes. Lock the door after us if you want, but we'll be quick. Murph — I need you to help me move Terry's body in here.'

'In here?' said Murph. 'Why?'

'Because Johnny knows where it is,' said Patrick. 'It could have evidence on it. Whatever about Terry, if he's laid a finger on anyone else . . . '

Murph and Patrick ran around to the sacristy.

'Right,' said Patrick, going to one side of the tarpaulin, crouching down. 'Grab his legs.'

Murph crouched down.

'Lift,' said Patrick.

Murph lifted and frowned. 'This is way heavier.' He looked down.

'I found some of Terry's tools when I came in here,' said Patrick, pushing against Murph, making him walk backwards. 'I was thinking that Johnny might have used one of them to hit him.

He might have wiped off the blood, but left his prints on them somewhere if he wasn't careful. So I threw the tools in with the body just in case.'

They carried the body around the side of the chapel. The door was still open. Laura was sitting by the wall where they had left her. Patrick took several steps backwards through the door and stopped. They put the body down. Patrick strode to the door. 'Right. Come on.'

He looked at Murph and pointed to Laura. 'Quick. Help her up.'

Murph walked over to Laura. Patrick took the key from the door, slipped back outside, and locked it behind him.

47

Patrick walked around the side of the chapel, opened the sacristy door, and walked in.

'Hello!' he said.

Murph's voice boomed from the other side of the confession boxes. 'What the fuck is going on? What the fuck are you doing?' He slammed his hands against it. 'Fucking answer me!'

'We're fucked!' said Laura. 'It's fucking Patrick. He killed Terry. And he's locking us in here so he can — '

'So he can what?' said Murph. He slammed his hands against the confession box. 'So you can what, you prick? Just get the fuck out of here. Just go. What do you think we're going to do?'

Patrick stood, motionless, his ear tilted towards them.

'Fucking answer us,' said Laura, her voice as close as Murph's, both of them now hammering on the confession box. 'Let us the fuck out and you can fuck off with yourself! No one's going to say anything to anyone! Just go!'

'Little Miss Sergeant's Daughter?' said Patrick. 'You were the most eager to go to the guards.'

'That was before this!' said Laura.

'Morality goes out the fucking window when your ass is on the line, is that it?' said Patrick.

'She's got kids at home,' said Murph, 'and they need to see their mammy again — '

'And I have never given so little a shit in my life about morality,' said Laura. 'So yeah . . . there you go.'

'You're something else,' said Patrick.

'I don't care what the fuck you think of me,' said Laura. 'I don't. I don't know what you're doing over there. But we'll sit here all week if we have to, and you can go wherever it is you want to go. And we'll stand up in any court of law and swear that we saw Terry Hyland fuck you off a cliff if it means you can walk off into the sunset.'

Murph started whispering to Laura. Patrick listened to their footsteps moving away from him, listened to the sound of tarpaulin being unwrapped.

Laura screamed. 'Clare!'

'Jesus Christ!' said Murph. 'You sick fuck.'

Patrick laughed. 'Were you looking for the tools? No. No tools . . . unless there's a judge's gavel in there. But that's not going to have much of an impact, physically.'

Murph's footsteps thundered towards the confession box. He hammered a fist against it. 'You just tell us whatever you want us to do and we'll do it.'

'I think I just want you to die,' said Patrick.

He opened the confession box door.

'Die?' said Murph. 'What the fuck are you talking about — 'die'?'

'Die,' said Patrick. 'Jesus Christ, Murph. The fire — it was me. I set the fire. You told me you were going to tell that story, you asked me to run it by you again, you asked me to show you how I'd made all that smoke. And, of course, that wasn't good enough for you. You had to go bigger and bolder. And that suited me down to the ground. I was fucking sick of you all, you fucking assholes. Good enough to help you with the entertainment, not good enough to be part of the night, though. Clare going crying to her fucking French teacher about what I was doing in the library and she goes to Consolata and she fires me, then, and how could I explain that to the mother, and then Jessie . . . and I'd listened to Jessie enough times, the two of us fucked in the head with all that went on and me helping her out so many times, hidden away, because I'm the freak all of a sudden when all she'd ever said was that the two of us were the same like we were the broken halves of the same child and then she's gone like everyone else and all she wants to do is get pasted, and stand me up, so she can hang out with you pricks, laughing at me behind my back, but I'm good enough for you now, amn't I?'

'Well, you got your accent back, didn't you, you prick?' said Murph.

'Patrick, what are you talking about?' said Laura. 'You were good enough for us after the — '

'After it!' said Patrick. 'After it!'

'But we've been friends for years!' said Laura. 'I don't get it! You saved us! You changed your mind in the end! So why are you — '

Patrick groaned. 'You're all so fucking nice! It's painful. I didn't fucking save you — I got caught! By Consolata. She — as she put it — 'gave me the gift of being a hero' to see if that

304

would straighten me out. And I did enjoy it. But not in a nice way. In a fuck-you kind of way. Obviously. Anyway . . . ' He reached into the confession box, took out a blue container of kerosene and unscrewed the lid. 'Let's try this again.'

'Try what again?' said Laura. 'What are you doing?'

Patrick poured the kerosene into the confession box, then all across the floor and on to the rolled-up altar carpet, and in a trail as he backed out through the sacristy door.

Laura and Murph smelled it at the same time. Laura screamed.

Patrick reached into his jacket and pulled out four loose pages from the notebook. One page had the same line repeated horn top to bottom: NONSENSE.

On the next page, the ink was diluted in places.

I MET MY DAMAGED REFLECTION AND THERE WAS NO MIRROR IN BETWEEN. I COULD REACH OUT AND TOUCH ANOTHER ME. SO WHAT SHARDS ARE MAKING ME BLEED?

The next page said:

WHAT BRIDE OF CHRIST ARE YOU? THE ONE STANDS AROUND SMOKING IN HER WEDDING DRESS. IN THE FIRES OF HELL.

The last page had one question:

305

He took the pages, twisted them tightly, bent down and dipped them in the kerosene on the floor. Then he walked over to the confession box, took out a lighter, flicked up a flame, and held it to the paper.

He stood, staring, as the flames took hold.

He watched his words burn. 'I confess?'

48

MRS LYNCH

Castletownbere
July 1991

Mrs Lynch stood in the tiny back yard, with a basket of wet laundry sheets at her feet. In front of her, a double sheet was folded over the washing line, letting sunlight through its threadbare patches — the scars of her painful writhings. Sunlight . . . through the places her heels scrambled against, through the places her knees would burn when her body was shunted forward.

She had always hidden her body, but that hadn't stopped men wanting what lay beneath the armour of her clothes, layers she had started to build since the first time her uncle had quietly opened her bedroom door and walked the floor to pull back her covers. Halfway across, there was one floorboard that creaked, and it was either that or the smell of whiskey breath that would waken her. It was never his touch. She was always awake before that, always had time enough to feel the terror, and over the years, to train herself to shut it down.

Patrick's father had a different approach. She

307

met him when he was sixteen years old and she was eighteen, gone from her family, slowly beginning to hope that one day — there was no rush — she could get married, one day, she could feel safe in a man's arms. Patrick's father lured her in with tenderness. But only one evening of it. As soon as she had given in to her hope, he did everything he could to prove to her that it was pointless.

It didn't matter that she had only ever presented herself to the world without enhancement or adornment; no makeup, no jewellery, no perfume, hair cut by a barber, eyebrows unplucked, nails clipped short, but bare. All she had ever been was scrubbed clean, looking younger than her years. Maybe that's all it was, she thought. She was scrubbed so clean that to dirty her was a special triumph.

★ ★ ★

It had been a month since Terry Hyland had first knocked on her door for a reason other than to fix something. When she opened it, he was standing on the street, looking at her like she had called him there. He broke the silence of her confusion by telling her he had something to say to her, asking her could he come in, and she let him, but she didn't know why. She brought him into the kitchen and put the kettle on out of politeness.

'I learned to read,' he said.

Mrs Lynch heard what he was saying, but couldn't match the expression on his face to the words. He was saying one thing, a good thing, but there was a darkness in his eyes that spoke only of bad things. A chill started a slow crawl across her back, then quickened, spreading out like tentacles when she saw Terry take out Patrick's notebook from his jacket pocket. She stared at the thing that she and her son had never spoken of, the thing she had taken from his desk drawer the night of the fire that had brought her to her knees by her bed to pray for his soul.

Terry held it up and tapped the air with it. 'He's some fucked-up prick.'

Mrs Lynch's gaze followed the notebook as he slipped it back into his pocket.

'And do you know who taught me?' said Terry. 'To read.'

The tick of the clock was the only other sound in the room.

'Mrs Brogan,' he said, nodding. He shrugged. 'I was doing a job in the house, and, sure, she could see straight away that I couldn't read. A woman like her would know all the tricks. She said there was no shame in it. She was fierce impressed a man my age had got so far without it, saying I must have a fierce memory because she knew I had to. You cover it up, I suppose. Cover it up.'

Mrs Lynch knew the value of silence, knew how words could make a man turn on you. Terry's eyes met hers and she caught the flicker of what some would see as nervousness, but she recognized it as the thrill of his sudden, opportunistic power and the sight of her and the silence of her proving to him that he could wield it without complaint.

★ ★ ★

Mrs Lynch knelt in the confession box, her rosary beads wrapped around her clasped hands, her head bowed.

'Bless me, Father, for I have sinned,' she said. 'I have a rage inside me my whole life. And I feel it like bones. And if it was taken out of me . . . like that, I'd be a heap on the floor. It keeps me upright. That's what it does at this stage — keeps me upright.'

She closed her eyes and breathed in air tinged with incense and furniture polish.

'I hate him, Father. I hate him. I hate my own child.' She looked up. 'I hate the child that I screamed for nineteen hours to bring into this world.'

She drifted in the silence that followed. She had been half-expecting to feel the shift in the air as Father Owens made the sign of the cross through the grille, the warmth of his breath as he delivered a penance to fit her sins. But there was no one on the other side of the grille. The other side wasn't even open.

She reached down and picked up the can of polish she had set on the kneeler and sprayed a fine mist of it on to the oak panel beside her. She removed a soft yellow cloth from the pocket of her apron and moved it in wide arcs across it, losing herself in the motion of making something shine in the dark place that swallowed up sins.

49

Edie stood in the middle of the bedroom, looking around, panicked.

'If I'm going to go to get help,' she said, 'If I'm going to leave you, I can't . . . leave you sitting here like — '

'You don't have time!' said Helen. 'We don't have time.'

'We do!' said Edie. 'We do. We can . . . ' She looked at Helen, panicked. 'I don't think I can do it. I don't think I can make it over there. To Val. What am I going to say to her? Dylan is there! What am I going to do? Burst into them in the middle of the night, and say — '

'Oh, God, Edie.'

'What?' said Edie. 'But . . . how is that going to . . . ' She looked around the room. 'OK, OK. Think. Think.'

'I have thought!' said Helen. 'Go. For the love of God — go.'

'I can't bear it!' said Edie. 'I can't bear the idea that he would come in here and do something to you! Because of me! And where are the others? Where are they? Why has no one come to . . . '

Helen looked at her. 'Because it's *you: you* are the only person who can do this.'

* * *

Patrick walked into the suite.

'I can see by your grave faces, you were only ... you were reading my notebook. I should have put those KEEP OUT! PRIVATE! stickers on it that used to come free with the cereal at the time.'

Edie grabbed the notebook from the bed and ran to Patrick, pushing it against his chest. 'Take it. Just take it. I don't care. We didn't read it. We've never seen it. Take it and go. I don't care about Terry. We'll deal with it.'

'Who?' said Patrick. 'You and Johnny?'

'Yes!' said Edie. Her eyes sparked with fear. 'Where — '

' — is Johnny?' said Patrick. 'Taking steps to rehabilitate himself.'

'What?' said Edie. 'What are you talking about?'

'Johnny's fine,' said Patrick. 'Don't worry about Johnny. But I'm a bit offended. Because I was under the impression that you didn't care too much about Johnny.'

'I never said that,' said Edie.

'The things we never say are often the real things, aren't they?' said Patrick. 'They're like little pools of water that can suddenly form into an ice cube, nice and solid, visible ... at the right temperature. And you can pop them out and everyone can see them. Or ... if the temperature is scorching ... inside you ... they can be mirages.' He paused. 'Do you care about me, Edie?'

Edie stared at him. Helen stared at a hummingbird on her duvet cover.

'I . . . yes,' said Edie.

'Really?' said Patrick.

She nodded. 'Yes.' She held out the notebook to him. 'Take this,' she said. 'It was thirty years ago.'

Patrick didn't move.

'Why won't you take it?' said Edie.

Patrick didn't reply.

'Why are you doing this to me?' said Edie. 'Are you trying to . . . why don't you take it?'

Patrick was looking through her.

'I'm losing my mind,' said Edie. She stood up and turned to Helen. 'I'm losing my fucking mind.' She raised the notebook over her head and slammed it on to the floor. It bounced and landed open, pages down. The impact cracked the old glue and a rush of pages slid from between the covers, spreading out across the floor.

'Did you find yourself in there?' said Patrick, glancing down.

'I don't want to talk about it,' said Edie.

'Is it 'unpleasant'?' said Patrick. 'Did you find yourself? Have you been to . . . you?' He smiled. 'Fucking look at me!' he roared.

Edie's head snapped up.

'Thank you!' said Patrick. 'You usually don't have a problem with that. Over your shoulder, from below . . . '

'Don't,' said Edie.

'Answer my question — did you find yourself?'

Edie nodded.

'Did you recognize yourself?' said Patrick.

Edie didn't reply.

Patrick turned to Helen. 'She didn't, did she? Did you break it to her?'

'What's the fucking point of all this?' said Edie, standing up, turning to him. 'What's the point?'

'Do you remember when you broke my arm?' said Patrick.

Edie frowned.

Patrick turned to Helen and nodded. 'She did.'

'I didn't break your arm,' said Edie. 'I — '

'Pulled me by the leg when I was sitting in a tree, and I fell, and I broke my arm. And you made me not tell anyone, and I didn't.' He turned back to Helen. 'And it never came up again! Not even recently! She has literally been lying naked inside an arm that she broke! Running her finger along the scar! And not a word! He looked at Edie. Did you think I'd forgotten? Seriously? Have you ever had your arm broken? It comes with a searing fucking time print branded on it. Especially when you're eight years old! Especially when the pretty new girl in school does it! Jesus. I couldn't have had any less friends, but imagine going in to school and announcing that Edie Kerr, this angel who has bestowed herself upon us, broke my arm — '

'It was an accident,' said Edie. 'I was only — '

'Pulling my leg?' said Patrick. He smiled. 'We do need a replacement Murph.'

'What?' said Helen. She locked eyes with Edie. 'No!'

They stared at Patrick, wide-eyed.

'No!' said Edie, storming over to him. 'No!'

She shoved his chest hard. 'No! Why? Why? Why? You fucking psychopath!'

'Finally!' said Patrick. 'Finally! I'll take it! I'll fucking take 'psychopath'! Jesus Christ, Edie. It was Hansel and Gretel. It was like laying down breadcrumbs and watching someone pick them up, eat them, and wander back to the fucking gingerbread house.' He shook his head. 'Despite all the red flags I raised. Actively raised, in fact, I didn't just raise them. I stabbed you in the face with the flagpoles.'

A breeze blew in from outside.

Edie frowned. 'Is that . . . smoke? Is that fire?'

Helen slammed her hands on to the covers. 'What's that smell?' she roared. 'What's that smell?'

Patrick looked at her. 'Do you want the Murph answer?'

50

Smoke was rising from behind the confession boxes. Murph ran over to the door to the left of the altar, into the porch, and pulled at it. 'Locked,' he said. 'Fuck.'

'Oh God,' said Laura. 'No. This can't be happening.'

'It's not,' said Murph.

'It fucking is!' said Laura. 'It is!'

'It's not,' said Murph. 'Fuck — this is all my fault. This is all my fault.'

'Stop,' said Laura. 'Shut up. Stop. It's not.' Her lower lip started to quiver. Her eyes filled with tears. 'We just need to get out. We have to get out.'

Murph grabbed her arms. 'I'm getting you out of here if it kills me. But it better fucking not.' He handed her the torch. 'Hold this.' Then he grabbed her face with both hands. 'I promise you. We're getting out. This is not how we're going to go. No way.' He put his hands on his head and looked around the chapel. 'Think. Think. If those fucking windows weren't so high up.'

'How come every other motherfucker seems to escape from the place?' said Laura. She started to laugh through her tears. 'Now I'm like you.'

'What?' said Murph.

'Nothing . . . just . . . the lads from the

industrial school. The Houdinis. Dad picking them up in town. I'm losing it.'

'No, no, no,' said Murph. 'Hold on. Hold on. The Rathbrook guy. Wasn't he talking about the land and his brother, appearing like some spectre or something, driving him demented? And before them — the pilgrims coming to the Mass rock. I was thinking — there was no way — '

'Sorry, but is this a story — '

'Shut up!' said Murph, shaking her. 'Listen to me! There was no way they were all climbing up the cliffs. The Rathbrook guy, and his brother appearing one side of the place one minute, the other side the next — and Dad used to tell me about the gun-running here during the War of Independence, how they had fake panels in the confession boxes where they stashed the rifles. And the industrial school lads — that's how they got away into town!'

'How?' said Laura. 'I don't get it! We're going to die. We're going to — '

'The little shits would say they were going to the chapel!'

'We're going to die — '

'There's a tunnel in here!' said Murph. 'There's a fucking tunnel in here somewhere. It's how the guns got in, it's how the lads got out.'

Laura's eyes widened.

'Yes,' said Murph.

They were suddenly illuminated as the flames caught hold of the confession box and the glow filled the chapel.

51

Edie ran for the French doors. Patrick lunged for her, but she side-stepped him, squeezing through the crack in the door, pulling the curtain out behind her, stalling him as he tried to follow. She started to run towards the chapel.

'They're gone!' shouted Patrick, running after her.

Edie stumbled, tears pouring down her face, righting herself, then staggering forward.

'It's too late!' said Patrick 'It's too late again!'

Edie's shoulders slumped, her legs weakened, and she was falling again when Patrick grabbed for her and sent her down onto the soaked ground. He rolled her on to her back. 'You're not a saviour, Edie. You're the save-ee. Have you not figured that out yet?' He held her down by her wrists. She struggled against him.

'How do you think you know everything about everyone?' said Edie. 'Since when do you — '

'Since ALWAYS,' said Patrick. 'Jesus, Edie. Just because something is not out there, presented for all the world to see, then it doesn't fucking exist for you.' He nodded. 'Yeah — I know that about you, don't I? I wasn't joining in with all your Spirituality Lite — your low-hanging fruit plucked from Helen's Tree of Life — I wasn't discussing your observations on the world with you (a) because I wanted you to shut the fuck up so I could fuck you and (b) not because I have no insight — but because I have all the insight. Do you know what happens when you're on the outside? You look in. You look hard and you look close because you're desperately trying to figure out what it is that these people have that you don't. It turns out — it's connection.'

Edie frowned.

'Oh, no — not to each other,' said Patrick. 'Not friendship. A connection with something . . . inside of you. Wires from minds and hearts and guts, all connected to this . . . motherboard. A word I hate: 'mother'.' He paused. 'I don't have a motherboard. Or it's a fucked-up-motherboard. Look — maybe it's got nothing to do with the woman. My father wasn't great either.'

'You haven't a clue!' said Edie, raising her head, the tendons on her neck popping.

'Oh, Edie,' said Patrick. 'You're as dim as you've always feared.'

'You don't know anything!' said Edie. 'You don't know anything about any of us.'

Patrick froze. 'Don't know anything about you?' He looked at her, incredulous. 'I AM you.'

'What?' said Edie. 'What are you talking about?'

'I am you when the world sees the best of me,' said Patrick. He tilted his head and flashed a brief smile. 'I am Helen when I care enough not to kill you in front of her. I am Murph when I laugh through your pain. I am Laura when I tell you the brutal truth that lies behind it. I'd only

319

be Johnny if I got caught for all this. And then I'd be Clare: deny, deny, deny'

He straddled her body, spreading his weight evenly, gripping her with his thighs. Then he wrapped his hands around her neck, and started to squeeze.

★　★　★

Edie looked into the dark seas of Patrick Lynch's eyes.

Everything else had been a rehearsal. She had loved her tiny theatre and audience of one, the applause of two hands, the two hands that were now around her neck, and oh, how not to have played a role all this time, because who, among all her roles could save her now? The beautiful girl? The privileged daughter? The dutiful wife? The filthy mistress? Not the loving mother. She wanted to die. And none of the others had the strength.

There was no one out of costume, walking out of a dark theatre at the end of the performance. They were all alive only on stage, under lights.

Her eyes closed.

Daddy, why, when I close my eyes, are there three things that anchor you to me: your wristwatch, your strong arms, the darker tan of your neck?

And Daddy, why did we never drive past Pilgrim Point again after that summer?

And why, Daddy, did we never fish in that pocket of sea again?

And why did I choose to settle where your

eyes no longer could?

Why, Daddy, when you told me that you would never leave me if I wasn't safe, there was a tiny arc of blood up along your neck, and darker blood in the bezel of your wristwatch, and a tiny whorl of a fingerprint in blood on the inside of your strong arms?

A soul weighs 21 grams.

Her eyes flickered.

How much does a secret weigh?

Edie looked into the dark seas of Patrick's eyes.

I am heavy with the weight of you. I am heavy with every secret of yours I kept, every secret of mine. As my soul flies, my secrets do too. I am light, but I have paid the price. I have paid the price to be light.

Her eyes closed.

52

Laura glowed in the fresh burst of flames. 'No,' she said, her eyes wide. 'No, no, no, no, no.' She was holding the torch limp by her side.

'Stay calm,' said Murph, sliding it from her grip. 'Stay calm. Not that creepily, though.' He shone the beam around the floor, then up the walls to where two of the confession boxes used to be. 'Jesus CHRIST!' he said, pointing to the spray paint. 'A bit fucking late.' He kept looking around. 'It had to have been accessed through one of the confession boxes — that's why there were so many of them.'

'What if it's under the altar?' said Laura.

'We're fucked,' said Murph. 'So it's not.' He arced the torch to the marks on the opposite wall. 'It's down there!' he said. 'It has to be!' He pointed to a stack of beams underneath. 'Quick, quick, quick. Tear them the fuck down.'

Smoke was billowing up from the corner, rising into the roof, drifting across it.

'Laura, get down that end. We'll lift them. Go, go, go.'

'Wait!' said Laura. 'Wait.' She got into position. 'OK . . . now go.'

Murph started to heave them off.

'Slow down!' said Laura. 'Slow down!'

'Tough,' said Murph. 'The smoke'll get us. Go, go, go.'

They started again, but Laura stopped, bent over, coughing.

'Get up t'fuck!' said Murph. 'We don't have time. Keep going. Come on.'

They started again. Behind them, the flames were spreading. Their eyes were red, and streaming.

'Stand back,' said Murph. 'I'm toppling the lot.' He crouched down to the bottom of the stack and yanked two beams towards him, stepping back as the beams above were sent clattering on to the floor. He bent down, and started sliding them forward.

'We've got it, we've got it,' he said. 'Motherfucker.'

The chapel was filling with smoke that was getting thicker and blacker, carrying a horrible stench with it. Murph looked at Laura standing at the other side of the fallen beams, bent over, coughing into the crook of her elbow.

'Cross over to me!' he said. 'Careful.' He started to cough. 'We're getting out of here, we're getting out.'

A burst of flames shot across the altar behind Laura, and sent her scrambling towards him, across the beams.

'No!' said Murph, standing up. 'Don't! They won't stay — '

Laura took two more steps, then looked up at Murph halfway through her third, her eyes bright with panic. Her foot fell between two beams that clamped it between them as she fell in the opposite direction, crying out as her ankle cracked, and again when she landed, her wrist smacking off a sharp edge. She lay on her back, moaning.

Murph was about to scramble across to her, but he stopped himself. He crouched down and pushed apart the beams that trapped her ankle. 'OK . . . Laura. I'm used to ignoring your moaning,' he said as he walked away. 'I know you're in agony, but I have to keep going here to get this fucking thing cleared, so I'm not even going to look at you, but you're going to roll over and crawl over to me like it's 1992 after a bottle of whatever that shite was and by the time I've got this thing open, you better be right befuckinghindme.'

He coughed into his arm and started pulling the beams away from the metal plate. Behind him, Laura roiled on to her stomach, and started to move towards him.

'Got it!' he said. 'Got it! You better be moving back there.' He paused. 'Title of your sex tape.'

Laura coughed and laughed and kept moving towards him. Murph hooked his fingers into the two metal rings, heaving off the top. There was a grate underneath. He got his fingers under the edges and pulled it up.

He felt a hand brush against his lower back. He turned around. Laura was lying on her side behind him, her face scrunched up in pain, her finger hooked into the waistband of his jeans.

'Right in the crack of my arse,' he said. 'That's my girl.'

Behind them, flames bloomed from the altar carpet and illuminated the chapel again. There was a heavy trail of blood along the beams behind Laura. Murph's eyes went wide. He lowered his hand gently on to her side. Laura looked up at him and smiled. He smiled back.

'Right,' said Murph. 'I'm dropping down into whatever the fuck is down here and then you're going to slide over and do the same. Except I'll be down there . . . waiting for a star to fall.'

53

Patrick arrived back at the door to the suite. It was locked. The curtains were drawn. He slammed his hand against the glass.

'You fucking bitch!' he said. He looked on the ground around him. Then he turned and ran over to a pile of earth, and picked up a rock from beside it, and lined up the sharpest edge. He went back and tapped it against the bottom corners of the right-hand door until it shattered.

He stepped through, swiping the curtain back angrily, pulling some of it away from the rail. He glanced at Helen's wheelchair, upturned to his right. To his left, there were trails of mud leading to the en suite bathroom door. He tried the handle. It was locked. He put his ear to the door.

'I didn't want you to see that — what happened with Edie,' said Patrick. 'I don't even know why.' He unzipped his jacket and took out his car keys. There was a supermarket trolley token hanging from his key ring. He crouched down at the en suite door. Under the keyhole was a metal safety lock with a groove at the centre. He slid the token in and turned it. The lock clicked open. He stood up and pushed in the door. Helen was sitting on the floor against the bath, the knees and the hem of her nightdress soaked in mud.

'Why?' sobbed Helen. 'Why did you have to

do that? Why? She would have lied for you. She promised you she would. You knew she would.'

Patrick made a face. 'Have you ever broken someone's heart?'

'No,' said Helen.

'At the beginning,' said Patrick, 'especially if it's a sudden and brutal end — the person whose heart you have broken will do anything to make the pain go away. They will promise you anything. And they'll keep those promises — through all the stages of grief . . . up to 'anger'. Because anger can go anywhere. And anger mutates. And if it turns into hatred? Well, a useful hatred is more powerful than a wasted love. And that's when it gets dangerous. Promises are the first thing a woman will burn on the bonfire of her ex.'

'What makes you think you broke her heart?' said Helen.

'Because I told her so many times how she ticked every single box on my wish list. And then she found my wish list.'

A frown flickered on Helen's face.

'I wouldn't ask either,' said Patrick. 'Now, let's get you back to bed.'

'Wh-what?' said Helen, struggling to control the sobs.

'Exactly that,' said Patrick. 'What's the best way to do this?' He looked through the doorway. 'The wheelchair?'

Helen was sobbing and nodding, wiping her eyes.

'I can walk.' said Helen. She started to get up. Patrick went over and gently took her elbow, helping her to her feet. She glanced up at him. He was looking straight ahead.

As they walked past the red emergency pull cord, Helen reached out and yanked it hard.

54

The alarm rang out, loud and piercing. Patrick dropped Helen to the ground, and stared down at her, his eyes wide.

'Oh, Helen,' he said. 'Oh, Helen, oh Helen, oh Helen.' He stepped over her, went into the bathroom, hit the reset button, and everything went quiet.

Helen lay sobbing on the floor. Patrick crouched down and pulled her up. She let her legs go limp.

'You're not making this easy,' he said, dragging her to the bed. He wedged her against it as he reached over and threw the duvet back wider. Then he rolled her up on to the bed, shifted her body across and settled her head on to the pillows. He sat down and rested his hand on the folded-down cover.

'I'm going to ignore that,' he said. 'They're irresistible, pull cords. I always want to pull one to see what happens.' He paused. 'Now, I know. Fuck all if someone can reach the reset button. Definitely fuck all if the owners of the establishment are dead.'

Helen sobbed quietly.

'Relax,' said Patrick. 'Relax. I'd hardly be making you comfortable if I was going to kill you.'

Helen's breath caught.

Patrick nodded. 'What kind of prick would I

be if I killed the Birthday Girl? In the wheelchair? With . . . ' He looked around. 'The candlestick?'

Helen followed his gaze to two tall, gold candlesticks on the cabinet inside the door, each with a gold hummingbird perched half way up. Patrick looked down at the wrapping paper on the floor below it.

'Was that your present from Edie?' said Patrick.

Helen nodded and cried.

'Why?' said Patrick.

Helen didn't reply.

'Why hummingbirds?' said Patrick.

Helen said nothing.

'I know why,' said Patrick. 'Beauty and healing. You and Edie.' He paused. 'Do you know the parable about the hummingbird? And the forest fire? When all the rest of the animals were standing around staring at the fire, panicking, this one tiny hummingbird flew back and forth to the flames, carrying a single droplet of water in his beak each time. No matter how seemingly limited his impact could be, no matter how open to ridicule he might have been, he fought the big fight. Moral of the story? Fire puts the shits up everyone.'

He reached over to the bedside table and picked up Helen's tenth-birthday photo. 'Haven't we all done things in our childhood we're not proud of?' he said. 'What do you think? Should we still be held accountable when we're older? Aren't we all different people now?' He pointed to the key rack in the photo — mounted on the kitchen wall behind her. Then he slid his finger back and forth under it. 'I wonder would any of these unlock a mystery?' He stopped at one key.

Helen went very still.

'Say you did something terrible as a child . . . ' said Patrick. 'Should that one thing define you for the rest of your life? Stop everything. Helen is done. Or Patrick is done.'

Helen didn't reply.

'Or,' said Patrick, 'is it as simple as some people are born evil? But then . . . define evil. What one person might call an act of evil, someone else might call an act of survival. And that survival impulse is strong.' He smoothed down Helen's cover. 'Here's what I think about evil. Evil is like cancer. We're all born with the potential for it, but it doesn't flare up in some people. Until something happens. Do you know that feeling when you do something terrible and it's like a clock stops? You are no longer that pure person you used to be, and you know you never will be again. And you can tell yourself you were the victim first, and what you did was only in response to someone else's actions. But that's not very spiritual, is it?'

Helen's eyes filled with tears.

'Spirituality is all about the self, isn't it?' said Patrick. 'So no matter how much you delude yourself, no matter how well you perform for the people around you, you know in your soul . . . in your SELF . . . that you have been destroyed . . . by your . . . self. And then the flood gates go down . . . to hold back the lifetime of tears you won't be able to bear crying. Or — and this is what I'm getting at — for some people, different

331

flood gates open. And they're the ones that release those microscopic cells into your body. And no light and no love and no hopes and no prayers can change a fucking thing.'

55

HELEN

Saturday, 30 July 1983
The Night of the Rape

He was a masked man, and he was in my
kitchen. The back door was open. The back door
was always open. My parents were out. I'm old
enough to be left on my own, but Miriam's
babysitting. She thinks I'm too old for a
babysitter too. So sometimes she goes out. Not
tonight. Tonight, I think she's sneaked a boy into
the guest room. She lets me use her Walkman if I
don't tell on her.

★   ★   ★

She's not in the kitchen. But the masked man is.
I fought him off. I fought really hard. And it's all
so quiet. It's like the sound of slaps. Lots of
slaps. And breathing that I know only I can hear.
I'm fighting him. I'm strong. But it's only
pyjama bottoms, and then it's only pants, and
it's all just elastic to pull down. And he does. Far
enough. And he tries to . . . he tries.

'You frigid fucking bitch,' and it's a whisper

but he's glancing up at the door behind me snarling at me in my ear the whole time. His eyes are bulging inside in the black mask. I don't know those eyes. I don't know who he is. He smells so bad. He smells of sea salt, and fish, and stale raincoats. He raises his hand to hit me, and then he stops, and jumps up, and jumps back away from me.

'Jesus Christ — look at you!' he's roaring. 'Look at you. You're after soaking yourself. You little bitch.'

He's standing at my feet, trying to zip up his pants.

'Shut the fuck up, will you? Shut the fuck up.'

I don't even know I'm crying. I don't even know. I can't hear anything except him, roaring. I can't even feel tears. Nothing. I can't feel my body.

'Get the fuck up,' he says. 'Get the fuck up off that floor.'

I do, and he comes right up to me, grabbing my arms, shaking me, shaking me, and my teeth are knocking together, and my head is loose on my neck.

'If you open your fucking mouth about this,' he says, 'I'll come back, and I'll fucking kill you. I'll come back and I'll kill your father, and I'll rape your fucking mother, and I'll kill her too. And I'll stab you all t'fuck! There'll be blood all over this floor. And I'll kill all your little friends and I'll bury them in the woods. And I'll rape you the next time. So you keep your fucking mouth shut.'

I'm nodding so much and he tries to shake me

but I'm stiff as a board and it's only my head that's knocking back and forth.

'I'll have my eye out for you the whole time,' he says. 'I don't miss a trick, girl. I'll be watching you when you go out that door to school in the morning, and. I'll be watching you all the way home.'

He stares at me with those bulging eyes.

My head is floating, and I don't feel well.

★ ★ ★

He turns to the wall and sees the key rack. There's a line of hooks in a piece of timber, with bunches of different keys. Mam used to write the names or the numbers on the little tag to keep track. He's looking at them and I try to run, back into the hall, to get to the front door, to get out, to get away, and he launches at me, and he grabs my wet leg, and he drags me back, and I fall, and he flips me over. And he's disgusted with me. He yanks me up, so I'm half-standing, and he shakes me a few times until I'm standing straight, and his eyes again, burning inside the holes. And they're absolute madness.

'Stop whingeing t'fuck!' he's saying, shaking, shaking, shaking me. 'I fucking told you,' he's saying. 'Do you hear me? I'll kill the lot of you. I'll kill the fucking lot of you.'

I can hear the rattle of the keys this time. I'm thinking it's my parents back. My parents aren't back. He's the one with the keys. He took them from the rack. He dangled them in front of my face. I can see the little boat, the blue boat, and I know what it is, I see it on the side of Clare's dad's trucks. I know who works there.

'Are these from next door?' he says to me. 'Kevin Crossan's place?' And the little boat is swinging back and forth, making me sick. 'Where your little friend lives? That skinny little dark-haired one?'

I couldn't say no.

56

Patrick reached over and pulled a fistful of tissues from the box beside Helen's bed and handed them to her.

'How did you know?' said Helen. 'How could you possibly have known that?'

'Sister Consolata told me,' said Patrick.

'What?' said Helen. 'How did she know? Why would she tell you?'

'Oh, the things that woman told me,' said Patrick. 'All through my life. And beyond her own.'

Helen frowned.

'You know I came to view Pilgrim Point as a favour to Edie, back in 2015. Well, that was interesting timing: it happened to be right after Father Owens died. Poor Father Owens was losing his marbles for years, no one realized. Leaving his diary about the place, sticking things in it that weren't meant to be there, not doing what the sick and the dying were asking of him, like — in Consolata's case — giving a letter to her solicitor to be given to Patrick Lynch on the occasion of her passing. So I was here for the viewing, and Father Owens' housekeeper gets wind of that, and drops the letter into the estate agent for me, probably thinking it's a 'Dear Patrick, Thank you for mowing the lawn — ' letter, and . . . fuck me. No. No, it was not.'

'What was it?' said Helen.

'I call it,' said Patrick, 'a tale of four fathers. There was a very bad father. And then there were three . . . I was going to say good fathers?' He paused. 'Anyway, I don't know, but . . . isn't mourning in the eye of the beholder? What can any of us do but mourn the loss of the person we knew? Or avenge it? The person I lost may not be the same person you killed. The hole left behind in a life may be a different shape to what you tore away to make it.'

Patrick studied Helen's face.

'I know you want me to understand what you're saying,' said Helen, 'and I want to, but — '

'You can't. I realize,' said Patrick. 'And I can't. I . . . You know she killed Murph's dog — Consolata. She killed Rosco. Hit him a few slaps of a shovel across the back of the head. I saw a little paw sticking out of a black rubbish bag in the shed in the convent one Saturday.'

'Why would she do that?' said Helen.

'Rosco was nosing about where he shouldn't have been,' said Patrick. 'Wouldn't let it go.'

'Wouldn't let what go?' said Helen.

'Nothing — I don't want to talk about Sister Consolata's secrets any more,' said Patrick. 'The good news is that *your* secret is safe with me. And here's why: there was carnage here tonight. There's a fire raging in the chapel. The fire brigade are going to be here any minute because someone is going to see smoke. I don't know how far I'm going to get. So we need a story. It can be Johnny went on a rampage. Paranoid,

338

drunken, coked-up Johnny at his wits' end, owing money everywhere, under pressure from Terry Hyland. But, then there's Dylan. Your godson, left behind with that legacy. So, it looks like Terry went on a rampage. Desperate, broke, drunken Terry finally snaps at the luxury of it all — so near and yet so far. Edie can go into the sea, running from Terry. Johnny could have been the hero who tried to save her and died trying.

He paused.

'Did Edie ever tell you about Jessie in the fire? That she wanted to die, that we watched her die? That she chose that. I was wondering if there wasn't a small part of you that was relieved? That you wouldn't have that sad, pretty face as a reminder every time you looked at her? I know. That's a hard one. I'm sure that one reared its head for you a few times. You probably signed up for a new spirituality course every time.'

Tears slid down Helen's face.

'So,' said Patrick, 'you're going to help me out here. All you need to do is tell the 'Terry Is the Bad Guy' story. And who's not going to believe Father Lynch? And definitely who's not going to believe . . . Poor Helen?'

★   ★   ★

Patrick started to stand up. Behind him, Helen caught a movement at the French door. She kept her eyes steady on Patrick. She didn't flicker. She reached out and grabbed his wrist. 'Wait.'

He stared down at her hand, and looked up at her.

'Can I read you something?' she said. 'It's short. It's about you.'

He frowned. 'About me?'

Helen nodded. 'The book is in my handbag.'

'I'm not falling for that.'

The shadow passed at the door again.

'You can take it out yourself,' said Helen. 'It's at your feet. The page is bookmarked.'

'Why do you want me to read it?' said Patrick.

'I want you to hear it,' said Helen.

'Why?'

She paused. 'I could give you so many good answers to that, answers that a different kind of person would fall for. But to be honest? I want to see your eyes.'

'I'm curious now.' He glanced down at the handbag, in front of the bedside table.

Behind him, the curtain, half-ripped from the curtain rail was moving centimetre by centimetre across the opening.

57

Patrick shunted forward an inch on the bed. Without lowering his head, he shoved his foot under the handbag and slid it up the bedside table until he was within reach of the long strap. Patrick took the book out and handed it to Helen. She opened it at the bookmark, and glanced up at him.

Behind him, the curtain was almost free of the shattered doorway.

'It's getting cold in here,' said Patrick, his body half-twisting towards it.

Helen grabbed his wrist again. 'Listen,' she said, pressing down on his hand, firm but gentle.

Patrick settled again.

Helen lowered her gaze to the book and read, drawing her finger across the page under every line. 'It doesn't matter, the nature of a child's wounds or their number or size, or their visibility, or depth, whether their flesh was bruised, or burned, cut or torn, whether their faces were reddened by the back of a hand, or the heat of shame.' She paused and looked up at Patrick, then down again at the book. 'It doesn't matter whether they were taken in ways that were never meant for a body so small. It doesn't matter whether they were poisoned by words that bound them to silence, or convinced them they were nothing or that they were everything, or that they wanted to give willingly what another person wanted to steal from them.' She paused and looked up at Patrick. Without lowering her gaze, and while her finger still moved under the lines across the page, she spoke the words, her eyes locked on to his. 'Because it is not our wounds that unite us damaged girls and boys. It's what came before — the perfection of a pure spirit. Yes, we were wounded, but first, we were as perfect as humans ever are. We still are — you know.'

Patrick let out a breath. 'What did my eyes do?'

'Nothing,' said Helen. 'Absolutely nothing.'

Behind him, the shadow was a solid black shape in the doorway, poised to step over the broken glass.

'I'm sorry about Murph,' said Patrick. 'You know he was in love with you.'

A frown flickered on Helen's face.

Behind Patrick, safely, quietly over the glass, stood Murph, his face blackened with smoke, shining with sweat.

Helen tilted her head. 'He was in love with me?'

Behind Patrick, Murph nodded. He raised his hands in front of his chest and made a heart shape with his fingers.

Tears welled in Helen's eyes.

'Edie told me,' said Patrick. 'He was meeting you for a drink, dressed up to the nines, ready to confess everything. And poor Murph. All this love stretching between you for twenty years like an elastic band. And he thought it would snap

342

when he finally plucked up the courage to tell you. But it snapped because you told him that you had MS.'

Helen's lip started to quiver and tears spilled down her face.

'He didn't even realize why he pulled back,' said Patrick. 'He didn't even realize that he chose not to love another woman who might leave this life too soon.' He paused. 'Poor Murph.'

Behind him, Murph nodded, tears sliding down his face, making pale trails in the smoky black.

'And you loved him too,' said Patrick.

Helen nodded. 'I did. I always did.'

'Except, according to Edie, you were too busy thinking you deserved nothing better than that prick who left you. And she could never figure that out, how someone as gorgeous as you, could settle for so little.'

Helen cried harder.

'Unfortunately, Murph is not brave,' said Patrick.

Behind him, Murph reached for the candlestick, and took it in both hands.

Patrick frowned. He inhaled deeply through his nose.

Behind him, Murph took a silent step forward, the candlestick raised.

'What is that smell?' said Patrick.

'Fire,' said Murph, swinging the candlestick down, slamming it hard against Patrick's temple. 'Fire, you prick.'

58

Sergeant Val James sat at her desk in the garda station, her mobile phone beside her, her computer open on PULSE — the garda's database. She entered a car registration number and got a hit on the registered owner: PATRICK LYNCH. She clicked on the Driver's Licence Insurance Production Record — a record of when any person driving the car had been asked to produce their driver's licence and insurance to a guard. There were two names listed for incidents in the previous year. She clicked on the first one: GRAHAM LANGERWELL who had been pulled over for speeding in Dublin the previous January. She clicked on his production record. On 20 March 2006, he had been caught speeding in a rental car in Kealkill, 50 kilometres east of Castletownbere.

Val fired up her laptop and opened a folder called House Sale, and clicked on a pdf. There was a coastal map that included Pilgrim Point. A small site next to it was shaded in grey. An arrow was drawn from it to the handwritten words:

*REGISTERED OWNER: LANGERWELL
HOLDINGS*

Val grabbed her phone, scrolled to SUSAN and texted her.

Are you out taxi driving too?

She added an eye-roll emoji and hit SEND. Her phone rang.

'Aren't we some fools?' said Susan.

'I'm here half an hour in the station waiting for him,' said Val. 'And it'll be, 'Oh, the battery died, Mam'.'

'Well,' said Susan, 'I can tell you there's nothing wrong with his battery. I know exactly where your son is, because I get all the goss.'

'Are your lot home?' said Val.

'They are,' said Susan, 'that's why I rang. Cian's after taking the bus out to Ardgroom. He got fed up waiting for you, but according to the lads, he's got his eye on some young one out that way and he hopped in for the spin.'

'I'll kill him,' said Val. 'Are they long gone? Did he forget he was to come to the station or what?'

'He must have,' said Susan. 'But they're not long gone. Hold on — one of the lads is shouting at me here. So — they reckon three lads are being dropped off in Urhan, two more in Eyeries, another lad in Kilcatherine — '

'The pup!' said Val. 'I'm not waiting up half the night for him to get a tour of Beara. Hopefully, I'll catch him on the road.' She pushed back her chair. 'I was actually texting to ask you a question on the QT. This is going back a few years now, before I was ever here. But did you, by any chance, handle the will for a transfer of one acre of land out at Pilgrim Point — it would have been Sister Consolata's will, and she died in 2006.'

'I did,' said Susan.

'I obviously looked into the land around ours when we were buying the place,' said Val, 'but I only got as far as the registered owner — Langerwell Holdings. I didn't take much notice. Do you know was there a beneficial owner?'

'What's this all about?' said Susan.

'Don't ask,' said Val.

'Okaaay,' said Susan. 'Yes. It was Patrick Lynch. He's from here — he used to work up above at the convent, so did his mother. So I suppose this was a token of Consolata's gratitude. Mind you, someone else was telling me the connection was Patrick's father — Consolata knew him from Cork city when she was starting out — some delinquent teen she'd been dealing with as part of her ministry or whatever you call that. Apparently, she brought him with her when she moved down here, got him into the industrial school to straighten him out.' She paused. 'I'm not sure how much good it did him. I know the wife kicked him out.'

'So maybe it was a token of guilt,' said Val.

Susan laughed. 'Consolata? Guilt? Easy to know you're not from around these parts.'

59

SISTER CONSOLATA

Pilgrim Point
30 July 1983
The Night of the Rape

Sister Consolata stood in the darkness of the convent laundry room, jaw clenched, lips tight like a pulled seam, Daniel Lynch stood opposite her, his eyes wild, his body trembling. He was wearing a grey T-shirt and jeans that were stained in blood that had been taken and lost in so many ways; pouring from deep wounds, cast from the blade of a knife, flicked from the broken bubbles of saliva it had mixed with, smeared then by tiny, clawing, desperate hands.

The buckle on his brown leather belt hung loose, jangling as his hips rocked. The top button of his jeans was open, and a small yellowy twist of his underpants was wedged into the V of his open fly.

'You watched her dance, didn't you?' said Sister Consolata.

A frown flickered on Daniel's face.

'You watched her,' said Sister Consolata, lifting her arms, and flapping them twice like a bird captured in slow motion, moving her hips in the same way; once, twice. 'You WATCHED her,' she roared. 'You WATCHED her.'

Daniel opened his mouth to say 'No'.

'And you WANTED her,' said Sister Consolata, each word snapping like a whip. 'Same as you want all the girls who move in the sunlight the way you want them to move in the dark.'

Daniel's eyes moved like trapped flies.

'How do you think it feels?' said Sister Consolata.

Daniel ground his entwined fingers against each other, his elbows moving in and out against his sides.

'How do you think it FEELS?' she roared.

'Sore,' he said. 'Sore, Sister.'

'For me!' she screamed, slamming her fist against her chest. 'For me!'

The trapped flies stilled, drawn to the only light in the room; the white band of her black veil.

Sister Consolata glared at him. 'And I the one brought you here, trailing the smell of a hundred foster homes behind you.'

Daniel pulled his hands from their grip.

Sister Consolata looked down at his left hand. 'And he's still wearing a wedding ring on his finger! You've some cheek, and you kicked out of the house years ago. And that poor child, pining for you like a dog at a window. So, you can swear to me now, on your son's life, that you won't come next, nigh, or near this town again?'

'I swear on Patrick's life that I won't come next, nigh, or near this town again.'

'And if I have to look them in the eye myself, and tell them you've died, I will.' Her eye was caught, and she looked down, pointing to his jacket pocket.

'What's that?' she said. 'Give that to me.'

'No, Sister.'

She looked at him, incredulous.

'I can't, Sister. You don't want to — '

'Give it to me!' She lunged forward, grabbing the corner of fabric, whipping it free from his pocket. A key came with it, landing with a light, metallic clank but Sister Consolata was focused on the fabric, straightening it out in her hands, seeing the shape of it, like a triangle, and it had a waistband with a little bow on it, and two holes for the legs, and it was so small. She looked up at him, her face lit with anger.

'You fool!' she hissed. 'You fool!' She threw the underwear at his feet. 'Put that back! Put it back in your pocket!' She glanced around. 'We need to . . . we need to . . . '

'Wh-what . . . '

'Whist!' she said, batting a hand at him. Then it was question after question — what way did you go, could anyone have seen you, where did you get the bike, could anyone have seen you there, don't lie to me or you'll be sorry, and he told her everything, apart from the details of his most horrible acts.

She turned to Daniel, staring with disgust into his fearful, pleading eyes.

'You can get rid of the bike, the clothes, the lot — bury them down by the grotto, where Jerry Murphy's been digging.'

Relief flooded Daniel's face.

'Now get down on your knees,' she said.

Daniel did as she asked.

Sister Consolata bowed her head. 'I confess . . . '

Daniel paused, rubbed the back of his sleeve under his nose.

Sister Consolata's head whipped up. 'I confess!' she roared.

60

Murph held Helen, sobbing in his arms. He pulled back, held his hands to her face, and kissed her firmly, gently.

He grabbed Helen's wheelchair, pulled it to the side of the bed, and helped her in. She went to the front door of the suite. Murph opened the door and shoved the wedge under it. Helen crossed the threshold on to the walkway.

'Don't go anywhere,' said Murph. He glanced back at Patrick, lying, bleeding and unconscious, on the scattered pages of his notebook. 'I'm going to lock this prick in the bathroom.'

As he dragged Patrick by the ankles past the shattered door, he heard the sound of a distant fire engine. He backed into the en suite and rolled Patrick into the recovery position. He stood up, stepped around him and, as he walked out the door, caught sight of the emergency pull cord from the corner of his eye. He reached out and pulled it.

He went to Helen. Her hands were over her ears.

'I've always wanted to do that,' said Murph. 'Right,' he said, 'there's a you to make safe in the inn. And a Laura in a tunnel with a broken ankle. I got her as far down as I could, but she made me go check on you. Mind you, at this stage, she probably got up and walked on it the rest of the way.' He gripped the handles of the wheelchair.

Helen glanced around at him, frowning. 'I can do it — it's fine.'

'Not at the speed I'm about to go,' said Murph.

★ ★ ★

In the darkness of the bathroom, Patrick's eyes flickered open. He winced, rolled on to his back. He touched his hand to the wound at the side of his head and pulled it away. He looked at the blood, disgusted, then got slowly to his feet. He tried the door handle, then kicked it.

He felt around the pockets of his jacket, and pulled his wallet from the inside. He went to the window and under the weak glow from the moonlight, slid out a store loyalty card. He went over to the door, crouched down, held on to the handle, and started to slide the card up and down in the gap between the door and the frame, getting more and more angry, pausing to slam his hand against the door before he started again.

Then he heard a click. Then he smiled.

61

Val James drove through town, past the late-night stragglers scattered down Main Street everywhere there was a porch to shelter from the rain. The phone was on speaker.

'Right, Susan — I'm off to catch my fugitive son,' she said.

'He's a juvenile, now, so go easy,' said Susan. 'And I'll rep him in court if I have to. Don't make me choose.'

'You know something,' said Val. 'There was a friend of Edie's up above tonight — a District Court Judge I came up in front of in Dublin when I was starting out.'

'I know Clare,' said Susan. 'She's from here. Scary bitch.'

'I'll never forget her — she tore strips off me for my evidence collection. I was mortified. I'll tell you one thing, though — it stayed with me. She says to me in this posh D4 accent: 'Gawr-da James. My father used to say to me 'Eyes ahead', which, of course, was his way of telling me not to dwell on the past.' And she says she doesn't want me to dwell on my mistakes, which was pretty decent of her, but she wants to drill that phrase into me for a different reason. She goes, 'So 'Eyes ahead', Garda James. And I'm not talking just about having your eyes on the evidence that lies before you at a crime scene. I mean — have

353

your eyes on that day in the future when you'll be presenting that evidence.' And here's the thing that really got me. She says, 'Your work will not always be life and death, Garda James. But it will always have a victim. And you want to be able to look out across a courtroom at that victim or their loved ones and know that you have done everything in your power to honour them.''

'So she's why you're the way you are,' said Susan. 'Did you say anything to her tonight? She's the wind beneath your wings?'

'I did not,' said Val. 'Guards are in one ear and out the other to judges. But I might get Edie to say something.' She drove through the last of the street lights and turned on her full beams. 'Right, I'm going to lose you. Talk to you tomorrow.' She hung up and hit the second preset button on the radio. Billie Eilish's voice filled the car, beautiful and haunting. There were no other cars on the road. When she got to the turn for Urhan, she drove past it, turned the car back around to face town, and parked on the gravel lay-by close to the ditch. She texted the bus driver.

Missed Cian in the square. Are you still in Urhan? Can you drop him off at the turn before Eyeries — I'm parked up. Thx.

She sat back, turned up the radio, and folded her arms. Her eyes were starting to close when she saw a car approaching, from town, being driven at high speed. She straightened in the seat. Her heart jumped when she saw the registration number. She turned her head as the black Audi passed,

Patrick Lynch at the wheel, something off about his face, caught in the glow of the lights on the console.

As soon as he was out of sight, Val started up the car, turned it around and drove towards Eyeries.

She grabbed the phone and texted the bus driver.

Scratch that. Duty calls. Would you mind dropping him to the house? I'll sort you out.

When she reached Eyeries Cross, she caught the glow of the tail lights as the Audi disappeared around the bend, heading in the direction of Kenmare. Her phone beeped. She glanced down and saw a thumbs-up emoji from the bus driver. Her shoulders relaxed as her foot hit the accelerator.

★   ★   ★

She followed the car on the straight, hilly road to Ardgroom. Rain was pouring down and she flicked her windshield wipers to maximum. She glanced down at her phone, checking for it to come back into coverage. When it kicked in, she hit 1 on her speed dial.

'Hey — it's me. The bus is dropping Cian home. Can you do me a favour? Can you check if the lights are back on at the inn?' She waited. 'What? Smoke? Jesus Christ. There was something fucked up going on there earlier. I knew it.

355

I'm in Ardgroom. I spotted one of the guests — one of their friends — on the road when I was waiting for Cian. He looked like he had blood on his face. Is that the sirens? Jesus Christ. I hope they're all right.' She listened. 'No, no — I won't, I won't. I'll just see if . . . oh, shit. He's after going tearing.'

She hung up and slammed her foot on the accelerator. The road was a series of straights, broken with pockets of tight bends. She was driving at 100 kilometres an hour but didn't pick up his tail lights again until they hit the church at Lauragh and she caught him on the road winding up out of the village. He had no choice but to slow on the steep, narrow incline ahead. She reached the top and rounded the bend, dropping her speed to 30 kilometres to take the hairpin bend that curved into another tight bend and another, the road barely wide enough for two cars to pass. To her left, only a crooked line of wire-panel fencing separated her from a one hundred foot drop into the valley below.

When she hit the straight, she squinted into the windshield — there was nothing but darkness on the long straight ahead. Then a flash of headlights struck her and she saw a car speeding towards her on the opposite side of the road . . . until it started curving, aiming at her side, forcing her towards the edge.

62

Patrick watched in the rear-view mirror as Val's car arced across the road and slammed into a fence post. He did a U-turn and stopped twenty feet horn her, switching off his headlights, watching as Val slowly raised her head. Her airbag was deflated. She turned and tried to open the driver's door. It wouldn't open. She leaned over and pushed open the passenger door. Patrick slammed his foot on the accelerator.

* * *

Val was squeezing through the door when Patrick appeared beside her, grabbing her, pulling her out, dragging her to the back of the car and to her feet. Before she could straighten, he wrapped his arms around her from behind, and started to pull her towards the fence.

'No, no,' no,' said Val, struggling against him. 'Don't!'

Patrick didn't reply.

'Go!' said Val. 'Go! What can I do?' She pushed back hard against him, rolling her shoulder back, dipping it, dropping out from under his grip. She stood in front of him, palms up, her gaze momentarily drawn to a sudden burst of blood from his head wound. She

357

pointed to it. 'Your head.'

Patrick touched it and Val darted to her right — out on to the road. She started to run. Patrick spun around and ran after her, wiping his hand back off his face, smearing the fresh blood through his hair.

Val's phone rang in her jacket pocket and she started to reach for it. Her steps faltered. Patrick shot forward, closing the distance in two strides, tackling her across the road, slamming her hard against the timber fencepost, then pulling her away from it and holding her by the collar of her jacket. He dragged her to the middle of the wire panel and pushed her against it.

'No, no, no,' said Val, slamming her fist against his forearm. 'No, no no.' She held her feet firm, her body solid. Patrick pushed harder and she staggered backwards. The wire panel started to bend with her weight.

'Don't,' said Val. 'Don't.' She shifted her hip around. Patrick kept pushing. Val bent her knees and pushed up against him. Her heels slid through the mud and the wet grass, sending stones skittering on to the tarmac. Patrick fell foward, hard, on top of her. The wire panel slowly started to bend backwards. The fencepost shifted in the wet soil. The panel dropped three inches. Val screamed. Patrick's face loomed over hers, the spring in the wire bouncing her under his chin. Behind her was a gaping valley, and under her, from her shoulder blades to the top of her head was the cold, fresh air that filled it.

Patrick pushed down hard on the wire at her shoulders and Val slid an inch backwards. She grabbed desperately at the wire. The fencepost shifted again. She could feel Patrick start to pull away from her and she threw her arms around his neck.

'Don't,' she said into his ear. 'If I go down, you go too.'

Patrick tried to pull away from her, but her grip was too strong. He crawled a few feet backwards, and she clung to him, until she could feel solid ground underneath her head. Patrick rose up on his knees, steadying his weight across them.

'Go,' said Val, releasing her grip on him. 'Just go.'

'You don't know what I've done,' said Patrick.

'You haven't killed me,' said Val.

Patrick paused, his gaze flickering down on her. They locked eyes. Then he pounced. Val squeezed her eyes tight. Patrick was frowning, momentarily teetering over her, his drop truncated: his pause had been like a starting pistol. By the time he tried to send his full weight down on her, Val's knee was bent under him, her boot wedged against his stomach.

The force of his weight, and his will, sent Patrick Lynch over her head and crashing down on to the rocks below.

TEN MONTHS LATER

63

Murph and Helen turned to each other. Murph let out a breath. Helen's eyes were filled with tears. Her laptop was open on iTunes. It was playing the tail end of a pod-cast.

'*And that was the final episode of the podcast, Girl Eleven, Girl Sixteen, by Mally James, named this year's Podcast of The Year by the Irish Times.*'

Murph wiped at Helen's tears with his big thumbs. She started to laugh.

Murph nodded. 'Yup — I've taken half your make-up off.'

Helen held her hand against his.

'That was tough going,' said Murph.

'It would have been tougher going if Val hadn't helped us out,' said Helen. 'Well, helped Dylan out, really.'

Murph nodded. 'Jesus Christ — can you imagine those details getting out? Edie . . . and Patrick. There isn't even a rumour going around about it — that's how fucked up the idea of it is to anyone. No one would believe it. Fair play to Val.'

'I admire the woman a lot,' said Helen. ''It wasn't the 'why', was it?'' she said.

'They dug the 'why' up out of the acre next door,' said Murph.

'Ah, Murph — you can't blame the parents on

everything,' said Helen. She paused. 'Poor Dylan.'

'He has you,' said Murph, 'And there's no better woman in my eyes.' He paused. 'And he has me, which is pretty shit because no one wants to live with the school principal.'

'I do,' said Helen.

'But you're desperate,' said Murph.

Helen laughed.

'Jesus, though, he's naive enough — Dylan.'

'Murph!' said Helen. 'That's not nice.'

'Ah, not naive,' said Murph. 'Young. He's all excited — Mally got a first for the podcast. And he's telling me people are saying I'm some kind of hero, and he thinks that's great. And I'm just thinking — '

'I know what you're thinking and stop it,' said Helen. 'Stop it.'

'But — '

'Laura would kill you and you know she would. Kill you.'

'But — '

'Murph,' said Helen, her hand on his back. 'This might be the only thing that could ever make me cross with you. I can't have you beat yourself up about this for the rest of your life. It was a freak accident. A jagged piece of timber, her femoral artery. It was too dark for you to see the extent of the wound. Even if you had, even if you had called an ambulance right away, there wasn't going to be a lot they could do. This was not your fault.'

'But — it was my idea to move the beams and I didn't think — '

'You both would have died, if you hadn't tried something,' said Helen. 'And if you'd died, I would have too. I know it's hard when you can't save the world. But, at least know how grateful I am that you saved me. You are my brave boy.' She kissed him.

They fell into a short silence.

Then Murph stood up. 'Come here, you beautiful creature.' He bent down to scoop her in to his arms.

Helen slapped him gently away. 'I can walk!' she said. 'I'm fine.'

'I don't care if you're having a good day!' said Murph. 'What if I'm having a bad one? What if I'm shitting it about starting in the school and being expected to be responsible and I want to feel like a man by carrying my beautiful princess to my lair?'

Helen laughed.

'Every time I get to have my wicked way with you,' said Murph, 'I think the same thing . . . '

Helen smiled at him. 'Aw . . . what?'

'She's faking the MS. There's not a thing wrong with that woman.'

★ ★ ★

At midnight, Murph stood on the balcony at the front of the house. He was dressed in jeans and a T-shirt, barefoot, looking out over the harbour, holding a glass of 1615 Pisco Torontel, then raising it.

'This is for you, lovely lady,' he said. 'In your honour. And you had lots of it. And you should be proud of yourself. And you died honourably. And kindly. And here we are — myself and Helen. And life is fucked up beyond measure and beautiful too and I'm quite pissed now, in fairness. I miss the fuck out of you. We'd barely seen each other in years — once or twice a year, tops — and after one night, you've made me miss you this much. It must be weird being up there with no one to fight with about telling the truth because you're with the angels.' He took a drink. 'So, Laura, this is for you . . . have I said that already? Have I mentioned the sponsored walk I'm going to organize in your honour? The Laura Hurley Memorial Walk . . . of Shame. Wear whatever you were wearing last night but with a slick of deodorant from the opposite sex.' He smiled. 'Come on . . . it's me.'

He turned to go back inside, then paused. He looked up at the stars.

'Are any of ye the lucky ones? Or are you just the boring ones? I'd like to speak to the lucky ones. It's about Helen Maguire.' He swayed back on his heels. 'Right,' he said, raising his glass. 'Lucky stars — thanks, in fairness. You finally kicked in.' He let out a breath. 'Love,' he said. 'You can't outrun the fucker.'

Epilogue

30 July 1983
The Night of the Rape

Helen stood mopping the kitchen floor. There was a loud knock on the back door. She jumped, and looked up to see her mother standing there — her expression a mix of anger and fear. Helen went over and unlocked the door.

'Why was that locked?' said her mother. 'Why are you mopping the floor at this time of night?'

'I spilled something,' said Helen.

'Something terrible's happened next door,' said her mother. 'Where's Miriam?'

★ ★ ★

Miriam stood, wide-eyed, at the window of the Maguires' guest bedroom, looking at the scene unfolding outside.

'I don't know what's going on!' she said. 'Jessie Crossan's gone off in the ambulance with her dad! And your dad's inside in their house.'

'I have to get out of here,' said Johnny, squeezing in beside her, reaching past her to push the window open.

'Are you mad?' said Miriam. 'Your dad's right

367

outside! He's talking to Edward Kerr. They look shook.'

★ ★ ★

Dr Weston leaned in to Edward. 'Never.' He shook his head. 'In all my years . . . ' He let out a breath. 'It's a miracle she's alive.' He raised his head. 'And he's not long gone, by my reckoning.' He paused. 'Look — between ourselves, there was a docket on the floor of the bedroom . . . it's from one of Vin Brogan's boats.'

Edward's eyes widened. Dr Weston nodded.

'What did you do with it?' said Edward.

Dr Weston patted his brown leather bag. 'You might want to have a word with Vin — I don't know what crew he's got on at the moment. But there's no way a man who's done what he's done to that child . . . there's no way he could have gone near town to get back on that boat . . . if it is one of the crew.' He pointed to his left. 'And he won't have gone that way — it's blocked off for whatever's going on in the morning. So unless the man's hiding away in a house somewhere, he's gone west.'

Edward nodded, then walked down the path, got into his car, and started the engine. He did a U-turn and drove down to the end of the back road, the last bend taking him down the short narrow lane on to Main Street.

The sound of the band and the cheering crowd on the square drifted through the open window, the pulse of the bass throbbing beneath it. He took the right-hand turn that curved around the playground and drove to the outskirts of town and up to the Brogans' house. When he got to the top of their steep driveway, he glanced up and saw a light glowing in the front bedroom.

★ ★ ★

Clare, Edie, and Laura were sitting on the floor at the foot of Clare's bed, playing the Game of Life, surrounded by sweets, and crisps, and drinks.

'It's my go,' said Clare.

'Oh,' said Edie. 'Sorry.' She handed her the dice.

Clare rolled them. 'Six and six!'

There was the sound of a horn beeping outside. Clare jumped up and went to the window.

'Oh, no! It's your dad,' she said, turning to Edie.

'What?' said Edie. 'No! I hope I don't have to go home.' She got up and went to the window. 'What if he found we didn't invite Jessie. That would make him so cross.'

Clare levelled her with a look. 'It's my house. So, it's not your fault. And why would he care?'

'He doesn't like people being excluded,' said Edie. 'He has this thing about it.'

'And we all know,' said Clare, 'if Jessie was here, we'd all be lined up on the bed having to watch her do all her 'routines'.'

Edie glanced over at Laura. Laura was looking at Clare.

'She would!' said Clare when they didn't respond. 'She's obsessed.'

'And why didn't you invite Helen?' said Edie.

'I wanted Helen to come,' said Clare, pointing towards Laura.

'Because Miriam needed the babysitting money,' said Laura. 'She heard us going on about tonight, and she came in after and said she'd beat the head off me if I ruined Regatta Saturday for her.'

'Would she not want to be out tonight?' said Edie.

'She says she's broke,' said Laura.

Clare gave them a patient look. 'She's obviously got some fella coming over to the house.'

Laura shot out a laugh. 'God help him.'

Edie was back looking out the window. She turned to Clare. 'Oh! Your dad's heading off in the car with my dad.'

'"And that was the Eleven O'clock News with Edie Kerr',' said Clare.

★ ★ ★

Vin Brogan sat in the passenger seat of Edward's car. They left the lights of town behind them as they drove the dark and winding road west. As they approached the convent, they saw head-lights on the opposite side of the road.

'Who's that?' said Vin. 'Slow down, slow down.'

Edward slowed, squinting through the wind-screen at a man running down the hill from a parked van. 'It's Jerry Murphy'

They drove up towards him, pulled in, and flashed the lights. Jerry changed course and came up alongside them.

'Jerry,' said Edward. 'Have you been out long?'

'That dog,' said Jerry, pointing back. 'I swear to God — '

'Have you seen anything, anyone unusual out this way?' said Edward.

Jerry lowered his head and leaned in the window. 'Vin! I've got that letter in the van for you.' He glanced at Edward. 'Jesus — you're looking fierce serious, the pair of you.'

'Jessie Crossan's been found — destroyed altogether,' said Vin. 'Raped in her bed. She's on her way to Bantry in the ambulance — '

'Jesus, Mary, and Joseph,' said Jerry, blessing himself. 'Liam and I were out in the van looking for the dog. Liam said he spotted him shooting out after a fella on a bike, heading up the side road to the convent.'

'Hop in,' said Vin. 'Will Liam be all right on his own in the van?'

'He will, of course,' said Jerry.

Edward drove past the van and did a U-turn, pulling up next to it it.

'Liam!' said Jerry.

Murph climbed over to the driver's side, and leaned out. 'How's it goin', lads?'

'Liam,' said Jerry, his elbow out the window, 'open the glove box, there, and hand me out that letter for Vin. Good man. Now, will you be all right here for a minute? I'll go on away up for Rosco with the lads, and I'll be back to you.'

'Sure, I'll come with you!' said Murph.

'You're fine out,' said Jerry. 'We'll be two ticks.'

He slapped his hand against the side of the car and Edward drove on, taking the next right. Vin held up his hand, and Jerry passed him the letter.

'Knock the lights off,' said Vin, turning to Edward.

They drove in darkness along the narrow road, parked and got out of the car. They heard a faint bark coming from the convent grounds.

Jerry rolled his eyes. 'If I'm gone for any length, this is where he thinks I've gone.' He took out a key, and opened the chapel gate. They walked through, and closed it behind them, staying close to the wall. As they moved towards the outbuildings, Rosco bounded around the side of one of them, and stood at the corner barking.

'Look!' said Vin. There was a bike lying on the grass, the spin of the back wheel slowing to a stop.

'What's that building?' said Edward.

'The laundry room,' said Jerry. They jogged down towards it, Jerry shooing Rosco back around the corner. They heard the raised voice of a woman as they reached the door. Jerry mouthed 'Consolata' at the others.

They crept closer. They exchanged glances when they heard a man praying.

'I confess to Almighty God and to you, my brothers and sisters — '

'That's him, the prick!' said Vin, darting forward, yanking the door open.

Daniel Lynch was on his knees, his hands joined together in prayer. He looked up, wide-eyed, at Vin, then at Edward and Jerry, behind him.

Vin glared at Sister Consolata. 'Is that what you think, you auld bitch? That he can pray it away?'

Sister Consolata stared at him, defiant, her back straight, her mouth in its tight line. Vin grabbed Daniel's arm and pulled him to his feet. Then he grabbed him by the neck, and held up his fist to him.

'Vin!' said Jerry. 'Vin! Take it easy, take it easy.'

Daniel, his eyes wide with panic, struggled against Vin's grip. Edward moved in, grabbing his other arm, and they dragged him past Jerry out on to the grass. Jerry stood, frozen, in the doorway, his eyes wide.

Vin grabbed Daniel by the neck again, and punched him, splitting the skin over his eye, sending him down on his knees, blood pouring across his face. Vin staggered backwards.

'Lads!' said Jerry from the doorway. 'Lads.'

Edward moved in then, pulling Daniel half off his knees, sending a powerful blow down on his jaw.

'For the love of God,' said Jerry, wincing, turning away, finding his gaze drawn to the floor of the laundry room where Sister Consolata was on her hands and knees reaching out for a small pair of bloodstained underpants. She froze, her hands on them, her eyes locked on Jerry's. His mouth opened, but no words came out. Then his hand flew back to the door frame and he grabbed it as he turned, using it to throw himself outside, ploughing through the space between Vin and Edward to where Daniel lay, curled in a ball, sobbing.

'You savage,' said Jerry, kicking Daniel hard in the ribs, kicking him again. 'Animal's too good for you.'

He kept kicking until he was pulled away. And every time one of the men fell back, another stepped in to take his place until they had kicked and beaten the last breath out of Daniel Lynch.

They stood over him, sweating, heaving for breath, spattered with blood.

Sister Consolata stood at Daniel's feet. Vin turned to her, running his hand over the top of his head, settling the thin loose strands of hair. 'Do you think you're God, Sister — is that it? Do you think your prayers can make men out of monsters? Do you think you can work miracles? Do you think you're some kind of saint?'

Sister Consolata stared at him, her eyes flaring — a gleaming black in the void.

'Telling me what a great fella Daniel Lynch is!' said Vin. 'How well he'd done since you brought him down here, how you could vouch for him and oh, sure, wouldn't he be a great asset for my boat? And me having to drag him away Friday night from standing around the pier, seeing what little girl's parents didn't have a close enough eye on her. And you knew! You were warned, weren't you?' He pointed at Jerry. 'Jerry found the letter you were sent. He found your letter, and he trying to gather up the history of the place and do it justice.' He paused. 'But you?' he said. 'Oh, no. Not a screed of justice in the world if it's not yourself doling it out. Sure, why would you pay any notice to a letter when you're God Almighty?'

He turned to Edward. He was staring, pale-faced, at Daniel's lifeless body on the grass. Vin reached into his back pocket, and pulled out the envelope. He handed it to him. 'Read this and it might make you feel better.'

Edward opened it and read.

Dr St John Burke
Finney Street
Cork City

PERSONAL
Sister Consolata
St James' Industrial School for Boys
Pilgrim Point
Beara
Co. Cork.

7 June 1971

Dear Sister Consolata
I acknowledge receipt of your letter of fifth May, re Daniel L. and regret to inform you that the boy who presented to me last week bore no resemblance to the remorseful and maturing young man of whom you spoke so highly. Moreover, he gave me cause for grave concern.

It is my professional opinion that Daniel L. should be monitored at all times. If resources cannot provide for such strict supervision, at a minimum, you must ensure that he never be left unaccompanied in the presence of pre-adolescent girls.

Regards

Dr St John Burke

Consultant Psychiatrist

Regina — I speak now as St John, your brother. The above is the text of the letter I will be formally sending you as School Manager of St James'.

Since you were a child, you and I spent many nights arguing over the beliefs we held dear, and I watched, albeit with great pride, your youthful passion and devotion. But I have a decade on you, dear sister — a decade spent in a world far removed from the cosseted one in which I left you, and the cloistered one to which you committed so soon thereafter.

With this latest post, you have finally been confronted with what had once been the touchpaper of our fiery debates — the raw human manifestation of society's ills: the abused, the insane, the discarded, the rejected, the criminal. But to live among them daily, to guard their dormitories by night, you are experiencing it at a brute intensity beyond any I have known.

I understand the efforts you have taken to rehabilitate Daniel, so it pains me greatly to say that there are some children who are beyond the help of both science and religion.

We are all passing through, Regina — on that we do agree. But I do wonder, does the very name Pilgrim Point contain in it a warning: I am for pilgrims. No one's time here shall ever be lasting. Those who wish to settle here will only ever be unsettled.

May you be a pilgrim there.
With love,
St John

Vin turned to Sister Consolata. 'At least we can all benefit from your blind eye now.'

They fell into silence. It was broken by the sound of barking. They turned to see Murph running away from them, and Rosco scampering across the grass towards him and bounding into his arms.

Murph kept running and never looked back.

Acknowledgements

There's a reason why I say the following two lines so often: Life is Beautiful and People are Gorgeous. Because it is, and they are. And I'm eternally grateful.

Here are two pages of gorgeous people:

My editor, Sarah Hodgson — you have been AMAAAZING. Thank you, thank you, thank you X a zillion; Assistant Editor, Finn Cotton — well, you're a star. Thank you for playing a blinder; Executive Publisher, Kate Elton, and all the talented team at HarperCollins — thank you for everything; CEO, Charlie Redmayne — thank you for being a champion of writers; Tony Purdue, Eoin McHugh, Patricia McVeigh, Jacq Murphy, Ciara Swift, and Nora Mahony from Harper Collins, Ireland — thank you, you superteam; Anne O'Brien — thank you for your copy-editing skills; Special Agent, Simon Trewin — thank you for everything.

I love researching — for the people I meet, the brains I get to pick, the knowledge and insight I gain, the new friends I make, and for the generosity of spirit that surrounds it all. People will often say they are honoured to be thanked at the back of a book. But, truly, the honour is all mine.

Very special thanks to: the wonderful, witty and wise, Elaine Moore, who I first discovered through her brilliant blog, www.wheellife.co.uk; Donal Lenihan, a true gent, who dealt so kindly and humorously with a rugby rookie; Hervé Blanchard; Professor Marie Cassidy; James Eogan; Liz Foley; René Gapert; Diarmuid McCarthy; Marney O'Donoghue; Brendan O'Driscoll, Brian O'Driscoll; Marie O'Halloran; Marc O'Sullivan; Paddy O'Sullivan; Stephen Pierce from Kerry Office Supplies; Bob Rotella, Catherine Ryan; Terry Reilly from Switch Distribution. Any errors are mine.

To my friends, who played such a huge part in bringing this book over the line. Among them, they so generously provided: brilliant conversation, joy, inspiration, laughter, reading, writing, feedback, rereading, shelter, transport, macarons, research, shoulders, prayers . . .

For their particularly outstanding contribution to *I Confess*, and my life, thank you to the generous, high-larious, selfless, insightful, creative genii, Paula Kavanagh (we will always have What Ifs) and Julie Sheridan (we will always have Limahl); for epic manoeuvres in the final stretch, huge thanks to Colin Weldon (well done, Weldon. Five stars!), Sue Booth-Forbes of Anam Cara Writers' and Artists' Retreat, David Browne, Rebekah Carroll, Eoin Colfer, David & Majella Geraghty, Sarah Hanley; Anne Harrington, Bernice Harrison, Ger Holland, Simon Kernick, Casey King, Derek Landy, PJ Lynch, Eoin McHugh, Ger McDonnell, Marian McDonnell, Jenny Murphy, Noleen Murphy & John Kevin Harrington, John Murry, Liz Nugent & Richard McCullough, Estella O'Brien, David O'Callaghan, John O'Donnell & Micheline Huggard, Vanessa O'Loughlin, Sue Swansborough,

Dick Tobin, Kevin Wignall, and Brian Williams.

Very special thanks to Mary Harrington Causkey at Eyeries Post Office — your kindness knows no bounds. And thank you to everyone at Eyeries Post Office — you are all stars.

I ventured forth to three special places in Beara to write *I Confess*. So thank you to Mark Golden & Mark Johnston, Louise O'Sullivan, Tom Dickenson, Mags McCarthy and all the staff at the Beara Coast Hotel, Castletownbere; David & Lorna Ramshaw, Ciara Feeley, Caroline O'Sullivan, and everyone at the Tea Room, Castletownbere; Cindy van Nulck and all the staff at Cindy's Gems, Eyeries.

To my beloved family — I adore you. I took off-the-radar to an extreme on this one, so thank you from the bottom of my heart for your understanding, love, and patience.

We do hope that you have enjoyed reading this large print book.

Did you know that all of our titles are available for purchase?

We publish a wide range of high quality large print books including:
Romances, Mysteries, Classics
General Fiction
Non Fiction and Westerns

Special interest titles available in large print are:
The Little Oxford Dictionary
Music Book
Song Book
Hymn Book
Service Book

Also available from us courtesy of Oxford University Press:
Young Readers' Dictionary
(large print edition)
Young Readers' Thesaurus
(large print edition)

For further information or a free brochure, please contact us at:
Ulverscroft Large Print Books Ltd.,
The Green, Bradgate Road, Anstey,
Leicester, LE7 7FU, England.
Tel: (00 44) 0116 236 4325
Fax: (00 44) 0116 234 0205

THE DROWNING CHILD

Alex Barclay

When Special Agent Ren Bryce is called to Tate, Oregon to investigate the disappearance of twelve-year-old Caleb Veir, she finds a town already in mourning. Two other young boys have died recently, but in very different circumstances. As Ren digs deeper, she discovers that all is not as it seems in the Veir household — and that while Tate may be a small town, it guards some very big secrets. Can Ren uncover the truth before more children are harmed?